2021年度辽宁省社会科学规划基金项目
“英文月亮短诗及其韵体汉译研究”（项目编号：L21BYY004）

101首英语月亮短诗及其汉译并注

王永胜　朱　红◎译著

安徽师范大学出版社
ANHUI NORMAL UNIVERSITY PRESS
· 芜湖 ·

图书在版编目(CIP)数据

101首英语月亮短诗及其汉译并注 / 王永胜,朱红译著 .—芜湖:安徽师范大学出版社,2023.9

ISBN 978-7-5676-6120-2

Ⅰ.①1… Ⅱ.①王… ②朱… Ⅲ.①英语诗歌—诗歌研究 Ⅳ.①I106.2

中国国家版本馆CIP数据核字(2023)第167077号

101首英语月亮短诗及其汉译并注

王永胜 朱 红◎译著

责任编辑:晋雅雯 责任校对:刘 翠

装帧设计:张德宝 姚 远 责任印制:桑国磊

出版发行:安徽师范大学出版社

芜湖市北京中路2号安徽师范大学赭山校区 邮政编码:241000

网 址:http://www.ahnupress.com/

发 行 部:0553-3883578 5910327 5910310(传真)

印 刷:江苏凤凰数码印务有限公司

版 次:2023年9月第1版

印 次:2023年9月第1次印刷

规 格:700 mm × 1000 mm 1/16

印 张:24

字 数:358千字

书 号:ISBN 978-7-5676-6120-2

定 价:86.00元

凡发现图书有质量问题,请与我社联系(联系电话:0553-5910315)

Preface
前　言

在群星璀璨、光芒四射的英文诗歌天空中，有一类篇幅短小的诗歌，它们关乎一个共同的意象——月亮。这些诗都以月亮为主题，或直接写月，或借月抒怀，读后令人深思。这些月亮短诗，有的出自名家，如珀西·比希·雪莱、托马斯·哈代等；有的出自非名家，如詹姆斯·乔伊斯、伊芙琳·斯科特等。笔者从各类英文媒体中精选出101首月亮短诗，对其展开翻译探索并作加注处理，以期帮助读者领略英语诗歌的魅力，享受诗歌美的审美乐趣。

本书精选的诗歌，大部分属于英文格律诗，少部分为英语现代诗，即自由体诗，但都具有短小精悍的特点，所以称之为“短诗”。它们以月亮为意象，从不同的角度映射出一定的主题思想。对这些诗的翻译所形成的汉语译文，简称“译诗”。由本书译者翻译、加工、处理过的译诗“可口”与否，那恐怕就是“众口难调”了。

这样说，不是在推脱诗歌译者的责任，实则因为诗歌翻译乃难中之难的事情。这里的所说的“英诗汉译”，不仅仅涉及英诗的“内容”，还涉及英诗的“形式”——格律翻译。英诗格律的多样性及英汉语言的差异性，使得英诗汉译较其他文体的汉译，难度更大。但英诗汉译领域仍然是“百花齐放、百家争鸣”。译者各有方法，有民族化译法、移植译法、格律化译法等；译诗形式亦多样，有汉语格律诗的形式、汉语自由体无韵诗歌的形式、汉语散文体的形式等。

英诗汉译是以原诗为基础的，要在观照英诗形式即格律的基础上，忠实英诗的内容，此乃英诗汉译的根本。因为形式是为内容服务的，无论形式多么完美，内容与原诗不符，甚至背离了原诗，也就失去了英诗汉译的意义，翻译的目的也就无从谈起。本书中的译诗基本上采用的是“节奏弹跳式自由体韵诗”（Free Verse with Sprung Rhythm）形式，也就是说，译诗形式并不严格紧扣汉语古体诗或近体诗的格律形式，但基本保留其押韵形式，即偶数行押韵，首行可押也可不押，并尽可能做到平声入韵，有时也押仄声韵，采取平仄通押的押韵方式，以求最大限度做到对原诗内容的“忠实”。这里的“节奏弹跳式”借用的是英国诗人杰拉尔德·曼利·霍普金斯提出的“Sprung Rhythm”（“弹跳韵式”或“弹跳节奏”），算是“洋为中用”了。

Prior to Hopkins, most Middle English and Modern English poetry was based on a rhythmic structure inherited from the Norman side of English literary heritage. This structure is based on repeating groups of two or three syllables, with the stressed syllable falling in the same place on each repetition. Hopkins called this structure “running rhythm”, and though he wrote some of his early verse in running rhythm, he became fascinated with the older rhythmic structure of the Anglo-Saxon tradition, of which Beowulf is the most famous example. Hopkins called his own rhythmic structure “sprung rhythm”. Sprung rhythm is structured around feet with a variable number of syllables, generally between one and four syllables per foot, with the stress always falling on the first syllable in a foot. It is similar to the “rolling stresses” of Robinson Jeffers, another poet who rejected conventional metre. Hopkins saw sprung rhythm as a way to escape the constraints of running rhythm, which he said inevitably pushed poetry written in it to become “same and tame.” In this way, Hopkins can be seen as anticipating much of free verse.

在霍普金斯之前，多数中世纪英语诗歌及现代英语诗歌所基于的韵式结构，是从英国文学遗产中诺曼人一方继承下来的。这种韵式结构的基础是重复的群组，每个群组由两个到三个音节构成，而且重音落在每一次重复中同样的位置上。霍普金斯称其为“奔跑韵式”（或“奔跑节奏”）。尽管霍普金斯早期的一些诗运用奔跑韵式写成，但他却对更为古老的“盎格鲁–撒克逊”传统的韵式结构着迷，古英语史诗《贝奥武甫》就是最为有名的一个例子。霍普金斯称自己的这种韵式结构为“弹跳韵式”（或“弹跳节奏”）。弹跳韵式围绕音步展开，每个音步的音节数量不固定，但每个音步一般由一到四个音节组成，且重音总是落在每个音步的第一个音节上。这种结构类似于鲁滨孙·杰弗斯创造的“滚动重音”。杰弗斯是另一位厌弃传统格律的诗人。霍普金斯将弹跳韵式视作挣脱奔跑韵式限制的一种方式。他认为，奔跑韵式势必将以此韵式写成的诗推向“同模和驯服”。这样看来，就可以说，霍普金斯预先写出了大量的自由体韵诗[①]。

就译诗而言，若以汉语停顿的次数，即所谓的“顿数”，来代替英诗音步的话，则每一顿数的汉字数量是不固定的（这一点跟汉语近体诗中严格的格律要求有所不同）。这样做的目的，就是最大可能地忠实于原诗的意象、内容和意义。

不同的译者对英诗原文内容的思考也会有所不同，无法在诗的理解上完全一致，所谓“诗无达诂”也。关于这一点，从美国现代派诗人比利·柯林斯为他的学生所写的一首现代诗《诗歌入门》（*Introduction to Poetry*）中，可见一斑，算是理解诗歌内容方面“以诗论诗”的典范。

I ask them to take a poem
and hold it up to the light
like a color slide

or press an ear against its hive.

I say drop a mouse into a poem

① 这段关于“弹跳韵式”（或“弹跳节奏”）的译文为本书译注者所译。

and watch him probe his way out,

or walk inside the poem's room
and feel the walls for a light switch.

I want them to waterski
across the surface of a poem
waving at the author's name on the shore.

But all they want to do
is tie the poem to a chair with rope
and torture a confession out of it.

They begin beating it with a hose
to find out what it really means.

我要求学生拿出一首诗，
对着光线举起来，
就像举起一张彩色幻灯片；

或者将一只耳朵贴近诗的蜂房。

我说的是，把一只老鼠扔进诗中，
看老鼠如何找到出口；

或者在诗的房间里走动，
摸索四周的墙壁，找到灯的开关。

我想要学生
在诗的表面滑水，

同时向岸边的诗作者招手。

可是，学生想做的
却是用绳子把诗绑到椅子上，
严刑拷打，逼其招供。

他们开始用软管带抽打，
要查出它到底有什么意义。

从上述对诗歌内容理解的角度考虑，本书著者尽最大可能在“观照”原诗的“意义”和“意象”的基础上，对英文原诗加以汉译探索。

本书遵循以下翻译原则：

1.人名、地名的翻译主要依据《世界人名翻译大辞典》（1993年第1版/2007年第2版）及《世界地名翻译大辞典》（2008年第1版）。个别的人名、地名的翻译，兼顾了流行的译法。

2.译诗在忠于英诗原文的基础上尽量杜绝“翻译腔”，以保持汉语语言的纯洁性和规范性。

3.译诗多采用“归化”的翻译方法，即充分观照汉诗的押韵特点，以求最大程度适合汉语读者的阅读习惯。

当然，“金无足赤，人无完人”，匆忙且蹒跚的步履难免会迈出“不和谐”的步伐。书中若有不当甚至错漏之处，还望读者指正。

王永胜　朱　红

2022年初

Contents
目　录

Chapter 01　Moon's Impressions on Different People
第一章　月之印象 / 001

001 Emily Elizabeth Dickinson　埃米莉·伊丽莎白·狄更生 / 003
The Moon Was but a Chin of Gold / 003
月儿只不过是个金下巴 / 005

002 Charlotte Smith　夏洛特·史密斯 / 007
Press'd by the Moon (Sonnet XLIV) / 007
受控于月儿（商籁体第44首） / 010

003 Lew R. Sarett　卢·R.萨雷特 / 011
Yellow Moon / 011
黄月亮 / 014

004 Jonathan Swift　乔纳森·斯威夫特 / 015
On the Moon / 015
关于月亮 / 017

005 Carl Sandburg　卡尔·桑德堡 / 019
Child Moon / 019
孩童望月 / 020

006 Charlotte Smith　夏洛特·史密斯 / 021
To the Invisible Moon (Sonnet LXXX) / 021
致藏匿的月儿（商籁体第80首） / 024

Chapter 02　Song of the Moon
第二章　月之歌谣 / 027

007 Claude McKay　克劳德·麦凯 / 029
Song of the Moon / 029
月亮之歌 / 031

008 Robert William Service 罗伯特·威廉·瑟维斯 / 033

Moon Song / 033

月亮之歌 / 037

009 Ernest Christopher Dowson 欧内斯特·克里斯托弗·道森 / 040

The Moon Maiden's Song / 040

月亮少女之歌 / 042

010 Lady Mary Wortley Montagu 玛丽·沃特利·蒙塔古夫人 / 043

A Hymn to the Moon / 043

月亮颂歌 / 046

011 Samuel Taylor Coleridge 塞缪尔·泰勒·柯尔律治 / 047

To the Autumnal Moon (Sonnet 18) / 047

致秋月（商籁体第18首） / 049

Chapter 03 Moon's Light Shining

第三章 月之光明 / 051

012 Sara Teasdale 萨拉·蒂斯代尔 / 053

Moonlight / 053

月光 / 054

013 Henry Wadsworth Longfellow 亨利·沃兹沃斯·朗费罗 / 055

Moonlight / 055

月光 / 058

014 Henry Wadsworth Longfellow 亨利·沃兹沃斯·朗费罗 / 061

Daylight and Moonlight / 061

日光与月光 / 063

015 Emily Elizabeth Dickinson 埃米莉·伊丽莎白·狄更生 / 065

The Road Was Lit with Moon and Star / 065

月亮和星星把路照亮 / 066

016 Alfred Tennyson 艾尔弗雷德·丁尼生 / 067

When on My Bed the Moonlight Falls / 067

月光洒落在我的床上 / 069

017 Thomas Hardy 托马斯·哈代 / 071

In the Moonlight / 071

月光之下 / 073

018 Alfred Edward Housman 艾尔弗雷德·爱德华·豪斯曼 / 075

White in the Moon the Long Road Lies / 075

月色中，长路铺展白茫茫 / 077

019 Emily Brontë 艾米莉·勃朗特 / 078

Moonlight, Summer Moonlight / 078

月光，夏夜的月光 / 080

020 Sarah Knowles Bolton 萨拉·诺尔斯·博尔顿 / 081

The Moonlight / 081

月光 / 083

021 Thomas Moore 托马斯·穆尔 / 084

While Gazing on the Moon's Light / 084

凝望月光之时 / 087

022 Maxwell Bodenheim 马克斯韦尔·博登海姆 / 089

Moonlight Bends over the Black Silence / 089

月光照亮黝黑的沉寂 / 090

023 Witter Bynner 威特·宾纳 / 092

A Thrush in the Moonlight / 092

月光下的画眉鸟 / 093

024 Adelaide Crapsey 阿德莱德·克拉普西 / 094

Moon Shadows / 094

月下之影 / 095

Chapter 04 Moon and Love

第四章 月与爱情 / 097

025 Thomas Hardy 托马斯·哈代 / 099

Shut Out That Moon / 099

将那月亮隔到外边 / 103

026 Walter Savage Landor 沃尔特·萨维奇·兰多 / 105

On an Eclipse of the Moon / 105

记一次月食 / 107

027 Thomas Moore 托马斯·穆尔 / 108

The Young May Moon / 108

五月的初月 / 110

028 Vachel Lindsay 韦切尔·林赛 / 112

The Moon is a Painter / 112

月亮是位好画家 / 115

029 Percy Bysshe Shelley 珀西·比希·雪莱 / 116

To the Moon / 116

致月儿 / 117

030 Evelyn Scott 伊芙琳·斯科特 / 118

The Naiad / 118

那伊阿得 / 119

031 James Joyce 詹姆斯·乔伊斯 / 120

What Counsel Has the Hooded Moon / 120

那头戴风帽的月亮给了你什么样的忠告 / 122

Chapter 05 Moon and Feelings

第五章 月与情感 / 123

032 Robert Frost 罗伯特·弗罗斯特 / 125

The Freedom of the Moon / 125

自由的月亮 / 127

033 Christina Georgina Rossetti 克里斯蒂娜·乔治娜·罗塞蒂 / 128

Is the Moon Tired? / 128

月儿累了吗? / 129

034 William Butler Yeats 威廉·巴特勒·叶芝 / 130

The Crazed Moon / 130

发了疯的月儿 / 132

035 Sara Teasdale 萨拉·蒂斯代尔 / 134

The Kind Moon / 134

好心肠的月亮 / 135

036 Charlotte Smith 夏洛特·史密斯 / 137

To the Moon (Sonnet IV) / 137

致月儿(商籁体第4首) / 140

037 Thomas Hardy 托马斯·哈代 / 141

The Moon Looks In / 141

月亮朝屋内看去 / 143

038 Emily Elizabeth Dickinson 埃米莉·伊丽莎白·狄更生 / 144

The Moon upon Her Fluent Route / 144

月儿自如地踏上了自己的路线 / 145

039 Robert Louis Stevenson 罗伯特·路易斯·史蒂文森 / 147

The Moon / 147

月儿 / 148

040 Dylan Thomas 迪伦·托马斯 / 150

Clown in the Moon / 150

月亮上的小丑 / 151

041 Sir Philip Sidney 菲利浦·锡德尼爵士 / 152

To the Sad Moon (Sonnet XXXI) / 152

致伤心的月亮（商籁体第31首） / 154

042 Sylvia Plath 西尔维亚·普拉思 / 156

The Moon and the Yew Tree / 156

月亮与紫杉树 / 159

043 Amy Lowell 埃米·洛厄尔 / 161

From China / 161

中国诗的灵感 / 162

Chapter 06 Moon and Things

第六章 月与万物 / 163

044 Ella Wheeler Wilcox 埃拉·惠勒·威尔科克斯 / 165

Moon and Sea / 165

月与海 / 166

045 Emily Elizabeth Dickinson 埃米莉·伊丽莎白·狄更生 / 167

Ah, Moon—and Star! / 167

啊，月亮——还有星星！ / 169

046 Emily Elizabeth Dickinson 埃米莉·伊丽莎白·狄更生 / 171

月亮与大海相距遥远 / 173

047 Siegfried Sassoon 西格弗里德·沙逊 / 174

A Poplar and the Moon / 174

一棵白杨与月亮 / 175

048 Vachel Lindsay 韦切尔·林赛 / 177

The Encyclopaedia / 177

百科全书 / 178

049 William Butler Yeats 威廉·巴特勒·叶芝 / 180

The Cat and the Moon / 180

猫与月儿 / 182

050 Vachel Lindsay 韦切尔·林赛 / 184

The Recreant Queens (To be tied to a pebble and thrown through a palace window) / 184

不忠的王后（要被绑上一块鹅卵石从宫殿窗户扔出去） / 186

Chapter 07 Gentle and Charming Moon

第七章 月柔月媚 / 189

051 William Wordsworth 威廉·华兹华斯 / 191

Strange Fits of Passion Have I Known / 191

我所熟悉的奇特之情阵阵闪现 / 194

052 William Henry Davies 威廉·亨利·戴维斯 / 196

The Moon / 196

月美人 / 198

053 Ella Wheeler Wilcox 埃拉·惠勒·威尔科克斯 / 199

The Old Moon in the New Moon's Arms / 199

新月怀抱中的旧月 / 201

054 William B. Tappan 威廉·B. 塔潘 / 202

Sweet Orb of Night / 202

黑夜迷人的眼 / 205

055 Henry David Thoreau 亨利·大卫·梭罗 / 206

The Moon / 206

月儿 / 208

056 Walter de la Mare 沃尔特·德拉梅尔 / 209

Silver / 209

银月 / 211

057 Walt Whitman 沃尔特·惠特曼 / 212

Look Down, Fair Moon / 212

俯身看吧，娇柔的月儿 / 213

058 D. H. Lawrence D. H. 劳伦斯 / 214

A White Blossom / 214

一朵白色的花 / 215

Chapter 08 Moonrise and Moonset

第八章 月升月落 / 217

059 Gerard Manley Hopkins 杰拉尔德·曼利·霍普金斯 / 219

Moonrise, June 19, 1876 / 219

1876年6月19日，月亮升起 / 221

060 D. H. Lawrence D. H. 劳伦斯 / 223

Moonrise / 223

月出 / 225

061 Thomas Hardy 托马斯·哈代 / 226

Seeing the Moon Rise / 226

看月儿升起 / 228

062 E. Pauline Johnson E·保利娜·约翰逊 / 229

Moonset / 229

月落时分 / 232

063 Carl Sandburg 卡尔·桑德堡 / 233

Moonset / 233

月落 / 234

Chapter 09 Full Moon and Waning Moon

第九章 月圆月缺 / 235

064 Sara Teasdale 萨拉·蒂斯代尔 / 237

Moon's Ending / 237

月渐隐至无影踪 / 238

065 Vachel Lindsay 韦切尔·林赛 / 239

Euclid / 239

欧几里得 / 241

066 Walter de la Mare 沃尔特·德拉梅尔 / 242

Full Moon / 242

满月 / 243

067 Carl Sandburg　卡尔·桑德堡　/　244

Under the Harvest Moon　/　244

秋收季节的满月之下　/　246

068 Elinor Morton Wylie　埃莉诺·莫顿·维利　/　247

Phases of the Moon　/　247

月相　/　249

069 Christina Georgina Rossetti　克里斯蒂娜·乔治娜·罗塞蒂　/　250

The Half Moon　/　250

半月　/　251

070 Sara Teasdale　萨拉·蒂斯代尔　/　253

The New Moon　/　253

新月　/　255

071 George Gordon Byron　乔治·戈登·拜伦　/　256

So We'll Go No More A-roving　/　256

我们不再漫游缠绵　/　257

072 Christina Georgina Rossetti　克里斯蒂娜·乔治娜·罗塞蒂　/　258

Lady Moon　/　258

月亮女士　/　259

073 Emily Elizabeth Dickinson　埃米莉·伊丽莎白·狄更生　/　260

Which is the Best—the Moon or the Crescent?　/　260

盈月或新月——哪个最佳？　/　262

074 Percy Bysshe Shelley　珀西·比希·雪莱　/　263

The Waning Moon　/　263

渐亏之月　/　265

075 Amy Lowell　埃米·洛厄尔　/　266

The Crescent Moon　/　266

小月牙儿　/　268

076 Rose Terry Cooke　罗斯·特里·库克　/　270

New Moon　/　270

新月　/　272

077 D. H. Lawrence　D. H. 劳伦斯　/　274

New Moon　/　274

新月　/　275

Chapter 10 What Different Creatures and Inanimate Objects Said about the Moon

第十章 月因物异 / 279

078 Vachel Lindsay 韦切尔·林赛 / 279

The Old Horse in the City / 279

城里老马眼中的月亮 / 280

079 Vachel Lindsay 韦切尔·林赛 / 282

What the Hyena Said / 282

鬣狗眼中的月亮 / 285

080 Vachel Lindsay 韦切尔·林赛 / 286

What the Snow Man Said / 286

雪人眼中的月亮 / 288

081 Vachel Lindsay 韦切尔·林赛 / 290

What the Scare-crow Said / 290

稻草人眼中的月亮 / 292

082 Vachel Lindsay 韦切尔·林赛 / 293

What Grandpa Mouse Said / 293

鼠爷爷眼中的月亮 / 295

083 Vachel Lindsay 韦切尔·林赛 / 297

What the Rattlesnake Said / 297

响尾蛇眼中的月亮 / 298

Chapter 11 What Different People Said about the Moon

第十一章 月因人异 / 299

084 Vachel Lindsay 韦切尔·林赛 / 301

What the Forester Said / 301

护林员眼中的月亮 / 302

085 Vachel Lindsay 韦切尔·林赛 / 304

A Sense of Humor (Spoken by the Author in his own person) / 304

一丝幽默之感（诗人自己眼中的月亮） / 306

086 Vachel Lindsay 韦切尔·林赛 / 308

The Soul of the Gambler (What the Ghost of the Gambler Said) / 308

赌徒的灵魂（赌徒的鬼魂眼中的月亮） / 310

087 Vachel Lindsay 韦切尔·林赛 / 312

What the Miner in the Desert Said / 312

沙漠矿工眼中的月亮 / 314

088 Vachel Lindsay 韦切尔·林赛 / 315

The Moon Is Compared to a City (What the Tired Reformer Said) / 315

月亮被比作一座城（疲惫的改革家眼中的月亮） / 317

089 Vachel Lindsay 韦切尔·林赛 / 318

The Moon Is a Knight in Armor (What the Soldier Said) / 318

月亮是穿戴盔甲的骑士（士兵眼中的月亮） / 320

090 Vachel Lindsay 韦切尔·林赛 / 321

Drying Their Wings (What the Carpenter Said) / 321

晾晒翅膀（木匠对孩子述说自己眼中的月亮） / 323

091 Vachel Lindsay 韦切尔·林赛 / 324

Yet Gentle Will the Griffin Be (What Grandpa Told the Children) / 324

但狮身鹰首兽也很温柔（爷爷对孩子们讲他眼中的月亮） / 326

092 Vachel Lindsay 韦切尔·林赛 / 327

The Beggar Speaks / 327

乞丐眼中的月亮 / 329

093 Vachel Lindsay 韦切尔·林赛 / 331

The Scissors-grinder (What the Tramp Said) / 331

磨剪刀匠人（流浪汉的述说） / 335

094 Vachel Lindsay 韦切尔·林赛 / 337

What the Young Rhymer Said / 337

年轻诗人眼中的月亮 / 339

095 Vachel Lindsay 韦切尔·林赛 / 340

The Strength of the Lonely (What the Mendicant Said) / 340

孤独者的实力（托钵修士眼中的月亮） / 341

096 Vachel Lindsay 韦切尔·林赛 / 343

What the Sexton Said / 343

教堂司事眼中的月亮 / 345

097 Vachel Lindsay 韦切尔·林赛 / 347

What Semiramis Said / 347

塞米勒米司眼中的月亮 / 349

098　Vachel Lindsay　韦切尔·林赛　/　350

What the Gray-winged Fairy Said　/　350

灰翅膀仙女眼中的月亮　/　351

099　Vachel Lindsay　韦切尔·林赛　/　352

What the Coal-heaver Said　/　352

添煤工眼中的月亮　/　354

100　Vachel Lindsay　韦切尔·林赛　/　355

A Net to Snare the Moonlight (What the Man of Faith Said)　/　355

网住月光（有信心之人眼中的月亮）　/　357

101　Vachel Lindsay　韦切尔·林赛　/　358

The Moon's the North Wind's Cooky (What the Little Girl Said)　/　358

月亮是北风的甜饼干（小女孩眼中的月亮）　/　360

Main Bibliography

主要参考文献　/　361

Epilogue

后　记　/　363

Chapter 01

Moon's Impressions on Different People

第一章

月之印象

001 Emily Elizabeth Dickinson
埃米莉・伊丽莎白・狄更生

◆ *The Poet's Profile* （诗人小档案）

埃米莉・伊丽莎白・狄更生（1830—1886）：美国女诗人，她的诗独具一格：诗行短小，一般没有标题，经常使用近似押韵的方式和一些非常规的大写及标点，主题多与死亡和永生相关。

◆ *The Moon Was but a Chin of Gold*

The Moon was but a Chin of Gold
A Night or two ago—
And now she turns Her perfect Face
Upon the World below—

Her Forehead is of Amplest Blonde—
Her Cheek—a Beryl hewn—
Her Eye unto the Summer Dew
The likest I have known—

Her Lips of Amber never part—
But what must be the smile
Upon Her Friend she could confer
Were such Her Silver Will—

And what a privilege to be

But the remotest Star—
For Certainty She take Her Way
Beside Your Palace Door—

Her Bonnet is the Firmament—
The Universe—Her Shoe—
The Stars—the Trinkets at Her Belt—
Her Dimities—of Blue—

◆ *Annotations* （原诗注释）

1. chin: *n.* the protruding part of the face below the mouth, formed by the apex of the lower jaw 颏；下巴

2. forehead: *n.* the part of the face above the eyebrows 额；前额

3. ample: *adj.* enough or more than enough; plentiful 足够的；充裕的；丰富的

4. blonde: *n.* fair or pale yellow （毛发）金黄色；浅茶褐色

5. cheek: *n.* either side of the face below the eye 脸颊

6. beryl: *n.* a transparent pale green, blue, or yellow mineral consisting of a silicate of beryllium and aluminium, sometimes used as a gemstone 绿柱石；绿玉

7. hew: *v.* chop or cut (something, especially wood or coal) with an axe, pick, or other tool （用斧、鹤嘴锄等）砍；劈；削；切；锯（尤指木头或煤）

8. like: *adj.* similar; resembling 与……相似的；相像

9. amber: *n.* hard translucent fossilized resin originating from extinct coniferous trees of the Tertiary period, typically yellowish in colour. It is found chiefly along the southern shores of the Baltic Sea and has been used in jewellery since antiquity 琥珀

10. confer: *v.* grant (a title, degree, benefit, or right) 授予（头衔、学位、利益、权利）(e.g. Moves were made to confer an honorary degree on her. 为授予她荣誉学位而采取了一些行动。)

11. privilege: *n.* something regarded as a rare opportunity and bringing particular pleasure 特殊荣幸；优待；特别待遇 (e.g. I had the privilege of giving the Sir George Brown memorial lecture. 我有幸作乔治·布朗爵士纪念演讲。)

12. bonnet: *n.* a woman's or child's hat tied under the chin, typically with a brim framing the face （有带）女帽；童帽

13. firmament: *n.* (poetic/literary) the heavens or the sky, especially when regarded as a tangible thing （诗/文）天空；太空；苍穹；苍天

14. trinket: *n.* a small ornament or item of jewellery that is of little value 廉价小装饰物；不值钱的首饰

15. dimity: *n.* a hard-wearing cotton fabric woven with stripes or checks （织有条纹或格子的耐磨的）棉布

◆ *A Lead-in Note* （简明导读）

狄更生在此诗中使用了一些非常规的大写和标点，此等风格很难对等性地在译诗中加以“观照”，只能在译诗中做常规性处理。此诗中，诗人以“她”代称月亮，用丰富的想象和夸张等手法对月亮做了形象化的描述。例如，月相的变化，在诗人看来，一会儿是“金下巴”，一会儿是“完美的脸庞”。在诗人眼中，月亮成了一位女子的象征，而这位女子给诗人留下了极其深刻的印象。

◆ 月儿只不过是个金下巴

月儿只不过是个金下巴——
就在一两个夜晚之前。
现在她将她完美的脸庞
转向人间——

她的前额——金黄色最细腻，
她的脸颊——切削过的绿宝石；
她那只眼睛啊，据我所知——
与夏夜露珠最为相似。

她琥珀色的唇从未开启，
但她能赠与朋友的，
必定是微笑
若这是她银白色的心愿——

成为一颗最为遥远的星星，
是何等殊荣——
你家宅邸大门旁边，
毫无疑问，她会取道而行。

她的帽子是苍穹，
宇宙是鞋——任她穿；
繁星——系于腰间；
她的衣裙——色彩蓝蓝。

002 Charlotte Smith
夏洛特・史密斯

◆ *The Poet's Profile* （诗人小档案）

夏洛特・史密斯（1749—1806）：英国浪漫主义女诗人及长篇小说家。夏洛特复兴了英国商籁体诗歌，为哥特式小说的规范作出了贡献，还写了一些政治感伤小说。夏洛特是一位成功的作家，在她一生的职业生涯中，出版过10部小说，3部诗集等作品。

◆ *Press'd by the Moon (Sonnet XLIV)*

Press'd by the Moon, mute arbitress of tides,
While the loud equinox its power combines,
The sea no more its swelling surge confines,
But o'er the shrinking land sublimely rides.
The wild blast, rising from the Western cave,
Drives the huge billows from their heaving bed;
Tears from their grassy tombs the village dead,
And breaks the silent sabbath of the grave!
With shells and sea-weed mingled, on the shore
Lo! their bones whiten in the frequent wave;
But vain to them the winds and waters rave;
They hear the warring elements no more:
While I am doom'd—by life's long storm oppress,
To gaze with envy on their gloomy rest.

◆ Annotations （原诗注释）

1. Press'd = Pressed

press: *v.* move or cause to move into a position of contact with something by exerting continuous physical force 压；榨；挤

2. arbitress: *n.* a female arbitrator 女仲裁人

3. tide: *n.* the alternate rising and falling of the sea, usually twice in each lunar day at a particular place, due to the attraction of the moon and sun 潮（汐）（e.g. They were driven on by wind and tide. 他们被风和潮水越冲越远。）

4. loud: *adj.* clamorous, insistent, and emphatic 大声喧闹的；强调的；坚持的

5. equinox: *n.* the time or date (twice each year) at which the sun crosses the celestial equator, when day and night are of equal length (about 22 September and 20 March) 二分时刻（春分或秋分）

6. surge: *n.* a sudden powerful forward or upward movement, especially by a crowd or by a natural force such as the waves or tide 汹涌（尤指人潮，波涛，潮汐等）（e.g. Flooding caused by tidal surges. 由潮汐猛涨而引起的洪水泛滥。）

7. o'er = over

8. sublime: *adj.* producing an overwhelming sense of awe or other high emotion through being vast or grand 宏伟的；令人敬畏的

9. blast: *n.* a strong gust of wind or air 一阵强风；一股强劲的气流（e.g. The icy blast hit them. 一阵寒风朝他们猛袭而来。）

10. billow: *n.* (Archaic) a large sea wave （古旧用法）巨大的海浪

11. heave: *v.* [no obj.] rise and fall rhythmically or spasmodically 起伏（e.g. His shoulders heaved as he panted. 他肩膀一起一伏地喘着气。）

12. grassy: *adj.* of or covered with grass （青）草的；长满草的

13. sabbath: *n.* (often the Sabbath) the holy day of week that is used for resting and worshipping God. For Jews this day is Saturday and for Christians it is Sunday. 安息日（犹太教定为星期六，基督教定为星期日）

14. mingle: *v.* mix or cause to mix together （使）混合；（使）相混 （e.g. The sound of voices mingled with a scraping of chairs. 说话声和椅子刮擦声混杂在一起。）

15. lo: *exc.* (archaic) used to draw attention to an interesting or amazing event （古旧用法）（用以引起对有趣或惊奇之事的注意）嗟夫；看；瞧 （e.g. And lo, the star, which they saw in the east, went before them. 嗟夫，东方所见之星行其前也。）

16. rave: *v.* to speak wildly, irrationally, or incoherentl y 咆哮；狂怒地说

17. warring: *adj.* (of two or more people or groups) in conflict with each other （两个或多个人、群体）交战的；敌对的；冲突的

18. element: *n.* a small but significant presence of a feeling or abstract quality 成分；性质 （e.g. It was the element of danger he loved in flying. 他喜欢的是飞行中的那份危险。）

19. doom'd = doomed

20. opprest = oppressed

21. gloomy: *adj.* causing distress or depression 使悲伤（或消沉）的 （e.g. a gloomy atmosphere 令人沮丧的气氛）

◆ *A Lead-in Note* （简明导读）

诗人夏洛特在参观英国苏塞克斯郡米德尔顿的一座墓地时，有感而发，写就此诗。米德尔顿是苏塞克斯郡一座临海的村庄，那里只有两三座房子。米德尔顿村的小教堂和大海之间原先有好几英亩的土地，但由于月亮的作用而产生潮汐现象，海水不断侵蚀，围起教堂墓地的墙壁已完全被冲垮了。很多坟墓破损，以前葬得好好的尸骨被冲刷了出来，所以“海滩上，尸骨与贝壳、海草相混杂”。月亮的引力令潮涨潮落，大海受控于“月儿”而变得“无所畏惧”，长年累月肆意冲刷着海滩。在诗人看来，月亮似乎是破坏之神，具有令人畏惧的威力。

◆ 受控于月儿（商籁体第44首）

潮汐受控于月儿——沉默的仲裁女，
春秋分也吵嚷着协同行使权力；
于是，大海不再局限于汹涌澎湃，
而是骑上退缩的陆地，无所畏惧。
西部洞穴那里生起狂野的强风，
催促着巨浪起床，床伏下又隆起。
碧草覆坟，风从中扯出村中死者，
打破了墓地宁静而平安的朝夕！
海滩上，尸骨与贝壳、海草相混杂；
看呐，波浪冲刷不停，尸骨似白玉！
可风再强劲，浪再狂吼，也是枉然，
挑衅之意再也听不见，他们已死。
但是，人生的暴风雨一直压着我，
令我沮丧，艳羡他们悲哀的安息。

003 Lew R. Sarett
卢・R. 萨雷特

◆ *The Poet's Profile* （诗人小档案）

卢・R. 萨雷特（1888—1954）：美国诗人、演讲家和教师。萨雷特生于芝加哥，出生时的名字叫卢・萨雷特斯基，其父母是波兰和立陶宛的移民。年纪尚小的时候，萨雷特就对自然及美洲印第安文化和传说感兴趣，这样的兴趣在他的生活和诗歌中有明显的体现。萨雷特出版过五部诗集：《很多很多的月亮》（1920）、《上帝的盒子》（1922）、《徐升之烟》（1925）、《逆月飞行》（1931）以及《卢・萨雷特诗选》（1941）。

◆ *Yellow Moon*

O yellow moon,
Drifting across the night
As a rakish pirate brig,
Tattered of rig
And ghostly white,
Goes floating down the black lagoon
Of a dead sea—
O pirate moon,
Out of your hatch and hold
Pour down your buccaneering beams,
Your pirates, swaggering and bold,
And bid them capture me;
O ghostly moon,

Carry me out to the farthest sweep
Of the slow tides of sleep;
Abandon me upon the gold
Of some enchanted strand,
Where the blue-flame comber gleams
And breaks upon the sand;
Oh, sail with me to a far land
Of unremembered dreams.

◆ Annotations （原诗注释）

1. o: *exc.* used to express surprise or strong emotion 哦；哟；啊；唉；哎呀（表示惊讶或强烈的情感）

2. rakish: *adj.* (especially of a boat or car) smart and fast-looking, with streamlined angles and curves （尤指车、船）流线型的；轻捷灵巧的

3. brig: *n.* a two-masted square-rigged ship, typically having an additional lower fore-and-aft sail on the gaff and a boom to the mainmast 双桅横帆船；双桅船；横帆双桅船

4. tatter: *v.* to make or become ragged or worn to shreds 扯碎；撕碎；使破烂

5. rig: *n.* the particular way in which a sailing boat's masts, sails, and rigging are arranged 帆装

6. ghostly: *adj.* of or like a ghost in appearance or sound; eerie and unnatural （外表或声音）似鬼的；古怪的；奇异的 （e.g. a frightening, ghostly figure with a hood 戴着头巾如鬼魅般的可怕身影）

7. lagoon: *n.* a stretch of salt water separated from the sea by a low sandbank or coral reef （由沙丘、珊瑚礁与海隔开的）咸水湖；潟湖

8. hatch: *n.* an opening in the deck of a boat or ship leading to the cabin or a lower level （船甲板上通往下面的）有盖舱口

9. hold: *n.* a large compartment or space in the lower part of a ship or aircraft in

which cargo is stowed （船或飞机）货舱

10. buccaneering: *n.* hijacking on the high seas or in similar contexts 劫持；海盗行为

11. swagger: *v.* walk or behave in a very confident and typically arrogant or aggressive way 昂首阔步；大摇大摆地走

12. bid: *v.* (bidding; past bid or bade; past participle bid) (archaic or poetic/literary) command or order (someone) to do something （古旧用法或诗/文用法）命令；吩咐 （e.g. I did as he bade me. 我按他的吩咐行事。）

13. sweep: *n.* (figurative) the range or scope of something （比喻用法）范围

14. sleep: *n.* (chiefly poetic/literary) a state compared to or resembling this, such as death or complete silence or stillness （主要为诗/文用法）休止；寂静；沉睡

15. enchant: *v.* (often be enchanted) fill (someone) with great delight; charm 使陶醉；使入迷 （e.g. Isabel was enchanted with the idea. 伊莎贝尔对那个想法着了迷。）

16. strand: *n.* (poetic/literary) the shore of a sea, lake, or large river （诗/文用法）海滨；海滩；湖滨；河岸 （e.g. A heron glided to rest on a pebbly strand. 一只鹭滑过天空，栖息在布满鹅卵石的岸边。）

17. comber: *n.* a long curling sea wave 卷浪

18. gleam: *v.* shine brightly, especially with reflected light （尤指反光的）发光；闪烁 （e.g. Her eyes gleamed with satisfaction. 她的眼中闪烁着满意的光芒。）

◆ *A Lead-in Note* （简明导读）

诗人萨雷特以黄月亮起兴，任想象的野马脱缰狂奔。月亮似海盗船，月色下众海盗“把我擒获掳去”。月亮又是幽灵的化身，“把我带到最遥远的地方”，并“在那儿金黄的沙滩上将我丢弃”。最后，诗人呼喊：“啊，与我一同航行到远方之地，那里的梦，无人会留下记忆。”在诗人的眼中，黄月亮具有无比的魔力，像一艘魔力之船，带着诗人驶向理想之地。

◆ 黄月亮

啊，黄月亮！
如海盗的流线型双桅船只，
漂过黑夜，
帆桅皆破碎的样子，
古怪而苍白，
沿着黑色的潟湖漂移，
那潟湖是一片死海。
啊，月亮，海盗的船只！
从你的货舱和舱口
将你劫持的光线倒出船体，
放出海盗，令昂首无畏的海盗
把我擒获掳去。
啊，月亮，幽灵的化身！
把我带到最遥远的地方，
那里潮水迟缓，一片安静。
在那儿金黄的沙滩上将我丢弃。
那片海滩令人沉醉：
蓝火苗般波浪闪耀着卷起，
拍打着沙滩。
啊，与我一同航行到远方之地，
那里的梦，无人会留下记忆。

004 Jonathan Swift
乔纳森·斯威夫特

◆ *The Poet's Profile*（诗人小档案）

乔纳森·斯威夫特（1667—1745）：英国讽刺作家、诗人。斯威夫特最为著名的作品是《格列佛游记》（1726），代表了讽刺文学的高峰。

◆ *On the Moon*

I with borrow'd silver shine
What you see is none of mine.
First I show you but a quarter,
Like the bow that guards the Tartar:
Then the half, and then the whole,
Ever dancing round the pole.

What will raise your admiration,
I am not one of God's creation,
But sprung, (and I this truth maintain,)
Like Pallas, from my father's brain.
And after all, I chiefly owe
My beauty to the shades below.
Most wondrous forms you see me wear,
A man, a woman, lion, bear,
A fish, a fowl, a cloud, a field,
All figures Heaven or earth can yield;

Like Daphne sometimes in a tree;
Yet am not one of all you see.

◆ Annotations （原诗注释）

1. borrow'd = borrowed

2. bow: *n.* a weapon for shooting arrows, typically made of a curved piece of wood joined at both ends by a taut string 弓（一种武器）

3. Tartar: *n.* (historical) a member of the combined forces of central Asian peoples, including Mongols and Turks, who under the leadership of Genghis Khan conquered much of Asia and eastern Europe in the early 13th century, and under Tamerlane (14th century) established an empire with its capital at Samarkand （历史上的用法）鞑靼人（包括蒙古人和土耳其人在内的中亚人联合部队的成员之一，13世纪早期在成吉思汗的率领下征服了亚洲大部分地区和东欧，14世纪在帖木儿的统治下建立了帝国，定都撒马尔罕）

4. pole: *n.* either of the two locations (North Pole or South Pole) on the surface of the earth (or of a celestial object) which are the northern and southern ends of the axis of rotation 地极；地极区域；（天体的）极

5. Pallas: *n.* (Greek Mythology) (also as "Pallas Athene") one of the names (of unknown meaning) of Athene or Athena （希腊神话）帕拉斯（雅典娜的名字之一，含义不详）

Athena: *n.* (Greek Mythology) a virgin goddess of wisdom, practical skills, and prudent warfare. She was born, fully armed, from the head of Zeus. Also called: "*Pallas Athena*" or "*Pallas*". 雅典娜（希腊神话中的贞洁女神，集智慧、实用技能、战事决策于一身。她全副武装从宙斯的头颅里蹦出来而降生。雅典娜也被称作"帕拉斯·雅典娜"或"帕拉斯"）

6. owe: *v.* (owe something to) have something because of (someone or something) 应把……归功于 （e.g. Champagne houses owe their success to brand image. 香槟酒店的成功要归功于品牌形象。）

7. shade: *n.* (usu. shades) (poetic/literary) a shadow or area of darkness （诗/文用法）阴影；阴暗处 （e.g. The shades of evening drew on. 夜幕降临。）

8. wondrous: *adj.* (poetic/literary) inspiring a feeling of wonder or delight; marvelous （诗/文用法）令人惊奇的；奇妙的

9. fowl: *n.* any other domesticated bird kept for its eggs or flesh, e.g. the turkey, duck, goose, and guineafowl 家禽

10. Daphne: *n.* (Greek Mythology) a nymph who was turned into a laurel bush to save her from the amorous pursuit of Apollo （在希腊神话中，达佛涅为了逃避阿波罗求爱而被变成月桂树）

◆ *A Lead-in Note* （简明导读）

此诗中，诗人以第一人称的视角描绘出月亮的“实质”。同时，诗人借助史实和古希腊罗马神话对月亮加以形象化的描述。月亮无所不能，甚至能“千变万化”。可以说，化身为月亮的诗人竭尽全力所作的一切都是为了“你”，但却无法赢得“你”的芳心，因“你”的眼中没有我。如果站在诗人“我”的角度，将“你”比作月亮的话，可谓：我本将心向明月，奈何明月照沟渠。

◆ 关于月亮

银色的光，是我借来之物；
你眼中所见，非我所属。
我最初让你看到的四分之一，
犹如弯弓，将鞑靼人守护。
接着是一半，随后是一轮，
一律绕着轴跃动，循环往复。

有何可提升你的敬佩之情？

我不是神造之物，
可跟帕拉斯相似，（我始终认为，）
我蹦出的地方，是父亲的脑部。
不管怎样，我的美在下方，
归于我的投影之术。
多数奇妙之形，我都能为你呈现出来——
男人，女人，熊，老虎；
鱼类，家禽，田，还有云，
以及天或地能造之物，
你像化身为树的达佛涅一样，
所看到的皆与我无关。

005 Carl Sandburg
卡尔·桑德堡

◆ *The Poet's Profile* （诗人小档案）

卡尔·桑德堡（1878—1967）：美国诗人及传记作家。桑德堡的诗收录在《芝加哥诗集》（1915）、《烟与钢》（1920）、《桑德堡诗歌全集》（1950）、《蜜与盐》（1963）四部诗集中。桑德堡也因1926年至1939年间完成的亚伯拉罕·林肯的传记而闻名。此传记共分为六卷，包括《亚伯拉罕·林肯：北美大草原岁月》（共两卷）及《亚伯拉罕·林肯：战争岁月》（共四卷）。

◆ *Child Moon*

The child's wonder
At the old moon
Comes back nightly.
She points her finger
To the far silent yellow thing
Shining through the branches
Filtering on the leaves a golden sand,
Crying with her little tongue, "See the moon!"
And in her bed fading to sleep
With babblings of the moon on her little mouth.

◆ *Annotations* （原诗注释）

1. wonder: *n.* a feeling of surprise mingled with admiration, caused by something beautiful, unexpected, unfamiliar, or inexplicable 惊奇；惊讶；惊叹；诧异 （e.g. He had stood in front of it, observing the intricacy of the ironwork with the wonder of a child. 他站在前面，带着孩子般的好奇，目不转睛地看着错综复杂的打铁工序。）

2. filter: *v.* pass (a liquid, gas, light, or sound) through a device to remove unwanted material 过滤（液体、气体、光或声音）（e.g. The eye filters out ultraviolet radiation. 眼睛可滤除紫外线。）

3. babbling: *n.* gibberish resembling the sounds of a baby 婴儿发出的咿哑声

◆ *A Lead-in Note* （简明导读）

在这个小女孩眼中，古老的月亮犹如饱经风霜的老奶奶，哼着无声的催眠曲。只要小女孩伸出小舌头叫着“看呐，月亮！”，她就会慢慢进入梦乡，或许还会做着关于月亮的甜蜜之梦。可见，月亮对孩子的吸引力巨大。

◆ 孩童望月

对于古老的月亮，
这个小女孩的惊奇之情
夜夜复现。
她将手指指向远方
那一轮遥远的、寂静的鹅黄。
从枝丫间倾泻而下，
透过叶的筛子，洒落一地黄沙。
她伸出小小的舌头，叫道：“看呐，月亮！”
随即躺在床上，渐入梦乡，
小嘴咿呀念着：月亮，月亮。

006 Charlotte Smith
夏洛特·史密斯

◆ *The Poet's Profile* （诗人小档案）

夏洛特·史密斯（1749—1806）：英国浪漫主义女诗人及长篇小说家。夏洛特复兴了英国商籁体诗歌，为哥特式小说的规范作出了贡献，还写了一些政治感伤小说。夏洛特是一位成功的作家，在她一生的职业生涯中，出版过10部小说，3部诗集等作品。

◆ *To the Invisible Moon (Sonnet LXXX)*

Dark and conceal'd art thou, soft Evening's queen,
And Melancholy's votaries that delight
To watch thee, gliding through the blue serene,
Now vainly seek thee on the brow of night—
Mild Sorrow, such as hope has not forsook,
May love to muse beneath thy silent reign;
But I prefer from some steep rock to look
On the obscure and fluctuating main,
What time the martial star with lurid glare,
Portentous, gleams above the troubled deep;
Or the red comet shakes his blazing hair;
Or on the fire-ting'd waves the lightnings leap;
While thy fair beams illume another sky,
And shine for beings less accursed than I.

◆ Annotations （原诗注释）

1. invisible: *adj.* concealed from sight; hidden 视力外的；看不清的；隐匿的（e.g. He lounged in a doorway, invisible in the dark. 他在门口闲待着，黑暗中看不清他的身影。）

2. conceal'd = concealed

concealed: *adj.* not accessible to view; hidden 看不见的；隐藏的

3. art: *v.* archaic or dialect 2nd person singular present of be （古旧用法及诗歌中用法）“be”的第二人称、单数、现在时形式

4. thou: *pron.* [second person singular] archaic or dialect form of you, as the singular subject of a verb （古旧用法或方言用法）（作动词的单数主语）你（同“you”）

5. soft: *adj.* sympathetic, lenient, or compassionate, especially to a degree perceived as excessive; not strict or sufficiently strict （尤指过于）心肠软的；仁慈的；富于同情心的；不够严厉的 （e.g. Julia's soft heart was touched by his grief. 朱莉娅仁慈的心被他的不幸打动。）

6. melancholy: *n.* a deep, pensive, and long-lasting sadness 忧思；愁思

7. votary: *n.* a devoted follower, adherent, or advocate of someone or something 忠实追随者；信徒；崇拜者；爱好者 （e.g. He was a votary of John Keats. 他是诗人济慈的崇拜者。）

8. delight: *v.* to take great pleasure or joy; (delight in) take great pleasure in 感到高兴；以……为乐

9. thee: *pron.* [second person singular] archaic or dialect form of you, as the singular object of a verb or preposition （古英语“thou”的宾格，同“you”）你；汝

10. glide: *v.* move with a smooth continuous motion, typically with little noise （尤指无声地）滑动 （e.g. A few gondolas glided past. 几艘小划船悄然划过。）

11. serene: *n.* (usu. as “the serene”) (archaic) an expanse of clear sky or calm sea （古旧用法）晴空；平静的大海 （e.g. Not a cloud obscured the deep se-

rene. 一片晴空，万里无云。）

12. brow: *n.* a person's forehead 额；脑门子

13. mild: *adj.* not keenly felt or seriously intended 微弱的；没劲的；没精打采的（e.g. She looked at him in mild surprise. 她略带惊奇地看着他。）

14. forsake: *v.* (past forsook; past participle forsaken) (chiefly poetic/literary) abandon (someone or something)（主要为诗/文用法）抛弃；遗弃（人或物）（e.g. He would never forsake Tara. 他永远不会抛弃塔拉。）

15. muse: *v.* be absorbed in thought 沉思；默想；冥想（e.g. He was musing on the problems he faced. 他正在冥想所面临的问题。）

16. thy: *poss. adj.* (also "thine" before a vowel) archaic or dialect form of your（元音前亦作"thine"）（古旧用法或方言用法）你（您）的（同"your"）

17. reign: *n.* the period during which a sovereign rules 统治期；（君主）在位期（e.g. The original chapel was built in the reign of Charles I. 原有的礼拜堂建于查尔斯一世当政时期。）

18. steep: *adj.* (of a slope, flight of stairs, or angle) rising or falling sharply; almost perpendicular（斜面、楼梯、角度）陡的；陡峭的；陡直的（e.g. She pushed the bike up the steep hill. 她把自行车推上陡峭的山坡。）

19. fluctuating: *adj.* having unpredictable ups and downs 上下摇动不定的

20. main: *n.* (the main) (archaic or poetic/literary) the open ocean（古旧用法或诗/文用法）大海；海洋；公海

21. lurid: *adj.* very vivid in colour, especially so as to create an unpleasantly harsh or unnatural effect 鲜艳得可怕的；耀眼的；绚丽的

22. glare: *n.* strong and dazzling light 刺眼的强光（e.g. Murray narrowed his eyes against the glare of the sun. 默里对着刺眼的阳光眯起了眼睛。）

23. portentous: *adj.* of or like a portent 预示性的；征兆似的（e.g. the envelope and its portentous contents 那个信封及其预示性的内容）

24. deep: *n.* (the deep) (poetic/literary) the sea（诗/文用法）海；海洋（e.g. denizens of the deep 海中动物）

25. blazing: *adj.* burning or shining very brightly 燃烧的；闪亮的

26. ting'd = tinged

27. illume: *v.* (poetic/literary) light up; illuminate （诗/文用法）点燃；照亮（e.g. Sparks from candles illume our faces. 蜡烛的火花照亮了我们的脸庞。）

28. accursed: *adj.* (poetic/literary) under a curse （诗/文用法）受诅咒的 （e.g. The Angel of Death walks this accursed house. 死神在这受诅咒的屋子里徘徊。）

◆ *A Lead-in Note* （简明导读）

诗人以拟人化手法和颇具象征意义的意象写出了“晚间”的温柔女王——月儿藏匿后所出现的情况。没有月儿的夜晚，有人开始“忧思”起来，到处寻找月儿。有人感到“轻微悲伤”，但仍没有放弃希望。但是，“我”的反应却不一样，“我却更喜欢从陡峭的礁石上边探查……”而就在“此时，你的银光投向另一片天空，照亮没有我这般倒霉之人的脸”。

◆ 致藏匿的月儿（商籁体第80首）

月儿——晚间的温柔女王，藏匿不见，
忧思的那些随从曾欣喜地放眼，
远望你缓缓地滑过蓝色的夜空，
却在夜晚的额前，徒劳将你找寻。
轻微悲伤还没有被希望所抛弃，
有你默默统领，或许还沉思一番。
可是在模糊而飘摇的大海之上，
我却更喜欢从陡峭的礁石上边
探查：那颗有预见性的火星何时
闪着耀眼光芒照亮汹涌的海面。
或看着红彗星摇着燃烧的头发，

或看着闪电跳跃在火红的浪尖。
此时，你的银光投向另一片天空，
照亮没有我这般倒霉之人的脸。

Chapter 02

Song of the Moon

第二章

月之歌谣

007 Claude McKay
克劳德·麦凯

◆ *The Poet's Profile* （诗人小档案）

克劳德·麦凯（1889—1948）：牙买加裔美国作家及诗人，美国“哈莱姆文艺复兴运动”的先锋，著有诗集《新罕布什尔之春》和《哈莱姆阴影》等。

◆ *Song of the Moon*

The moonlight breaks upon the city's domes,
And falls along cemented steel and stone,
Upon the grayness of a million homes,
Lugubrious in unchanging monotone.
Upon the clothes behind the tenement,
That hang like ghosts suspended from the lines,
Linking each flat to each indifferent,
Incongruous and strange the moonlight shines.

There is no magic from your presence here,
Ho, moon, sad moon, tuck up your trailing robe,
Whose silver seems antique and so severe
Against the glow of one electric globe.

Go spill your beauty on the laughing faces
Of happy flowers that bloom a thousand hues,

Waiting on tiptoe in the wilding spaces,
To drink your wine mixed with sweet drafts of dews.

◆ Annotations （原诗注释）

1. dome: *n.* (poetic/literary) a stately building（诗/文用法）雄伟的建筑物

2. cement: *v.* fix with cement 用水泥固定

3. lugubrious: *adj.* looking or sounding sad and dismal （看起来或听起来）悲哀的；忧郁的

4. monotone: *n.* a continuing sound, especially of someone's voice, that is unchanging in pitch and without intonation 单调；单调音 （e.g. He sat and answered the questions in a monotone. 他坐着用单调的声音回答问题。）

5. tenement: *n.* (especially in Scotland or the US) a room or a set of rooms forming a separate residence within a house or block of flats （尤指苏格兰或美国的）住房；租户

6. flat: *n.* a set of rooms for living in, typically on one floor of a large building and including a kitchen and bathroom（尤指一幢大楼里同一个楼面上带有厨房和浴室的）公寓

7. indifferent: *adj.* having no particular interest or sympathy; unconcerned 不感兴趣的；冷淡的；不同情的；不关心的

8. incongruous: *adj.* not in harmony or keeping with the surroundings or other aspects of something 不协调的；不调和的；不一致的；不适宜的

9. ho: *exc.* an expression of surprise, admiration, triumph, or derision （表示惊奇、赞赏、胜利或嘲笑）嗬 （Ho! I'll show you. 嗬！我给你看。）

10. severe: *adj.* very plain in style or appearance （风格或外表）非常朴素的

11. glow: *v.* give out steady light without flame （没有火焰地）发光 （e.g. The tips of their cigarettes glowed in the dark. 他们的烟头在黑暗中闪光。）

12. wilding: *adj.* growing wild; not cultivated 野生的；非耕种的

13. space: *n.* an area of land which is not occupied by buildings 空地 （e.g.

She had a love of open spaces. 她很喜欢开阔的地方。)

14. draft = draught

draught: *n.* a portion of liquid to be drunk, esp. a dose of medicine 饮品；药剂

15. dew: *n.* tiny drops of water that form on cool surfaces at night 露；露滴；露水 （e.g. The grass was wet with dew. 草地被露水打湿了。)

◆ *A Lead-in Note* （简明导读）

诗人先以第三人称的视角交代场景，即月光下的都市，那是钢筋混凝土的丛林，灰暗且无生气。接着，诗人以第二人称的视角，直接与月亮展开对话。诗人劝告月亮去往应该去的地方，那里有幸福之花绽放出的张张笑脸，“正踮起脚尖等待在旷野中，欲饮你的美酒，再兑些甘露”。

这首《月亮之歌》歌颂的是月亮的美好和永恒。岁月变更，斗转星移，不变的是月亮及其光芒，可谓“人生代代无穷已，江月年年望相似”。

◆ 月亮之歌

月光折断于城市的建筑，
再摔落——顺着钢筋石头的混凝物，
落到千家万户灰暗的房子上，
房子里始终死气沉沉，悲哀凄楚。
落到宅后的衣服上，
衣服挂在一根根线下，如幽灵悬浮。
线连千家，月照万舍——千家万舍
彼此冷漠，互不协调，隔阂生疏。

你出现于此，毫无魔力。
嗬，月，伤心的月！收起你拖尾的袍服。
对于闪耀着电光的星球而言，

你那银光袍服似乎老旧，过于朴素。

去吧，把你的美，洒向幸福之花
绽放出的张张笑脸，色调不计其数；
正踮起脚尖等待在旷野中，
欲饮你的美酒，再兑些甘露。

008 Robert William Service
罗伯特·威廉·瑟维斯

◆ *The Poet's Profile* （诗人小档案）

罗伯特·威廉·瑟维斯（1874—1958）：英裔加拿大诗人和作家，被人称为“育空河吟游诗人”（育空河发源于加拿大西北部育空地区）。他出生于苏格兰的兰开夏郡，但在美国西部和加拿大度过了很长一段时间。

◆ *Moon Song*

A child saw in the morning skies
The dissipated-looking moon,
And opened wide her big blue eyes,
And cried: “Look, look, my lost balloon!”
And clapped her rosy hands with glee:
“Quick, mother! Bring it back to me.”

A poet in a lilied pond
Espied the moon's reflected charms,
And ravished by that beauty blonde,
Leapt out to clasp her in his arms.
And as he'd never learnt to swim,
Poor fool! that was the end of him.

A rustic glimpsed amid the trees
The bluff moon caught as in a snare.

"They say it do be made of cheese,"
Said Giles, "and that a chap bides there. . .
That Blue Boar ale be strong, I vow—
The lad's a-winkin' at me now."

Two lovers watched the new moon hold
The old moon in her bright embrace.
Said she: "There's mother, pale and old,
And drawing near her resting place."
Said he: "Be mine, and with me wed,"
Moon-high she stared . . . she shook her head.

A soldier saw with dying eyes
The bleared moon like a ball of blood,
And thought of how in other skies,
So pearly bright on leaf and bud
Like peace its soft white beams had lain;
Like Peace! . . . He closed his eyes again.

Child, lover, poet, soldier, clown,
Ah yes, old Moon, what things you've seen!
I marvel now, as you look down,
How can your face be so serene?
And tranquil still you'll make your round,
Old Moon, when we are underground.

◆ *Annotations* （原诗注释）

1. dissipate: *v.* (of something such as a cloud or queue) disperse or scatter 使（云或队伍等）消散；散去

2. balloon: *n.* a brightly coloured rubber sac which is inflated with air and then

sealed at the neck, and used as a child's toy or a decoration 气球

3. rosy: *adj.* (especially of a person's skin) coloured like a pink or red rose, typically as an indication of health, youth, or embarrassment （尤指人的皮肤）玫瑰色的；（浅）玫瑰红的；肤色红润的；脸红的（尤指作为健康、年轻或尴尬的标志） (e.g. The memory had the power to make her cheeks turn rosy. 回忆能使她的脸色转为红润。)

4. glee: *n.* great delight 欢快；欣喜 (e.g. His face lit up with impish glee. 他的脸上闪露着顽皮的喜色。)

5. lilied: *adj.* covered or decorated with lilies 百合花覆盖的；用百合花装饰的

6. espy: *v.* (poetic/literary) catch sight of （诗/文用法）看到；看见；瞥见 (e.g. She espied her daughter rounding the corner. 她看见她女儿正绕过拐角。)

7. charm: *n.* (usu. charms) an attractive or alluring characteristic or feature 诱人之处；迷人之处 (e.g. the hidden charms of the city 这座城市暗藏的迷人之处)

8. ravish: *v.* (often be ravished) (poetic/literary) fill (someone) with intense delight; enrapture （诗/文用法）使狂喜；使陶醉；使入迷；使销魂 (e.g. Ravished by a sunny afternoon, she had agreed without even thinking. 陶醉于阳光明媚的午后，她不假思索地同意了。)

9. clasp: *v.* hold (someone) tightly 紧握；紧抱 (e.g. He clasped Joanne in his arms. 他双臂紧抱乔安妮。)

10. rustic: *n.* (often derogatory) an unsophisticated country person （常作贬义用法）乡下人；乡巴佬；土包子

11. bluff: *adj.* (of a cliff or a ship's bows) having a vertical or steep broad front （悬崖）垂直的；（船头）宽而垂直的

12. snare: *n.* a trap for catching birds or mammals, typically one having a noose of wire or cord （捕捉鸟兽的）陷阱；罗网

13. chap: *n.* a man or a boy （主要为英国英语非正式用法）男人；男孩

14. bide: *v.* (archaic or dialect) remain or stay somewhere （古旧用法或方言

用法）停留；居住 （e.g. How long must I bide here to wait for the answer? 我必须在这里待多久才能等到答复?）

15. boar: *n.* (also wild boar) a tusked Eurasian wild pig from which domestic pigs are descended, exterminated in Britain in the 17th century 野猪

16. ale: *n.* (chiefly Brit.) any beer other than lager, stout, or porter （主要为英国用法）(除陈啤酒、浓烈黑啤酒或黑啤酒之外的）麦芽啤酒

17. vow: *v.* solemnly promise to do a specified thing 宣誓；立誓；发誓 （e.g. He vowed that his government would not tolerate a repeat of the disorder. 他郑重宣告他的政府绝对不能容许再次发生混乱。）

18. lad: *n.* (informal) a boy or young man (often as a form of address) （非正式用法）少年；男青年

19. wink: *v.* close and open one eye quickly, typically to indicate that something is a joke or a secret or as a signal of affection or greeting 眨眼；眨眼示意 (尤用来表示说笑、讳言或作为传情、打招呼的示意） （e.g. He winked at Nicole as he passed. 当他经过时，他对尼科尔眨了眨眼。）

20. old moon: *n.* the moon in its last quarter, before the new moon 下弦月

21. embrace: *n.* an act of holding someone closely in one's arms 拥抱；怀抱 (e.g. They were locked in an embrace. 他们紧紧地抱在一起。）

22. pale: *adj.* (of a person's face complexion) having less colour than usual, typically as a result of shock, fear, or ill health （脸或脸色）苍白的 （e.g. She looked pale and drawn. 她看上去苍白憔悴。）

23. wed: *v.* get married 结婚 （e.g. They wed a week after meeting. 他们见面一个星期之后结婚。）

24. blear: *v.* make dim; blur 使模糊；使朦胧 （e.g. He bleared his eyes with books. 他因书看得太多而使视力模糊。）

25. pearly: *adj.* resembling a pearl in lustre or colour 有珍珠光泽的；珠色的 (e.g. The pearly light of a clear, still dawn. 晴朗、静谧清晨的珠灰色天光。）

26. bud: *n.* a compact knob-like growth on a plant which develops into a leaf, flower, or shoot 芽；蓓蕾

27. clown: *n.* (archaic)an unsophisticated country person; a rustic （古旧用法）乡下人；乡巴佬

28. marvel: *v.* be filled with wonder or astonishment 感到惊讶（或好奇）(e.g. She marvelled at Geoffrey's composure. 她对杰弗里的镇定感到惊异。)

29. serene: *adj.* calm, peaceful, and untroubled; tranquil 安详的；宁静的 (e.g. Her eyes were closed and she looked very serene. 她闭着眼看上去很平静。)

30. tranquil: *adj.* free from disturbance; calm 平静的；镇静的 (e.g. The sea was tranquil. 海面很平静。)

31. round: *n.* a tour of inspection, typically repeated regularly, in which the safety or well-being of those visited is checked 巡行；巡视；巡逻；巡诊 (e.g. The doctor is just making his rounds in the wards. 医生正在查病房。)

◆ *A Lead-in Note* （简明导读）

月亮仿佛一位饱经风霜的老者，目睹了数不尽的世间炎凉和人生百态，但升落照旧，盈亏依然——“啊，下弦月，下一次升起，你会安详如初，而我们却已入土而去。”千年万年之后，月亮依然唱着那首千古不衰的歌谣，俯视这变幻莫测的尘世。

◆ 月亮之歌

早晨的天空下，一个女孩儿
看见了月亮，飘离消失的样子。
她圆睁蓝色的大眼睛，
叫道：“看，看呐！我的气球飞走了。”
她拍着红润的小手，快活起来：
“快呀，妈妈！帮我取回来。”

在一个开满百合的池塘里，一位诗人

看见水中倒映出月亮迷人的影子。
那个金黄色的美人令他疯狂，
诗人纵身跃下，紧拥她到臂弯里。
但是，他这个可怜的蠢人，
从未学过游泳，那里成了他的丧命之地。

在树间，一个乡巴佬瞥见了
高悬的月亮，如同卡在陷阱里。
“他们都说月亮是奶酪做的，”
贾尔斯说。“住在那儿的是个小老弟……
我发誓，那里蓝野猪牌麦芽啤酒很浓——
那家伙正向我眨眼示意。”

一对情侣看着新月将下弦月
揽到自己明亮的怀抱里。
女孩说：“那是苍老的母亲，头发灰白，
就要接近她的安息之地。”
男孩说：“做我的人，嫁给我吧！”
月亮高悬，女孩凝视着……摇头不语。

一个士兵就要死去，看到了
模糊的月亮，如一团血球体。
他想，在别处的天空中，
柔和、明亮的月光，似珍珠
安详地照在叶子和蓓蕾上。
安详！……他闭上了双眼——又一次。

女孩，诗人，乡巴佬，情侣，士兵，
哦，没错，下弦月，这些皆为你眼中所视！

你俯视下方时，我感到惊讶：
你的表情怎能这般安详无比？
啊，下弦月，下一次升起，你会安详
如初，而我们却已入土而去。

009 Ernest Christopher Dowson
欧内斯特·克里斯托弗·道森

◆ *The Poet's Profile* （诗人小档案）

欧内斯特·克里斯托弗·道森（1867—1900）：英国诗人及小说家，经常跟“颓废”派成员中的奥斯卡·王尔德及奥布里·比尔兹利保持联络。他的两本诗集：《道森韵体诗集》（1896）和《装饰》（1899），主题都是有关无聊倦怠和厌烦人世方面的。

◆ *The Moon Maiden's Song*

Sleep! Cast thy canopy
Over this sleeper's brain,
Dim grow his memory,
When he wake again.

Love stays a summer night,
Till lights of morning come;
Then takes her winged flight
Back to her starry home.

Sleep! Yet thy days are mine;
Love's seal is over thee:
Far though my ways from thine,
Dim though thy memory.

Love stays a summer night,
Till lights of morning come;
Then takes her winged flight
Back to her starry home.

◆ *Annotations* （原诗注释）

1. maiden: *n.* (archaic or poetic/literary) a girl or young woman, especially an unmarried one （古旧用法或诗/文用法）少女；（尤指未婚的）年轻妇女

2. thy: *poss. adj.* (Also "thine" before a vowel) archaic or dialect form of your （元音前亦作"thine"）（古旧用法或方言用法）你（您）的（同"your"）

3. canopy: *n.* (figurative) something hanging or perceived as hanging over a person or scene （比喻用法）（人或景色上方的）笼罩物 （e.g. the canopy of twinkling stars 闪烁群星的天穹）

4. dim: *adj.* not clearly recalled or formulated in the mind （记忆或想法）不清晰的；模糊的 （e.g. She had dim memories of that time. 她对那时还有模糊的记忆。）

5. thee: *pron.* archaic or dialect form of you, as the singular object of a verb or preposition （古英语"thou"的宾格，同"you"）你；汝

6. thine: *poss. pron.* (form of "thy" used before a vowel) archaic form of yours; the thing or things belonging to or associated with the e （元音之前同"thy"）（古旧用法）你的（同"yours"）；（"thou"的物主代词）你（您）的东西

◆ *A Lead-in Note* （简明导读）

此诗出自道森的独幕诗剧《此时此刻的皮埃罗》(The Pierrot of the Minute)。剧中有两位主人公：月亮少女和具有伤心小丑形象的男丑角皮埃罗。临近剧终之际，月亮少女退场，有人唱起了《月亮少女之歌》。不管是梦境还是现实，这一晚，皮埃罗很幸福。因为这是一个有爱的夜晚，虽然"爱神只待一个夏夜，晨光展露时就离开"。

◆ 月亮少女之歌

睡吧！用你上空的华盖
罩住这位沉睡者的脑袋，
他的记忆就会变得模糊——
当他再一次醒来。

爱神只待一个夏夜，
晨光展露时就离开。
她拍打着翅膀飞走，
飞回星光闪闪的邸宅。

睡吧！但你我的时光相融。
爱的印迹在你身上放光彩——
尽管我离你的距离遥远，
尽管你的记忆模糊起来。

爱神只待一个夏夜，
晨光展露时就离开。
她拍打着翅膀飞走，
飞回星光闪闪的邸宅。

010 Lady Mary Wortley Montagu
玛丽·沃特利·蒙塔古夫人

◆ *The Poet's Profile* （诗人小档案）

玛丽·沃特利·蒙塔古夫人（1689—1762）：英国作家、诗人、杂文家，她的作品主要以书信体著称。同时她还作为一个女权论者、旅行家而为人所知。

◆ *A Hymn to the Moon*

Thou silver deity of secret night,
Direct my footsteps through the woodland shade;
Thou conscious witness of unknown delight,
The Lover's guardian, and the Muse's aid!
By thy pale beams I solitary rove,
To thee my tender grief confide;
Serenely sweet you gild the silent grove,
My friend, my goddess, and my guide.
E'en thee, fair queen, from thy amazing height,
The charms of young Endymion drew;
Veil'd with the mantle of concealing night;
With all thy greatness and thy coldness too.

◆ *Annotations* （原诗注释）

1. hymn: *n.* a religious song or poem, typically of praise to God or a god （赞美

上帝或神的）圣歌；赞美诗

2. arbor or arbour: *n.* a shady garden alcove with the sides and roof formed by trees or climbing plants trained over a wooden framework 凉亭；棚架

3. deity: *n.* a god or goddess (in a polytheistic religion) （多神教中的）神；女神

4. woodland: *n.* (Also as "woodlands") land covered with trees 林地；林区 (e.g. large areas of ancient woodland 一大片古林地)

5. shade: *n.* (poetic/literary) a shadow or area of darkness （诗/文用法）阴影；阴暗处 (e.g. The shades of evening drew on. 夜幕降临。)

6. muse: *n.* (Muse) (in Greek and Roman mythology) one of nine goddesses, the daughters of Zeus and Mnemosyne, who preside over the arts and sciences 缪斯（指希腊和罗马神话中掌管文艺和科学的九位女神之一，九女神为宙斯和尼莫茜尼之女。）

7. aid: *n.* a person or thing that is a source of help or assistance 帮手；帮助者；辅助物；辅助手段

8. thy: *poss. adj.* (also "thine" before a vowel) archaic or dialect form of your （元音前亦作"thine"）（古旧用法或方言用法）你（您）的（同"your"）

9. rove: *v.* travel constantly without a fixed destination; wander 流浪；漫游

10. thee: *pron.* [second person singular] archaic or dialect form of you, as the singular object of a verb or preposition （古英语"thou"的宾格，同"you"）你；汝

11. tender: *adj.* requiring tact or careful handling 微妙的；棘手的；难处理的；敏感的

12. confide: *v.* [reporting verb] tell someone about a secret or private matter while trusting them not to repeat it to others 吐露（秘密或私事）；倾诉 (e.g. He confided his fears to his mother. 他向他母亲吐露了他心中的恐惧。)

13. serene: *adj.* calm, peaceful, and untroubled; tranquil 安详的；宁静的

14. sweet: *adj.* (of a person or action) pleasant and kind or thoughtful （人或行为）惹人喜爱的；和蔼的；体贴的 (e.g. A very sweet nurse came along. 一位非

常和蔼可亲的护士走了过来。)

15. gild: *v.* to cover with or as if with a thin layer of gold 使有金子般的色彩(e.g. The morning sun gilds the sky. 朝阳把天空染成金色。)

16. grove: *n.* a small wood, orchard, or group of trees 树丛；小树林；果园(e.g. an olive grove 一小片橄榄树林)

17. E'en = Even

18. charm: *n.* (usu. as "charms") an attractive or alluring characteristic or feature 诱人之处；迷人之处 (e.g. the hidden charms of the city 这座城市暗藏的迷人之处)

19. Endymion: *n.* (Greek Mythology) a remarkably beautiful young man, loved by the Moon (Selene). According to one story, he was put in an eternal sleep by Zeus for having fallen in love with Hera, and was then visited every night by Selene. 恩底弥翁（希腊神话中的一个十分英俊的少年，为月之女神塞勒涅所爱。据一则故事描述，由于恩底弥翁与赫拉相爱，宙斯使其沉睡不醒，继而塞勒涅每晚都来探望他。)

20. Veil'd = Veiled

21. mantle: *n.* (figurative) a covering of a specified sort （比喻用法）覆盖物；罩；幕 (e.g. The houses were covered with a thick mantle of snow. 房屋上盖着厚厚的一层雪。)

◆ *A Lead-in Note* （简明导读）

这是一首唱给月亮的颂歌。月亮是银白色的女神，引领诗人“穿过阴暗处的林地”。借着月光，诗人“孤独地漫游”，对月“倾诉微妙难解的伤心事”。月亮，无论你多么高高在上、冷漠无情，你也无法抵挡年轻的恩底弥翁迷人的魅力，“纵然你是娇美的女王，亦被吸引下凡”。

◆ 月亮颂歌

你是银色女神，保守着暗夜的秘密；
引领我的脚步，穿越树林的幽深。
你有意见证的快乐无人知晓，
你守护着爱侣，辅佐女神缪斯！
借着你灰白的光，我孤独地漫游；
向你倾诉我温存的惆怅。
你甜蜜而静谧，将无声的丛林染成金黄——
我的朋友、女神、向导，皆为你。
纵然你是娇美的女王，亦被吸引下凡，
因年轻的恩底弥翁具有迷人的魅力。
在轻纱朦胧，茫茫的玄夜里
你闪耀着伟大的光芒，却冷若冰霜。

011 Samuel Taylor Coleridge
塞缪尔·泰勒·柯尔律治

◆ *The Poet's Profile* （诗人小档案）

塞缪尔·泰勒·柯尔律治（1772—1834）：英国诗人、评论家和哲学家，与威廉·华兹华斯合著的《抒情歌谣集》（1798）开启英国浪漫主义文学的先河，其中包括《古舟子咏》。

◆ *To the Autumnal Moon (Sonnet 18)*

Mild Splendour of the various-vested Night!
Mother of wildly-working visions! hail!
I watch thy gliding, while with wat'ry light
Thy weak eye glimmers thro'a fleecy veil;
And when thou lovest thy pale orb to shroud
Behind the gather'd blackness lost on high;
And when thou dartest from the wind-rent cloud
Thy placid lightning o'er th' awaken'd sky.

Ah, such is Hope! As changeful and as fair!
Now dimly peering on the wistful sight;
Now hid behind the dragon-wing'd Despair:
But soon emerging in her radiant might
She o'er the sorrow-clouded breast of Care
Sails, like a meteor kindling in its flight.

◆ Annotations（原诗注释）

1. autumnal: *adj.* like or connected with autumn 秋季的；秋天的

2. splendour: *n.* great light or luster; brilliance 光辉；光彩

3. vest: *v.* (poetic/literary) dress (someone)（诗/文用法）给……穿衣服（e.g. The Speaker vested him with a rich purple robe. 议长给他穿上华丽的紫色长袍。）

4. hail: *exc.* (archaic) expressing greeting or acclaim（古旧用法）（表示问候或欢呼）欢迎；好啊

5. thy: *poss. adj.* (Also "thine" before a vowel) archaic or dialect form of your（元音前亦作"thine"）（古旧用法或方言用法）你（您）的（同"your"）

6. glimmer: *v.* shine faintly with a wavering light 发出闪烁的微光（e.g. pools of glimmering light 发出荧荧微光的池塘）

7. fleecy: *adj.* (especially of a cloud) white and fluffy（尤指云）洁白蓬松的；如絮的

8. thou: *pron.* [second person singular] archaic or dialect form of you, as the singular subject of a verb（古旧用法或方言用法）（作动词的单数主语）你（同"you"）

9. lovest = loves

10. orb: *n.* (poetic/literary) an eyeball; an eye（通常作"orbs"）（诗/文用法）眼球；眼睛

11. shroud: *v.* (figurative) cover or envelop so as to conceal from view（比喻用法）隐蔽；隐藏；笼罩（e.g. mountains shrouded by cloud 被云彩笼罩的山）

12. gather'd = gathered

13. on high: in or to heaven or a high place 在（向）天堂；在（向）高空；在（向）高处（e.g. a spotter plane circling on high 侦察机在高空盘旋）

14. dartest = darts

dart: *v.* move or run somewhere suddenly or rapidly 急冲；飞奔；突然行进（e.g. She darted across the street. 她突然冲过马路。）

15. rend: *v.* (past and past participle rent) tear (something) into two or more pieces 撕裂；扯碎

16. placid: *adj.* (of a person or animal) not easily upset or excited （人或动物）平和的；温和的 （e.g. This horse has a placid nature. 这匹马性情温和。）

17. o'er = over

18. th' = the

19. wistful: *adj.* having or showing a feeling of vague or regretful longing 留恋的；惆怅的；怅惘的；依依不舍的 （e.g. a wistful smile 怅然一笑）

20. wing'd = winged

21. might: *n.* great and impressive power or strength, especially of a nation, large organization, or natural force （尤指国家、组织、自然力等）强大力量；威力；势力 （e.g. a convincing display of military might 令人信服的军事力量的显示）

22. kindle: *v.* light or set on fire 点燃

◆ *A Lead-in Note* （简明导读）

此诗中，诗人采用了拟人化的手法，形象地勾勒出秋月这一意象。此诗讴歌了秋月的美好和伟大。

◆ 致秋月（商籁体第18首）

多姿的夜神闪烁柔和的光辉，
大地圣母忙乱地劳作——真辛苦！
我看着你悄然游动，慵倦的娇眼，
从云雾轻纱里透出似水清辉。
忽而，你把苍白脸盘藏入，
叠叠乌云的后边，在高空隐去；
忽而，又从吹散的乱云间射出，

将夜晚唤醒，柔光在夜空遍布。

啊，这是希望之神！变幻却公允。
时而眼神朦胧，观迷茫之景象，
时而屈从于恶龙般绝望之神，
顷刻间爆发出强大的力量，
冲破忧虑之神愁云密布的心，
如飞燃的流星一般，扬帆起航。

Chapter 03

Moon's Light Shining

第三章

月之光明

012 Sara Teasdale
萨拉·蒂斯代尔

◆ *The Poet's Profile* （诗人小档案）

萨拉·蒂斯代尔（1884—1933）：美国杰出的抒情诗人，她的诗收录于《〈特洛伊的海伦〉及其他诗歌集》（1911）、《江河入海》（1915）、《爱歌》（1917）、《火焰与影子》（1920）及《奇异的胜利》（1933）等中。萨拉·蒂斯代尔以具有浪漫色彩的抒情诗篇赢得了大众的钦佩，她的诗主要围绕一名女子对美、对爱情，以及对死亡不断变换的视角而展开。1918年，蒂斯代尔获得哥伦比亚大学诗歌学会奖，这一奖项就是普利策诗歌奖的前身。

◆ *Moonlight*

It will not hurt me when I am old,
A running tide where moonlight burned
Will not sting me like silver snakes;
The years will make me sad and cold,
It is the happy heart that breaks.

The heart asks more than life can give,
When that is learned, then all is learned;
The waves break fold on jewelled fold,
But beauty itself is fugitive,
It will not hurt me when I am old.

◆ *Annotations*（原诗注释）

1. jeweled: *adj.* adorned, set with, or made from jewels 用宝石装饰的；镶宝石的；宝石制成的（e.g. a jewelled dagger 镶宝石的匕首）

2. fugitive: *adj.* (figurative) quick to disappear; fleeting（比喻用法）转瞬即逝的；易消失的；短暂的（e.g. He entertained a fugitive idea that Bella needed him. 他想贝拉会需要他，但这念头稍纵即逝。）

◆ *A Lead-in Note*（简明导读）

诗人说："等我老时，不会受伤。"但年轻时候的伤，仍令诗人心痛和肠断。人老之际，豁然明了"人心索取太多，人生给予却有限"。

◆ 月光

等我老时，不会受伤，
因为长长的浪奔腾，映射着月光，
不会像银蛇把我撕咬。
可岁月会令我心痛、冷若冰霜，
快乐之人亦断肠。

人心索取太多，人生给予却有限。
领会了这一点，就明白了一切。
波涛击碎层层珠翠，
可美本身转瞬失芳香，
等我老时，不会受伤。

013 Henry Wadsworth Longfellow
亨利·沃兹沃斯·朗费罗

◆ *The Poet's Profile* （诗人小档案）

亨利·沃兹沃斯·朗费罗（1807—1882）：美国诗人和翻译家。朗费罗写了很多具有音乐感的抒情诗篇，还写过神话和传奇故事。其代表作有《海斯布罗斯残骸》(1841)、《村中铁匠》(1841）和《海华沙之歌》(1855)。

◆ *Moonlight*

As a pale phantom with a lamp
Ascends some ruin's haunted stair,
So glides the moon along the damp
Mysterious chambers of the air.

Now hidden in cloud, and now revealed,
As if this phantom, full of pain,
Were by the crumbling walls concealed,
And at the windows seen again.

Until at last, serene and proud
In all the splendor of her light,
She walks the terraces of cloud,
Supreme as Empress of the Night.

I look, but recognize no more

Objects familiar to my view;
The very pathway to my door
Is an enchanted avenue.

All things are changed. One mass of shade,
The elm-trees drop their curtains down;
By palace, park, and colonnade
I walk as in a foreign town.

The very ground beneath my feet
Is clothed with a diviner air;
While marble paves the silent street
And glimmers in the empty square.

Illusion! Underneath there lies
The common life of every day;
Only the spirit glorifies
With its own tints the sober gray.

In vain we look, in vain uplift
Our eyes to heaven, if we are blind;
We see but what we have the gift
Of seeing; what we bring we find.

◆ *Annotations* （原诗注释）

1. phantom: *n.* a ghost 幽灵；鬼魂 （e.g. a phantom who haunts lonely roads 经常在荒野路上出没的鬼魂）

2. ascend: *v.* go up or climb 登上；攀登 （e.g. She ascended the stairs. 她上了楼。）

3. ruin: *n.* the remains of a building, typically an old one, that has suffered much

damage or disintegration n 被损毁之物；倾圮的建筑物；废墟；遗迹；残余

4. haunted: *adj.* (of a place) frequented by a ghost （地方或场所）幽灵出没的；闹鬼的

5. chamber: *n.* (poetic/literary or archaic) a private room, especially a bedroom（诗/文用法或古旧用法）私室（尤指卧室）

6. air: *n.* the free or unconfined space above the surface of the earth 天空；空间；空中

7. crumble: *v.* break or fall apart into small fragments, especially over a period of time as part of a process of deterioration 崩溃；瓦解 （e.g. their crumbling ancestral home 他们将要倒塌的祖屋）

8. serene: *adj.* calm, peaceful, and untroubled; tranquil 安详的；宁静的 （e.g. Her eyes were closed and she looked very serene. 她闭着眼看上去很平静。）

9. proud: *adj.* imposing; splendid 雄伟的；壮丽的 （e.g. Bulrushes emerge tall and proud from the middle of the pond. 水烛壮观地挺立于池塘中央。）

10. splendor: *n.* great light or luster; brilliance 光辉；光彩

11. terrace: *n.* each of a series of flat areas made on a slope, used for cultivation 阶地；梯田

12. supreme: *adj.* (of authority or an office, or someone holding it) superior to all others （权力、机构、掌权人）最高的 （e.g. a unified force with a supreme commander 由最高指挥官统帅的统一军队）

13. enchant: *v.* put (someone or something) under a spell 对（人或物）施魔法；用妖术迷惑

14. elm: *n.* a tall deciduous tree which typically has rough serrated leaves and propagates from root suckers 榆树

15. colonnade: *n.* a row of columns supporting a roof, an entablature, or arches 柱廊

16. divine: *adj.* devoted to God; sacred 敬神的；神圣的 （e.g. divine liturgy 神圣的圣餐仪式）

17. marble: *n.* a hard crystalline metamorphic form of limestone, typically white

with mottlings or streaks of colour, which is capable of taking a polish and is used in sculpture and architecture 大理石

18. glimmer: *v.* shine faintly with a wavering light 发出闪烁的微光 （e.g. pools of glimmering light 发出荧荧微光的池塘）

19. illusion: *n.* a thing which is or is likely to be wrongly perceived or interpreted by the senses 幻觉；错觉

20. spirit: *n.* a fairy or sprite; a supernatural being 鬼怪；妖精；幽灵；神灵

21. glorify: *v.* describe or represent as admirable, especially unjustifiably or undeservedly 美化

22. tint: *n.* a shade or variety of colour 色彩；色调 （e.g. The sky was taking on an apricot tint. 天空呈现出一抹杏黄色。）

23. sober: *adj.* muted in colour 颜色素淡的

◆ *A Lead-in Note* （简明导读）

诗人先是对月亮及月光下景色展开想象，接着描写了月光下诗人的感受，最后上升到了一个“哲学高度”——“任凭我们怎么观看，如何仰望，都是徒劳一场——如果双目失明。”我们的双眼能够看到东西，那只是我们的天赋。但是，如果我们视而不见，所视之物将毫无意义，因此我们的双眼要善于发现。

◆ 月光

灰白的月儿如幽灵提着灯笼，
将某座闹鬼废墟的阶梯攀登。
就这样，她穿过空中一间又一间神秘
而潮湿的私密暗室滑行。

时而藏身云层，时而露出面目，

仿佛是在痛苦中煎熬的幽灵——
一会儿掩埋在坍塌的墙壁里，
一会儿又在窗户上露出真容。

到了最后，她将所有辉光释放
到宁静和壮丽之中。
她走在云朵的梯田里，
如夜晚女皇，昂首挺胸。

我观望着，但已不再有什么
熟悉的物体映入我的眼帘。
我门前那条熟悉的小路
也被施以魔法，有了神通。

一切都变了——那大片的阴暗
是榆树拉下的幕屏。
我经过殿宇、公园、廊柱，
如同在异乡穿行。

我脚下地面上那层空气
也神圣起来，变得与以往不同。
大理石铺成了大街，不声不响，
在广场上闪着微光，广场空空。

纯属幻觉！月光之下
是日常生活中的一切，普普通通。
只不过是幽灵以自身的色调，
美化了素淡而灰白的容颜。

任凭我们怎么观看，如何仰望，
都是徒劳一场——如果双目失明。
我们看到的，只因我们有天赋
能看得到；我们所发现的，却如影随形。

014 Henry Wadsworth Longfellow
亨利·沃兹沃斯·朗费罗

◆ *The Poet's Profile* （诗人小档案）

亨利·沃兹沃斯·朗费罗（1807—1882）：美国诗人和翻译家。朗费罗写了很多具有音乐感的抒情诗篇，还写过神话和传奇故事。其代表作有《海斯布罗斯残骸》（1841）、《村中铁匠》（1841）和《海华沙之歌》（1855）。

◆ *Daylight and Moonlight*

In broad daylight, and at noon,
Yesterday I saw the moon
Sailing high, but faint and white,
As a schoolboy's paper kite.

In broad daylight, yesterday,
I read a poet's mystic lay;
And it seemed to me at most
As a phantom, or a ghost.

But at length the feverish day
Like a passion died away,
And the night, serene and still,
Fell on village, vale, and hill.

Then the moon, in all her pride,

Like a spirit glorified,
Filled and overflowed the night
With revelations of her light.

And the Poet's song again
Passed like music through my brain;
Night interpreted to me
All its grace and mystery.

◆ *Annotations* （原诗注释）

1. faint: *adj.* (of a sight, smell, or sound) barely perceptible （景象、气味、声音）微弱的；依稀的

2. mystic: *adj.* of or relating to religious mysteries or occult rites and practices 神秘的；玄妙的

3. lay: *n.* a short lyric or narrative poem meant to be sung （演唱用）短抒情（或叙事）诗

4. at (the) most: not more than 至多 （e.g. The walk took four minutes at the most. 这段路最多步行四分钟。）

5. phantom: *n.* a ghost 幽灵；鬼魂

6. at length: (literary) after a long time 很长一段时间以后；最后 （e.g. "I'm not sure,' he said at length. "我还是没把握。"他最后说道。）

7. feverish: *adj.* displaying a frenetic excitement or energy 狂热的；亢奋的；躁动不安的 （e.g. The next couple of weeks were spent in a whirl of feverish activity. 随后的两周是在紧张忙乱中度过的。）

8. serene: *adj.* calm, peaceful, and untroubled; tranquil 安详的；宁静的 （e.g. Her eyes were closed and she looked very serene. 她闭着眼看上去很平静。）

9. vale: *n.* a valley (used in place names or as a poetic term) （用于地名或诗歌）谷；溪谷

10. spirit: *n.* a fairy or sprite; a supernatural being 鬼怪；妖精；幽灵；神灵

11. glorified: [attrib.] (especially of something or someone ordinary or unexceptional) represented in such a way as to appear more elevated or special （尤指普通人或事）被拔高了的；被美化了的 （e.g. All Peter will be is a sort of glorified secretary. 彼得将来只会成为那种表面风光的秘书。）

12. grace: *n.* a characteristic or quality pleasing for its charm or refinement 优雅；优美

13. mystery: *n.* the condition or quality of being secret, strange, or difficult to explain 神秘性；神秘；隐秘性；不可思议性 （e. g. Much of her past is shrouded in mystery. 她过去的许多经历都笼罩在神秘之中。）

◆ *A Lead-in Note* （简明导读）

此诗中，诗人写出了在白昼和黑夜下月的不同状态。大白天的日光下，“月儿高挂而行，暗淡中呈白色调”，很不显眼。那位诗人的神秘诗篇，在大白天“如幽灵或鬼魂般”，令人难懂。一旦黑夜降临，“月儿自豪登场，似幽灵美化了一番”，此时的月儿焕发了光彩。月光照亮了一切，包括“那位诗人的作品又飘过我脑海，如音乐般”。此时，诗人明白了诗中所有的魅力和谜团。日光虽然十分强大，令一切一览无余，但月光更具魅力，更具表现力，更具亲和力，更能令月光下的一切焕发光彩。

◆ 日光与月光

我看到了月儿，就在昨天
正午时分，日光炎炎。
月儿高挂而行，暗淡中呈白色调，
如小男生玩的纸风筝一般。

就在昨天，日光炎炎，

我读了一位诗人的神秘诗篇。
在我看来，那首诗充其量
如幽灵或鬼魂般。

但最终，炽热的白昼
如激情消退而不回还。
黑夜，平和且宁静，
降临村庄、溪谷和小山。

接着，月儿自豪登场，
似幽灵美化了一番。
她把昭示一切的光亮
注入黑夜而溢出——如水般。

那位诗人的作品
又飘过我脑海，如音乐般。
黑夜向我做出了诠释，
诠释了诗中所有的魅力和谜团。

015 Emily Elizabeth Dickinson
埃米莉·伊丽莎白·狄更生

◆ *The Poet's Profile* （诗人小档案）

埃米莉·伊丽莎白·狄更生（1830—1886）：美国女诗人，她的诗独具一格：诗行短小，一般没有标题，经常使用近似押韵的方式和一些非常规的大写及标点，主题多与死亡和永生相关。

◆ *The Road Was Lit with Moon and Star*

The Road was lit with Moon and star—
The Trees were bright and still—
Descried I—by the distant Light
A Traveller on a Hill—
To magic Perpendiculars
Ascending, though Terrene—
Unknown his shimmering ultimate—
But he indorsed the sheen—

◆ *Annotations* （原诗注释）

1.magic: *adj.* very effective in producing results, especially desired ones 神奇的；奇妙的 （e.g. Confidence is the magic ingredient needed to spark recovery. 信心是点燃痊愈希望的神奇因素。）

2. perpendicular: *n.* a straight line at an angle of 90° to a given line, plane, or surface 成直角的线；垂线

3. terrene: *adj.* occurring on or inhabiting dry land 发生于（或居住于）陆地的

4. shimmer: *v.* shine with a soft tremulous light 发微光（e.g. The sea shimmered in the sunlight. 阳光照射下，海水闪着微光。）

5. ultimate: *n.* (the ultimate) the best achievable or imaginable of its kind 最好的事物；最终的事物（e.g. the ultimate in decorative luxury 豪华装饰的极点）

6. indorse: *v.* declare one's public approval or support of 公开赞同（或支持）；认可（e.g. The report was endorsed by the college. 报告得到了学院的认可。）

7. sheen: *n.* a soft lustre on a surface 光泽；光辉

◆ A Lead-in Note （简明导读）

月亮和星星是光明的使者，照亮了旅行者前方的路。月亮和星星具有某种力量，令"一位旅行者，在山脊上——如变魔术，直挺挺攀登而上——尽管身处凡尘之上"。不管终点的光有多么微弱，"可他认准了微光——不放"。有众星捧月，月亮之光才具有魔力，给了旅行者攀登人生巅峰的希望和勇气。

◆ 月亮和星星把路照亮

月亮和星星把路照亮——
树木静立，映出光亮——
借着遥远的光——我如此形容。
一位旅行者，在山脊上——
如变魔术，直挺挺攀登
而上——尽管身处凡尘之上，
尽管终点微微闪光，模糊不清——
可他认准了微光——不放。

016 Alfred Tennyson 艾尔弗雷德·丁尼生

◆ *The Poet's Profile* （诗人小档案）

艾尔弗雷德·丁尼生（1809—1892）：英国维多利亚时代最受欢迎及最具特色的诗人，1850年获"桂冠诗人"称号。他的长诗《悼念》（1850）是英国文学中最伟大的挽歌之一。

◆ *When on My Bed the Moonlight Falls*

When on my bed the moonlight falls,
I know that in thy place of rest
By that broad water of the west,
There comes a glory on the walls;

Thy marble bright in dark appears,
As slowly steals a silver flame
Along the letters of thy name,
And o'er the number of thy years.

The mystic glory swims away;
From off my bed the moonlight dies;
And closing eaves of wearied eyes
I sleep till dusk is dipt in gray;

And then I know the mist is drawn

A lucid veil from coast to coast,
And in the dark church like a ghost
Thy tablet glimmers to the dawn.

◆ *Annotations* （原诗注释）

1. thy: *poss. adj.* (also "thine" before a vowel) archaic or dialect form of your （元音前亦作"thine"）（古旧用法或方言用法）你（您）的（同"your"）

2. glory: *n.* high renown or honour won by notable achievements （重大成就带来的）名望；荣耀 （e.g. To fight and die for the glory of one's nation 为了国家的荣耀而战死。）

3. marble: *n.* a hard crystalline metamorphic form of limestone, typically white with mottlings or streaks of colour, which is capable of taking a polish and is used in sculpture and architecture 大理石

4. steal: *v.* to move, happen, or elapse stealthily or unobtrusively 溜走；悄悄地发生

5. o'er = over

6. mystic: *adj.* of or relating to religious mysteries or occult rites and practices 神秘的；玄妙的

7. eaves: *n.* the part of a roof that meets or overhangs the walls of a building 屋檐

8. weary: *v.* cause to become tired 使疲劳；使疲倦 （e.g. She was wearied by her persistent cough. 不停的咳嗽使她感到疲倦不堪。）

9. dip: *v.* (dipped, dipped or dipt; dipping) (dip something in/into) put or let something down quickly or briefly in or into (liquid) （在液体中）浸；蘸 （e.g. He dipped a brush in the paint. 他把画笔在颜料中蘸了一下。）

10. mist: *n.* a cloud of tiny water droplets suspended in the atmosphere at or near the earth's surface limiting visibility (to a lesser extent than fog; strictly, with visibility remaining above 1 km) （能见度大于1公里的）薄雾；轻雾；霭 （e.

g. The peaks were shrouded in mist. 山峰笼罩在雾霭中。)

11. lucid: *adj.* (poetic/literary) bright or luminous （诗/文用法）光辉的；明亮的 （e.g. Birds dipped their wings in the lucid flow of air. 鸟儿羽翼轻灵，翱翔于明朗的空中。)

12. veil: *n.* a piece of fine material worn by women to protect or conceal the face 面纱；面罩 （e.g. a white bridal veil 新娘的白色面纱）

13. glimmer: *v.* shine faintly with a wavering light 发出闪烁的微光 （e.g. pools of glimmering light 发出荧荧微光的池塘）

◆ *A Lead-in Note* （简明导读）

月光洒落诗人的床榻之际，诗人思念起已故的老友，不由得黯然神伤起来。也许，诗人借着月光来到了教堂，来到了老友长眠的地方；也许，在月光下诗人神游起来，老友的荣光浮现。但是，“神秘的荣光一点点游走，月光渐移，离开了我的床”。于是，诗人睡去，“直至黄昏融入一片灰茫茫”。

◆ 月光洒落在我的床上

月光洒落在我的床上，
我知道，在你安息的地方，
在西方那片宽阔的水域附近，
四壁出现了荣光。

大理石在黑暗中闪亮，
一团银色火焰静谧燃起光，
沿着组成你名字的字母燃起，
悬浮在你走过岁月的数字上方。

神秘的荣光一点点游走，

月光渐移，离开了我的床。
闭上疲惫的眼睛，我睡去，
直至黄昏融入一片灰茫茫。

于是我知道，轻雾洒落，
一层薄纱连起海岸，透着光芒。
黑暗的教堂中，你的眼
如幽灵般微微闪烁，直至露出曙光。

017 Thomas Hardy
托马斯·哈代

◆ *The Poet's Profile* （诗人小档案）

托马斯·哈代（1840—1928）：英国长篇小说家及诗人。他的作品多数描述了人们对苦难生活和命运作弄所施加的冷漠力量的抗争。其代表作有《卡斯特桥市长》（1866）、《德伯家的苔丝》（1891）和《无名的裘德》（1896）等。

◆ *In the Moonlight*

"O lonely workman, standing there
In a dream, why do you stare and stare
At her grave, as no other grave where there?"

"If your great gaunt eyes so importune
Her soul by the shine of this corpse-cold moon,
Maybe you'll raise her phantom soon!"

"Why, fool, it is what I would rather see
Than all the living folk there be;
But alas, there is no such joy for me!"

"Ah—she was one you loved, no doubt,
Through good and evil, through rain and drought,
And when she passed, all your sun went out?"

"Nay: she was the woman I did not love,
Whom all the other were ranked above,
Whom during her life I thought nothing of."

◆ *Annotations* （原诗注释）

1. grave: *n.* a place of burial for a dead body, typically a hole dug in the ground and marked by a stone or mound 墓穴；坟墓

2. workman: *n.* a man employed to do manual labour 男工；工人

3. gaunt: *adj.* (of a person) lean and haggard, especially because of suffering, hunger, or age （尤指人因苦难、饥饿或衰老而）瘦削和憔悴的

4. importune: *v.* ask (someone) pressingly and persistently for or to do something 向（某人）强求；向（某人）不断要求 （e.g. If the £190,000 had never been paid, he would have been importuned by his creditors. 如果他没有支付这190,000英镑，就会被债主缠着讨债。）

5. corpse: *n.* a dead body, especially of a human being rather than an animal 死尸；（尤指人的）尸体

6. raise: *v.* cause (a ghost or spirit) to appear 使（鬼魂）出现；招来（神灵） （e.g. The piece raises the ghosts of a number of twentieth–century art ideas. 这一作品使人联想起20世纪许多艺术观念。）

7. phantom: *n.* a ghost 幽灵；鬼魂 （e.g. a phantom who haunts lonely roads 经常在荒野路上出没的鬼魂）

8. alas: *exc.* (chiefly poetic/literary or humorous) an expression of grief, pity, or concern （主要为诗/文用法或幽默用法）哎呀；唉（表示悲痛、遗憾或关心） （e.g. Alas, my funds have some limitations. 唉，我资金有限。）

9. drought: *n.* a prolonged period of abnormally low rainfall; a shortage of water resulting from this 长期干旱；旱灾

10. nay: *adv.* (archaic or dialect) no （古旧用法或方言用法）不 （e.g. Nay,

I must not think thus. 不，我可不能那样想。）

11. rank: *v.* have a specified rank or place within a grading system （在序列中）居指明的地位

◆ *A Lead-in Note* （简明导读）

拥有之时，你不知道珍惜。一旦失去，你却倍感珍惜。但是，已经于事无补了。伊人已去，尸骨已寒。冷冷的月光下，你死死盯着她的坟墓，又有何用？月光下，你盯了好久，身心俱疲："要是凭借这死尸般寒冷的月光，你憔悴的大眼睛对她的灵魂纠缠不放，或许会招来她的魂灵，用时不会太长。"她在世时，你没有在意，没有珍惜，"因别的女子都会把她比下去，有她相伴时，我没把她放眼里。"月光，冷冷的月光，照亮了你所不了解的人心，照亮了你所不知道的内情。这样，月光就具有了洞察力。

◆ 月光之下

"喂，孤独的工友，你站在那里出神
为何一刻不停地
盯着她的坟墓，好似偌大的坟园里葬着她一个？"

"要是凭借这死尸般寒冷的月光，
你憔悴的大眼睛对她的灵魂纠缠不放，
或许会招来她的魂灵，用时不会太长。"

"嗨，傻瓜！我宁愿在此看她的坟，
也不愿在那儿与活着的各位相逢。
唉，我已无缘碰到如此欣喜的事情。"

"啊，你曾爱过她，毫无疑问。

安乐与患难改不了你的心。
她这一死，你人生的阳光无处寻？”

“非也——她是我未曾爱过的女子，
我总觉得别人都比她强，
有她相伴时，我未曾将她放眼里。”

018 Alfred Edward Housman
艾尔弗雷德·爱德华·豪斯曼

◆ *The Poet's Profile* （诗人小档案）

艾尔弗雷德·爱德华·豪斯曼（1859—1936）：英国诗人和古典学者，著有诗集《什罗普郡少年》。该诗集为系列怀旧诗，多以民谣形式写成。

◆ *White in the Moon the Long Road Lies*

White in the moon the long road lies,
The moon stands blank above;
White in the moon the long road lies
That leads me from my love.

Still hangs the hedge without a gust,
Still, still the shadows stay:
My feet upon the moonlit dust
Pursue the ceaseless way.

The world is round, so travellers tell,
And straight though reach the track,
Trudge on, trudge on, 'twill all be well,
The way will guide one back.

But ere the circle homeward hies
Far, far must it remove:

White in the moon the long road lies
That leads me from my love.

◆ Annotations （原诗注释）

1. blank: *adj.* (of a surface or background) unrelieved by decorative or other features; bare, empty, or plain （表面或背景）无装饰的；空白的

2. hedge: *n.* a fence or boundary formed by closely growing bushes or shrubs （矮树）树篱

3. gust: *n.* a brief, strong rush of wind 一阵强风；一阵狂风

4. pursue: *v.* (of a person or way) continue or proceed along (a path or route) （人或道路）沿着（小道或路线）前进或延伸

5. ceaseless: *adj.* constant and unending 不停的；不绝的；不断的 （e.g. The fort was subjected to ceaseless bombardment. 堡垒不断地受到炮击。）

6. track: *n.* a rough path or minor road, typically one beaten by use rather than constructed （尤指踩踏出来而非铺设的）小道；小径

7. trudge: *v.* walk slowly and with heavy steps, typically because of exhaustion or harsh conditions （尤指在疲劳状态或恶劣环境中）步履艰难地走

8. 'twill = it will

9. ere: *prep. & Conj.* (poetic/literary or archaic) before (in time) （诗/文用法或古旧用法）在……之前 （e.g. We hope you will return ere long. 我们希望你很快回来。）

10. hie: *v.* (archaic) go quickly （古旧用法）急行；赶往；赶紧去 （e.g. I hied down to New Orleans. 我赶往新奥尔良。）

◆ A Lead-in Note （简明导读）

趁着月色赶路，白茫茫的长路会“引领我前行，别离爱人情亦浓”。因为这次离别，外出闯荡，漫漫长路的终点处是出发时的家乡——有爱人守候

的家乡。要知道，“旅行者说，世界呈环状”，只要“艰难向前，艰难向前，一切都会好，脚下的路会引领其返程”。所以，出发吧，出发是为了再一次回到起点。但是，回到起点前，你“需走很远、很远的路程”。月光是你一路上的指路明灯，指引着你前进，最终达到终点，实现理想。

◆ 月色中，长路铺展白茫茫

月色中，长路铺展白茫茫，
月儿高挂孤零零。
月色中，长路铺展白茫茫，
引领我前行，别离爱人情亦浓。

树篱静静的，无强风吹过；
影子静静的，静静的，静静无声。
我踏上洒满月光的尘土，
迈步向前，一刻不停。

旅行者说，世界呈环状，
尽管沿着路途笔直而行。
艰难向前，艰难向前，一切都会好，
脚下的路会引领其返程。

兜这个大圈子回家以前，
需走很远、很远的路程：
月色中，长路铺展白茫茫，
引领我前行，别离爱人情亦浓。

019 Emily Brontë
艾米莉·勃朗特

◆ *The Poet's Profile* （诗人小档案）

艾米莉·勃朗特（1818—1848）：英国小说家，著名诗人，世界文学名著《呼啸山庄》的作者。这部小说奠定了她在英国文学史及世界文学史上的地位。

◆ *Moonlight, Summer Moonlight*

'Tis moonlight, summer moonlight,
All soft and still and fair;
The solemn hour of midnight
Breathes sweet thoughts everywhere,

But most where trees are sending
Their breezy boughs on high,
Or stooping low are lending
A shelter from the sky.

And there in those wild bowers
A lovely form is laid;
Green grass and dew-steeped flowers
Wave gently round her head.

◆ *Annotations* （原诗注释）

1. 'Tis = It is

2. fair: *adj.* light in color, especially blond 浅色的

3. solemn: *adj.* formal and dignified 正式的；庄严的

4. breathe: *v.* to exhale or emit 呼出；发散出

5. breezy: *adj.* pleasantly windy 有微风的

6. bough: *n.* a main branch of a tree 树枝；大树枝 （e.g. apple boughs laden with blossom 开满了花的苹果树枝）

7. on high: in or to heaven or a high place 在（向）天堂；在（向）高空；在（向）高处

8. stoop: *v.* bend one's head or body forwards and downwards 低头；俯身；弯腰

9. lend: *v.* to provide, esp. in order to assist or support 提供

10. shelter: *n.* a place giving temporary protection from bad weather or danger 遮盖物；躲避处；避难所

11. bower: *n.* a pleasant shady place under trees or climbing plants in a garden or wood 树阴处

12. form: *n.* the body or shape of a person or thing （人或物）形体；体型；身材

13. steep: *v.* soak or saturate (cloth) in water or other liquid 泡（衣服）；使（衣服）湿透

◆ *A Lead-in Note* （简明导读）

在诗人的眼中，月光，尤其是夏天夜晚的月光，无限美好。夏夜的月光，令人心驰神往，许多美妙的想法也因夏夜的月光而产生。夏夜的月光是映射出希望的月光，是带来希望的爱情之光。

◆ 月光，夏夜的月光

月光，夏夜的月光，
轻柔静谧，洁白明亮。
在最黑暗的午夜时分，
种种美妙的想法，到处飘荡。

但大多数树木，
或是枝叶高扬，纷飞舒展
或是静立低垂，都在给予着
一个躲避天空的庇护所。

在那里无人的庇荫处，
一个窈窕身影显现——可爱漂亮。
绿草和洒满露珠的鲜花
围绕在她头部，轻轻摇晃。

020 Sarah Knowles Bolton 萨拉·诺尔斯·博尔顿

◆ *The Poet's Profile* （诗人小档案）

萨拉·诺尔斯·博尔顿（1841—1916）：美国女作家及诗人。博尔顿从十五岁起就开始发表作品，并一直把写作作为自己的职业，作品涵盖诗歌、儿童文学以及传记。她的作品反映了她的个人信仰，那就是通过信念和勤奋，人有能力使自己的世界变得更加美好。

◆ *The Moonlight*

What is the moonlight to me?
An infinite rest;
The subtle and sweet melody
Of song unexpressed.

What is the moonlight to me?
The peace of a river:
Companionship of a sea
That surges forever.

What is the moonlight to me?
Satisfaction completest;
A precious and dear memory
Of all that is sweetest.

What is the moonlight to me?
A tryst and a union;
A promise for futurity;
A soulful communion.

◆ *Annotations* （原诗注释）

1. infinite: *adj.* limitless or endless in space, extent, or size; impossible to measure or calculate 无限的；无穷的；无边的；难以估量的；无数的

2. subtle: *adj.* (especially of a change or distinction) so delicate or precise as to be difficult to analyse or describe （尤指变化或差别）微妙的；细微的；难以描述的；难以分析的

3. melody: *n.* a sequence of single notes that is musically satisfying 旋律

4. unexpressed: *adj.* (of a thought or feeling) not communicated or made known （思想或感情）未表达的；未表露的

5. companionship: *n.* a feeling of fellowship or friendship 同伴关系；友谊

6. surge: *v.* a sudden powerful forward or upward movement, especially by a crowd or by a natural force such as the waves or tide 汹涌（尤指人潮、波涛、潮汐等）

7. tryst: *n.* (poetic/literary) a private, romantic rendezvous between lovers （诗/文用法）（情人的）约会；幽会

8. union: *n.* a marriage 结婚；婚姻 （e.g. Their union had not been blessed with children. 他们的婚姻没有子女。）

9. futurity: *n.* renewed or continuing existence 来世

10. soulful: *adj.* expressing or appearing to express deep and often sorrowful feeling 感情深切的；真诚悲切的 （e.g. She gave him a soulful glance. 她深情地看了他一眼。）

11. communion: *n.* the sharing or exchanging of intimate thoughts and feelings, especially when the exchange is on a mental or spiritual level （思想感情的）交流；神交；谈心

◆ *A Lead-in Note* （简明导读）

本诗的前两节具有一定的象征意义，后两节则含有更为具体的人生体验。对于诗人萨拉而言，月光有着丰富的内涵，但它带给诗人更多的是甜蜜的体验和亲切的回忆。

◆ 月光

于我而言，月光为何？
无尽头的休止；
隐含于歌中的
微妙而甜美旋律。

于我而言，月光为何？
河流的平和、静谧。
河流陪伴大海身旁，
大海波涛汹涌不止。

于我而言，月光为何？
完美无瑕的满意经历；
所有甜蜜无比体验中
宝贵而亲切的回忆。

于我而言，月光为何？
一场约会，一场团聚，
一个来世的诺言，
一个心灵沟通的机遇。

021 Thomas Moore
托马斯·穆尔

◆ *The Poet's Profile* （诗人小档案）

托马斯·穆尔（1779—1852）：爱尔兰诗人、音乐家、歌手、歌词作者及艺人。穆尔最为知名的抒情诗歌当属《吟唱少年》和《夏日里最后一朵玫瑰》。他把爱尔兰的历史、民间故事、人物传奇编织进诗歌当中，唤起读者对爱尔兰绿色岛国风光的向往。

◆ *While Gazing on the Moon's Light*

While gazing on the moon's light,
A moment from her smile I turn'd,
To look at orbs that, more bright,
In lone and distant glory burn'd.
But too far
Each proud star,
For me to feel its warming flame;
Much more dear
That mild sphere,
Which near our planet smiling came;
Thus, Mary, be but thou my own,
While brighter eyes unheeded play,
I'll love those moonlight looks alone
That bless my home and guide my way.

The day had sunk in dim showers,
But midnight now, with lustre meet,
Illumined all the pale flowers,
Like hope upon a mourner's cheek.
I said (while
The moon's smile
Play'd o'er a stream, in dimpling bliss,)
"The moon looks
On many brooks,
The brook can see no moon but this;"
And thus, I thought, our fortunes run,
For many a lover looks to thee,
While oh! I feel there is but one,
One Mary in the world for me.

◆ *Annotations* （原诗注释）

1. gaze: *v.* look steadily and intently, especially in admiration, surprise, or thought （尤指因为羡慕、吃惊或思考）盯着看；凝视

2. turn'd = turned

3. orb: *n.* (poetic/literary) an eyeball; an eye （诗/文用法）眼球；眼睛

4. glory: *n.* the splendor; bliss of heaven 光辉；光彩；天堂的荣耀（或福祉）

5. burn'd = burned

6. proud: *adj.* imposing; splendid 雄伟的；壮丽的 （e.g. Bulrushes emerge tall and proud from the middle of the pond. 水烛壮观地挺立于池塘中央。）

7. sphere: *n.* (chiefly poetic/literary) a celestial body （主要为诗/文用法）天体

8. thou: *pron.* [second person singular] archaic or dialect form of you, as the singular subject of a verb （古旧用法或方言用法）（作动词的单数主语）你（同"you"）

9. unheeded: *adj.* heard or noticed but disregarded 未受注意的；被忽视的（e.g. My protest went unheeded. 我的抗议没有引起任何注意。）

10. bless: *v.* (of a priest) pronounce words in a religious rite, to confer or invoke divine favour upon; ask God to look favourably on （牧师）为……祈神赐福；为……祈神保佑

11. shower: *n.* a brief and usually light fall of rain, hail, sleet, or snow 阵雨；冰雹（或雨夹雪等）的一阵；阵雪

12. lustre: *n.* a gentle sheen or soft glow, especially that of a partly reflective surface 光泽；光辉

13. meet: *adj.* (archaic) suitable; fit; proper （古旧用法）适当的；合适的；恰当的（e.g. It was not meet for us to see the king's dishonour. 令国王蒙羞的事我们是不便看见的。）

13. illumine: *v.* (poetic/literary) light up; brighten （诗/文用法）照明；照亮（e.g. He moved her lamp so that her face was illumined. 他移了移她的台灯，这样就照亮了她的脸庞。）

14. mourner: *n.* a person who attends a funeral as a relative or friend of the dead person 哀悼者；送葬者

15. Play's = Played

16. o'er = over

17. dimple: *v.* produce a dimple or dimples in the surface of (something) 使（物体表面）有浅凹；使（物体表面）起涟漪（e.g. A sucking swirl dimpled the water. 一阵上吸的漩涡使得水面泛起涟漪。）

18. bliss: *n.* perfect happiness; great joy 完美的愉悦感；福分；欣喜（e.g. She gave a sigh of bliss. 她幸福地长舒了一口气。）

19. brook: *n.* a small stream 小溪

20. fortune: *n.* (fortunes) the success or failure of a person or enterprise over a period of time or in the course of a particular activity 时运

21. thee: *pron.* [second person singular] archaic or dialect form of you, as the singular object of a verb or preposition （古英语"thou"的宾格，同"you"）

你；汝

22. oh: *exc.* used to express a range of emotions including surprise, anger, disappointment, or joy, or when reacting to something that has just been said （表示惊讶、愤怒、失望、高兴等感情）噢；啊；哦；唉；哎呀

◆ *A Lead-in Note* （简明导读）

诗人以月光起兴，以浅显的语言，道出了对爱人玛丽深深的眷恋之情。诗人运用类比的手法，将自己比作只映“此月”的“此溪”，将玛丽比作有“众星捧”的“此月”。“此溪”只映“此月”，而月光则是两者间的牵引，起到“黏合剂”的作用。

◆ 凝望月光之时

凝望月光之时，
我的眼神片刻偏离了月儿的笑意，
偏向了更加明亮的眼眸，
那眼眸燃放光芒，遥远而孤寂。
但那都是些壮观的恒星，
遥不可及，
我无法感受其火焰之温。
那个柔和的球体
更加亲切可爱，
靠近我们的星球，一路走来，笑容可掬。
因此，玛丽啊，你非我莫属，
更明亮的眼，我毫不在意。
我只爱那月光般的容貌，
那容貌赐我以家，引领我不偏离。

日落西山，阵雨模糊了视线，
但到了午夜时分，辉光适宜，
照亮了所有的暗淡之花，
如同哀悼者脸颊浮现出希冀。
我说（眼前，
月儿的笑意
映在溪流上，喜悦的涟漪荡漾）：
“月儿映在众溪
水面之上，
但此溪之上，只有此月映涟漪。”
因此我想，你我的时运正是如此安排，
许许多多有情者倾心于你。
啊！我只感到一个人在眼前，
我的世界里只有一个玛丽。

022 Maxwell Bodenheim
马克斯韦尔·博登海姆

◆ *The Poet's Profile* （诗人小档案）

马克斯韦尔·博登海姆（1892—1954）：美国诗人及小说家。1922年，博登海姆在芝加哥遇到了美国作家本·赫克特，并与他结成文学上的朋友，他们共同创办了《芝加哥文学时报》（1923—1924）。博登海姆后来去了纽约。在纽约，他以“格林威治村波西米亚之王”而著称。在20世纪20年代的“爵士乐时代”，博登海姆的作品为他赢得了国际声誉。

◆ *Moonlight Bends over the Black Silence*

Moonlight bends over the black silence,
Making it bloom to wild-flowers of sound
That only green things can hear.
A wind sprawls over an orchard,
Frightening its silent litany to sound.
A thread of star-light has fallen to this tree
And curls among its leaves, tangling them to silence . . .
Standing amidst these things, Beloved,
We feel the words our hearts cannot form.

◆ *Annotations*（原诗注释）

1. bend over: to lean over; to bend from the waist 俯身；弯腰

2. bloom: *v.* produce flowers; be in flower 开花；在开花；处于花期

3. sprawl: *v.* spread out over a large area in an untidy or irregular way 混乱（或无条理）地大面积铺开（e.g. The town sprawled along several miles of cliff top. 城镇在山崖顶上不规则地延伸了好几英里。）

4. orchard: *n.* a piece of enclosed land planted with fruit trees 果园

5. litany: *n.* a series of petitions for use in church services or processions, usually recited by the clergy and responded to in a recurring formula by the people 连祷文

6. curl: *v.* sit or lie with the knees drawn up 蜷曲（e.g. She curled up and went to sleep. 她蜷缩着睡着了。）

7. tangle: *v.* to mix together or intertwine in a confused mass（使）缠结；（使）乱作一团

◆ *A Lead-in Note*（简明导读）

月光具有何等威力？月光照亮无声的黝黑之所，打破了沉寂的氛围，有了声响："沉寂开了花，一种叫声音的野花。"此时，风刮起，果树不再沉默。但是，"一丝星光溅落此树，缠绕在叶间开始蜷缩，叶子于是不声不响……"情由境生，一对情侣的内心之语，未经思索，不由自主地脱口而出。月光亮起，月光替我们说出了千言万语。

◆ 月光照亮黝黑的沉寂

月光照亮黝黑的沉寂，
沉寂开了花，一种叫声音的野花，
那声音只有绿色之物听得见。
一阵风刮过果园，漫无方向，

惊扰了果树默默的祈祷，转而念念有声。
一丝星光溅落此树，
缠绕在叶间开始蜷缩，叶子于是不声不响……
心上人啊，伫立其间，
欲说之语，彼此还来不及组织。

023 Witter Bynner
威特·宾纳

◆ *The Poet's Profile* （诗人小档案）

威特·宾纳（1881—1968）：美国诗人、作家、学者及翻译家。1907年，他出版了第一本诗集《哈佛颂》（后来书名改成《年轻的哈佛》）。1929年与中国学者合作，翻译并出版了《群玉山头：唐诗三百首》（The Jade Mountain: A Chinese Anthology, Being Three Hundred Poems of the T'ang Dynasty, 618-906），这是该诗集的第一部英文全译本，曾多次再版，影响深远，堪称唐诗英译的经典之作。

◆ *A Thrush in the Moonlight*

In came the moon and covered me with wonder,
Touched me and was near me and made me very still.
In came a rush of song, like rain after thunder,
Pouring importunate on my window-sill.

I lowered my head, I hid it, I would not see nor hear,
The birdsong had stricken me, had brought the moon too near.
But when I dared to lift my head, night began to fill
With singing in the darkness. And then the thrush grew still.
And the moon came in, and silence, on my window-sill.

◆ *Annotations* （原诗注释）

1. thrush: *n.* any of numerous migratory songbirds of the widely distributed family Turdidae, usually having brownish upper plumage and a spotted breast and noted for a clear melodious song （有褐灰色斑点的）画眉鸟；歌鸫

2. wonder: *n.* a surprising event or situation 奇迹 （e.g. It is a wonder that losses are not much greater. 损失没有增加很多，真是个奇迹。）

3. importunate: *adj.* persistent, especially to the point of annoyance or intrusion 蛮缠的；纠缠不休的 （e.g. importunate creditors 纠缠不休的债权人）

4. window-sill: a ledge or sill forming the bottom part of a window 窗沿；窗台

◆ *A Lead-in Note* （简明导读）

月光给诗人以安慰，可画眉鸟的歌声无休无止，充盈夜晚的黑暗之处，令诗人烦躁不安，将诗人“击垮”。但是，月光犹如诗人心中心仪的女士，与诗人喃喃私语，令诗人欣慰，成了诗人心灵的慰藉。

◆ 月光下的画眉鸟

月亮进来，让我惊叹不已，
靠近我，抚摸我，让我静静休息。
画眉鸟的歌声涌进来，如雷鸣后的雨珠，
倾注窗台之上，无休无止。

我低下头躲藏，不愿看也不愿听，
但歌声把我击垮，令月亮往我眼前紧逼。
等我有胆量抬起头，歌声开始充盈
夜晚的各个黑暗之所。随后，画眉鸟开始沉寂。
月亮进来，于是我的窗台上一片静谧。

024 Adelaide Crapsey
阿德莱德·克拉普西

◆ *The Poet's Profile* （诗人小档案）

阿德莱德·克拉普西（1878—1914）：美国女诗人。对节奏和格律的关注使她创制了一种独特的五行诗变体形式——五行形式的22音节诗，这种诗歌形式受到了日本俳句和日本短歌的影响。

◆ *Moon Shadows*

Still as
On windless nights
The moon-cast shadows are,
So still will be my heart when I
Am dead.

◆ *Annotations* （原诗注释）

1. still: *adj.* not moving or making a sound 静止的；不动的；寂静的 （e.g. She sat very still, her eyes closed. 她闭着双眼静静地坐着。）

2. cast: *v.* cause (light or shadow) to appear on a surface 投射（光或影）（e.g. The moon cast a pale light over the cottages. 苍白的月华洒落在农舍上。）

◆ *A Lead-in Note* （简明导读）

这首自由体短诗极具伤感和压抑的色彩。静谧的月光投射下来，月下的影子相对静止不动，令诗人感到了可怕的静谧：那月亮是静止的，月光也是静止的，月下之影更是静止的，这愈发衬托出诗人内心的悲哀。

◆ 月下之影

我的内心，
在无风的夜晚，
如月下之影一般静谧，
静谧得如同我
死去一般。

Chapter 04

Moon and Love

第四章

月与爱情

025 Thomas Hardy
托马斯·哈代

◆ *The Poet's Profile* （诗人小档案）

托马斯·哈代（1840—1928）：英国长篇小说家及诗人。他的作品多数描述了人们对苦难生活和命运作弄所施加的冷漠力量的抗争。其代表作有《卡斯特桥市长》（1866）、《德伯家的苔丝》（1891）和《无名的裘德》（1896）等。

◆ *Shut Out That Moon*

Close up the casement, draw the blind,
Shut out that stealing moon,
She wears too much the guise she wore
Before our lutes were strewn
With years-deep dust, and names we read
On a white stone were hewn.

Step not out on the dew-dashed lawn
To view the Lady's Chair,
Immense Orion's glittering form,
The Less and Greater Bear:
Stay in; to such sights we were drawn
When faded ones were fair.

Brush not the bough for midnight scents

That come forth lingeringly,
And wake the same sweet sentiments
They breathed to you and me
When living seemed a laugh, and love
All it was said to be.

Within the common lamp-lit room
Prison my eyes and thought;
Let dingy details crudely loom,
Mechanic speech be wrought:
Too fragrant was Life's early bloom,
Too tart the fruit it brought!

◆ *Annotations*（原诗注释）

1.shut sb./sth. out to stop sb./sth. from entering a place 使……不能进入（某处）；挡住；遮住（e.g. I drew the curtains to shut out the light. 我拉上窗帘遮挡光线。）

2. casement: *n.* (chiefly poetic/literary) a window （主要为诗/文用法）窗户

3. blind: *n.* a screen for a window, especially one on a roller or made of slats 窗帘（尤指卷帘或百叶窗）（e.g. She pulled down the blinds. 她拉下窗帘。）

4. stealing: *adj.* avoiding detection by moving carefully 潜行；偷偷摸摸地移动

5. guise: *n.* an external form, appearance, or manner of presentation, typically concealing the true nature of something （尤指掩饰本性的）外观；外表；表现形式；伪装

6. lute: *n.* a plucked stringed instrument with a long neck bearing frets and a rounded body with a flat front, rather like a halved egg in shape 诗琴；琉特琴

7. strew: *v.* cover (a surface or area) with untidily scattered things 乱盖；乱铺(e.g. The table was strewn with books and papers. 桌上乱放着书和文件。)

8. hew: *v.* make or shape (something) by cutting or chopping a material such as wood or stone （把木头或石头等原材料）砍成；劈成；削成 （e.g. a seat hewn out of a fallen tree trunk 从倒下的树干上砍出一个座椅）

9. Lady's Chair: It refers to Cassiopeia, a beautiful circumpolar constellation. In Greek mythology, Cassiopeia the Queen once was known as the Lady of the Chair, which was supposed to represent the wife of Cepheus seated in a chair and holding up both arms. 这里指的是仙后星座，一个漂亮的围绕天极的星座。希腊神话中，卡西俄珀亚王后曾因"椅子上的女士"而著称。人们认为"椅子上的女士"代表的是克普斯的妻子，她两只胳膊举起，坐在椅子上。

10. Orion: *n.* (Greek Mythology) a giant and hunter who was changed into a constellation at his death; (Astronomy) a conspicuous constellation (the Hunter), said to represent a hunter holding a club and shield. It lies on the celestial equator and contains many bright stars, including Rigel, Betelgeuse, and a line of three that form Orion's Belt （希腊神话）俄里翁（死后化为星座的巨人猎手）；（天文学）猎户星座

11. Less and Greater Bear: Also known as the Little Bear and the Great Bear, here they refer to the Ursa Minor and the Ursa Major

Ursa Minor: *n.* a northern constellation (the Little Bear), which contains the north celestial pole and the pole star Polaris （天文学）小熊星座

Ursa Major: *n.* one of the largest and most prominent northern constellations (the Great Bear) （天文学）大熊星座

12. glittering: *adj.* shining with a shimmering or sparkling light 发出微光的；闪烁的

13. brush: *v.* push (something) away with a quick movement of the hand 推开；拂开 （e.g. She brushed a wisp of hair away from her face. 她把垂在脸上的一绺头发拂开。）

14. bough: *n.* a main branch of a tree 树枝；大树枝 （e.g. apple boughs laden with blossom 开满了花的苹果树枝）

15. scent: *n.* a distinctive smell, especially one that is pleasant 气味；香味

16. lingering: adj. lasting for a long time or slow to end 犹存的；苟延残喘的

（e.g. There are still some lingering doubts in my mind. 我心中仍存疑虑。）

17. sentiment: *n.* a feeling or emotion 感觉；情感 （e.g. an intense sentiment of horror 强烈的恐惧感）

18. common: *adj.* ordinary; of ordinary qualities; without special rank or position 普通的；平凡的；平民的；无特殊级别（或地位）的 （e.g. the dwellings of common people 平民住宅）

19. prison: *v.* (poetic/literary) imprison （诗/文用法）禁锢；限制

20. dingy: adj. gloomy and drab 阴暗的；单调的 （e.g. a dingy room 一间昏暗的房屋）

21. loom: *v.* appear as a shadowy form, especially one that is large or threatening （尤指大型、可怕之物）阴森地逼近 （e.g. Vehicles loomed out of the darkness. 汽车从黑暗中阴森森地出现了。）

22. mechanic: *adj.* resembling the action of a machine 机械的；老一套的

23. wrought: *adj.* made or fashioned in the specified way 用特定方式制作的；有特定风格的 （e.g. well-wrought pop 制作精良的流行乐）

24. fragrant: *adj.* having a pleasant or sweet smell 芬芳的；香的

25. bloom: *n.* a flower, especially one cultivated for its beauty （尤指供观赏的）花

26. tart: *adj.* sharp or acid in taste 酸的 （e.g. a tart apple 一个酸苹果）

◆ *A Lead-in Note* （简明导读）

随着时间的推移，一切都会发生改变，爱情也是如此。托马斯·哈代在此诗中探索的也是这方面的问题。

月亮见证了诗人的爱情，如今，爱情不在了，月亮犹在。因此，诗人不愿见到月亮，只因那月亮会勾起诗人那段痛苦而甜蜜的爱情。

◆ 将那月亮隔到外边

关上窗户，拉下窗帘，
将那偷偷夜行的月亮隔到外边。
她的装束太像从前，
我们的诗琴却因岁月的久远
铺满了灰尘，而我们熟知的姓名
也被刻到了白石头上面。

莫踏上洒满露珠的草地
去把仙后星座观看，
莫仰望猎户座那闪烁的外表，
也莫将大小熊星座尽收眼前。
待在屋内吧——如此景物曾吸引我们，
可如今，褪去的，当时正娇艳。

莫在午夜拂弄树枝，触发
余留的香气而令其飘散，
唤醒曾飘向我和你的
那些同样甜蜜的情感。
彼时，生活似乎是欢笑一场，爱情
据说也是欢笑不断。

灯照亮这普普通通的屋子，
它囚禁了我的思想和双眼。
让单调的琐事残酷地逼近吧，

不假思索地去运用语言。
人生早绽之花过于芬芳，
其果实又太酸、太酸。

026 Walter Savage Landor
沃尔特·萨维奇·兰多

◆ *The Poet's Profile* （诗人小档案）

沃尔特·萨维奇·兰多（1775—1864）：英国诗人、作家和散文家。他一生创作了大量题材各异的作品，大体可以分成四类：散文、抒情诗、政论文（包括讽刺诗）和拉丁文作品。其代表作有《格比尔》和《文人与政治家的假想对话》等。

◆ *On an Eclipse of the Moon*

Struggling, and faint, and fainter didst thou wane,
O Moon! and round thee all thy starry train
Came forth to help thee, with half-open eyes,
And trembled every one with still surprise,
That the black Spectre should have dared assail
Their beauteous queen and seize her sacred veil

◆ *Annotations* （原诗注释）

1. eclipse: *n.* an obscuring of the light from one celestial body by the passage of another between it and the observer or between it and its source of illumination （天体的）日食/月食

2. didst: *v.* (archaic) second person singular past of do （古旧用法）"do"的过去时第二人称单数形式

3. thou: *pron.* [second person singular] archaic or dialect form of you, as the singular subject of a verb （古旧用法或方言用法）（作动词的单数主语）你（同"you"）

4. wane: *v.* (of the moon) have a progressively smaller part of its visible surface illuminated, so that it appears to decrease in size （月亮）亏缺

5. o: *exc.* used to express surprise or strong emotion 哦；哟；啊；唉；哎呀（表示惊讶或强烈的情感）

6. thee: *pron.* [second person singular] archaic or dialect form of you, as the singular object of a verb or preposition （古英语"thou"的宾格，同"you"）你；汝

7. thy: *poss. adj.* (also "thine" before a vowel) archaic or dialect form of your（元音前亦作"thine"）（古旧用法或方言用法）你（您）的（同"your"）

8. starry: *adj.* full of or lit by stars 布满星星的；星光照耀的 （e.g. a starry sky 繁星点点的天空）

9. train: *n.* a retinue of attendants accompanying an important person 随从；扈从

10. spectre: *n.* a ghost 鬼怪；幽灵

11. assail: *v.* make a concerted or violent attack on （协同地或猛烈地）攻击或袭击

12. beauteous: *adj.* (poetic/literary) beautiful （诗/文用法）漂亮的；美丽的

13. sacred: *adj.* connected with God (or the gods) or dedicated to a religious purpose and so deserving veneration 与上帝（或神）相关的；奉献给上帝（或神）的；神圣的

14. veil: *n.* a piece of fine material worn by women to protect or conceal the face 面纱；面罩 （e.g. a white bridal veil 新娘的白色面纱）

◆ *A Lead-in Note* （简明导读）

诗人用诗化的语言，形象地展示了月食的过程。实际上，这次月食的记

录已经具有了一定的象征意义。月亮是一位蒙着神圣面纱的美丽女王，是拜倒在其“石榴裙”下的“众星”的爱情女神。他们怎么能容忍“那个黑色幽灵”将她“玷污”？可以想到，一场捍卫爱情女神的争斗不可避免。

◆ 记一次月食

挣扎之中，你暗淡，愈发暗淡，开始衰减。
啊，月亮！你周围所有的随从都半睁着眼，
闪着星光，一个个都要帮你，走上前来——
他们个个都无声地颤抖，吃惊中发现：
那个黑色幽灵竟然胆大妄为，袭击了
他们美丽的女王，夺取了她蒙着神圣面纱的脸。

027 Thomas Moore
托马斯·穆尔

◆ *The Poet's Profile* （诗人小档案）

托马斯·穆尔（1779—1852）：爱尔兰诗人、音乐家、歌手、歌词作者及艺人。穆尔最为知名的抒情诗歌当属《吟唱少年》和《夏日里最后一朵玫瑰》。他把爱尔兰的历史、民间故事、人物传奇编织进诗歌当中唤起读者对爱尔兰绿色岛国风光的向往。

◆ *The Young May Moon*

The young May moon is beaming, love.
The glow-worm's lamp is gleaming, love.
How sweet to rove,
Through Morna's grove,
When the drowsy world is dreaming, love!
Then awake! —the heavens look bright, my dear,
'Tis never too late for delight, my dear,
And the best of all ways
To lengthen our days
Is to steal a few hours from the night, my dear!

Now all the world is sleeping, love,
But the Sage, his star-watch keeping, love,
And I, whose star,
More glorious far,

Is the eye from that casement peeping, love.
Then awake! —till rise of sun, my dear,
The Sage's glass we'll shun, my dear,
Or, in watching the flight
Of bodies of light,
He might happen to take thee for one, my dear.

◆ *Annotations* （原诗注释）

1. beam: *v.* (of a light or light source) shine brightly （光或光源）照耀（e.g. The sun's rays beamed down. 阳光照射下来。）

2. glow-worm: *n.* a bioluminescent larva or a wingless wormlike female of certain insects, especially fireflies and beetles of the family Phengodidae 萤火虫

3. rove: *v.* travel constantly without a fixed destination; wander 流浪；漫游

4. grove: *n.* a small wood, orchard, or group of trees 树丛；小树林；果园 （e.g. an olive grove 一小片橄榄树林）

5. drowsy: *adj.* sleepy and lethargic; half asleep 困倦的；瞌睡的；昏昏欲睡的；假寐的 （e.g. The wine had made her drowsy. 葡萄酒使她昏昏欲睡。）

6. 'Tis = It is

7. lengthen: *v.* make or become longer 使变长

8. sage: *n.* a profoundly wise man, especially one who features in ancient history or legend （尤指古代历史或传说中的）圣人；圣贤

9. but: *prep.* except; apart from; other than 除了 （e.g. We were never anything but poor. 我们一直就是穷而已。）

10. far: *adv.* by a great deal 大大地；极大地 （e.g. The reality has fallen far short of early expectations. 现实与早先的预期相去甚远。）

11. casement: *n.* (chiefly poetic/literary) a window（主要为诗/文用法）窗户

12. peep: *v.* look quickly and furtively at something, especially through a narrow opening （尤指从缝隙中）偷看；窥探 （e.g. His door was ajar and she

couldn't resist peeping in. 他的门半开着，因此她忍不住向里偷看。）

13. shun: *v.* persistently avoid, ignore, or reject (someone or something) through antipathy or caution （因厌恶或谨慎）避免；避开；回避 （e.g. He shunned fashionable society. 他回避上流社会。）

14. thee: *pron.* [second person singular] archaic or dialect form of you, as the singular object of a verb or preposition （古英语“thou”的宾格，同“you”）你；汝

15. or: *conj.* otherwise (used to introduce the consequences of something not being done or not being the case) 否则；不然

◆ A Lead-in Note （简明导读）

五月的初月是正值年轻时光的月亮。这样的月亮所发出的光辉，年轻的情侣怎能错过！于是，诗人在诗中一再呼唤自己的爱人（也许就是诗中提到的莫娜）到月下共度好时光，以至于“我的爱人，绝佳之道——延长白昼时光，就是从夜晚偷来几个小时，不为人知晓！”在诗的最后一节中，高高在上的圣人成了陪衬，突出了诗人所爱之人的“闪亮”。

◆ 五月的初月

爱人啊，五月的初月开始照耀。
爱人啊，萤火虫的灯闪烁缥缈。
穿过莫娜家那片小树林，
一路漫游，多么美妙！
爱人啊，此时全世界昏沉进入梦乡。
我的爱人，那就醒来吧——天空皎皎；
我的爱人，不管夜多深，你我都有快乐来追寻。
我的爱人，绝佳之道——
延长白昼时光，

就是从夜晚偷来几个小时，不为人知晓！

爱人啊，全世界现在已入眠；
爱人啊，我和圣人却都不困倦。
圣人观看着星星，
而我观看的星星，更为明亮、遥远。
爱人啊，那颗星就是自窗户向外窥视的眼眸。
我的爱人，那就醒来别睡——直至太阳露笑脸；
我的爱人，我们要避开圣人的窗户。
我的爱人，否则在观看一束一束光线
飞逝而过的过程中，
圣人可能凑巧把你当作一颗星，一闪一闪。

028 Vachel Lindsay
韦切尔·林赛

◆ *The Poet's Profile* （诗人小档案）

韦切尔·林赛（1879—1931）：美国诗人及现代歌唱诗歌的奠基人。林赛的作品收集在《〈威廉·布思将军进入了天堂〉及其他诗集》(1913)、《〈刚果河〉及其他诗集》(1914)、《每一个灵魂都是一个轮回》(1929)等中。

◆ *The Moon is a Painter*

He coveted her portrait.
He toiled as she grew gay.
She loved to see him labor
In that devoted way.

And in the end it pleased her,
But bowed him more with care.
Her rose-smile showed so plainly,
Her soul-smile was not there.

That night he groped without a lamp
To find a cloak, a book,
And on the vexing portrait
By moonrise chanced to look.

The color-scheme was out of key,
The maiden rose-smile faint,
But through the blessed darkness
She gleamed, his friendly saint.

The comrade, white, immortal,
His bride, and more than bride—
The citizen, the sage of mind,
For whom he lived and died.

◆ *Annotations* （原诗注释）

1. covet: *v.* yearn to possess or have (something) 渴望；觊觎；垂涎；贪求

2. toil: *v.* work extremely hard or incessantly 苦干；辛勤劳动

3. gay: *adj.* brightly coloured; showy; brilliant 明亮的；绚丽的；灿烂的 （e.g. a gay profusion of purple and pink sweet peas 大量绚丽的紫色和粉红色的豌豆花）

4. devoted: *adj.* having been consecrated; dedicated 献身的；专注的

5. bow: *v.* cause (something) to bend with age or under a heavy weight 压弯；压倒；使俯身

6. care: *n.* a feeling of or occasion for anxiety 忧虑；担心

7. grope: *v.* feel about or search blindly or uncertainly with the hands 摸索（e.g. She got up and groped for her spectacles. 她起床摸索着找眼镜。）

8. cloak: *n.* an outdoor over-garment, typically sleeveless, that hangs loosely from the shoulders 斗篷；大氅；披风 （e.g. She is wearing a red cloak with a hood. 她穿着一件红色带兜帽的披风。）

9. vexing: *adj.* extremely annoying or displeasing 使人烦恼的；使人恼火的（e.g. the most vexing questions for policy-makers 对政策制定者来说最烦恼的问题）

10. chance: *v.* do something by accident or without design 偶然；碰巧（e.g. He was very effusive if they chanced to meet. 他们若是巧遇，他总会表现得热情过头。）

11. maiden: *n.* (archaic or poetic/literary) a girl or young woman, especially an unmarried one （古旧用法或诗/文用法）少女；（尤指未婚的）年轻妇女

12. faint: *adj.* (of a sight, smell, or sound) barely perceptible （景象、气味、声音）微弱的；依稀的

13. blessed: *adj.* made holy; consecrated 神圣的；神圣化的

14. gleam: *v.* shine brightly, especially with reflected light （尤指反光的）发光；闪烁（e.g. Light gleamed on the china cats. 瓷猫身上闪着光。）

15. saint: *n.* a person acknowledged as holy or virtuous and typically regarded as being in heaven after death 圣人；道德高尚的人；至善的人

16. comrade: *n.* a person who shares one's interests or activities; a friend or companion 志同道合者；朋友；伙伴

17. citizen: *n.* a native, inhabitant, or denizen of a particular place （特定地区）土生土长的人；住户；居民

18. sage: *n.* a profoundly wise man, especially one who features in ancient history or legend （尤指古代历史或传说中的）圣人；圣贤

◆ *A Lead-in Note*（简明导读）

诗中，"他"为"她"画像。画成之后，她虽对画像满意，却为他提出了更高的要求，因为"她玫瑰般笑容显露无遗，她心灵的笑容却不在场"。一次偶然的机会，月亮登场，无意中照亮了画家创作中的不足，却使她的肖像完美起来："她圣洁而友善，闪着光"。此时，"她"也许指画像中的她，也许指刚刚登场的月亮，也许就是月亮与画家心爱的她的融合体。

◆ 月亮是位好画家

他渴望为她画像。
趁她绚丽未减，他干劲不降。
她满心欢喜看着他
专心投入的模样。

到了最后，画像令她称心，
却严苛有加，使他忧虑万丈。
她玫瑰般笑容显露无遗，
她心灵的笑容却不在场。

那晚他没有点灯，摸索起来，
要摸一本书，还有一件大氅。
月升的那一刻，他偶然间
将目光落到那幅令他忧虑的画像。

那色彩的搭配，没有了基调；
玉女那玫瑰般笑容暗淡无芳。
但此时，透过神秘莫测的黑暗，
她圣洁而友善，闪着光。

这位伙伴洁白，不会老去，
是他的新娘，甚至胜过新娘——
不离不弃，启迪心智：
他为她而生，为她而亡。

029 Percy Bysshe Shelley
珀西·比希·雪莱

◆ *The Poet's Profile* （诗人小档案）

珀西·比希·雪莱（1792—1822）：英国文学史上最有才华的抒情诗人之一，被誉为“诗人中的诗人”，与乔治·戈登·拜伦一起被称为英国浪漫主义诗歌的“双子星座”。他的著名作品包括政治诗歌《麦布女王》（1813年），诗剧《解放了的普罗米修斯》（1820），论文《诗辩》（1821），以及悼念济慈的挽诗《阿东尼斯》（1821）。

◆ *To the Moon*

Art thou pale for weariness
Of climbing heaven and gazing on the earth,
Wandering companionless
Among the stars that have a different birth, —
And ever changing, like a joyless eye
That finds no object worth its constancy?

◆ *Annotations* （原诗注释）

1. art: *v.* (archaic, poetic or dialect) 2nd person singular present of be （古旧、诗歌或方言用法）“be”的第二人称、单数、现在时形式

2. thou: pron. [second person singular] archaic or dialect form of you, as the singular subject of a verb（古旧用法或方言用法）（作动词的单数主语）你（同“you”）

3. weariness: *n.* temporary loss of strength and energy resulting from hard physi-

cal or mental work 疲倦；困乏；消沉；厌倦

4. constancy: *n.* the quality of being enduring and unchanging 坚定不移；不屈不挠；始终如一；恒久不变 （e.g. the constancy of the tradition 此传统的持久）

◆ *A Lead-in Note* （简明导读）

此诗中，诗人雪莱以浪漫主义的手法，将月亮拟人化成一位“曲高和寡”的女子。该女子有着与众星不同的出身，因而“漫游其中，无一可为伴”。她的眼睛一眨一眨的，却显得很不开心，因她没有发现一个值得长相厮守的人。

◆ 致月儿

你面色苍白，难道一点儿都不疲倦？
你爬上天空将大地俯瞰。
繁星闪烁，却与你出身不同——
你漫游其中，无一可为伴。
你圆缺不停，如眼闪动却无喜悦之情，
因值得长相厮守的，你一个都没有发现。

030 Evelyn Scott
伊芙琳·斯科特

◆ *The Poet's Profile* （诗人小档案）

伊芙琳·斯科特（1893—1963）：美国女长篇小说家、剧作家及诗人。作为一位现代主义者及具有尝试性的作家，她是20世纪二三十年代一位重要的文学人物，有时候使用笔名“欧内斯特·苏扎”和“埃尔西·邓恩”进行写作。

◆ *The Naiad*

The moon rises,
Glistening,
Naked white,
Out of her stream.

Wet marble shoulders
Shake star drops on the clouds.

◆ *Annotations* （原诗注释）

1. naiad or Naiad: *n.* (in classical mythology) a water nymph said to inhabit a river, spring, or waterfall （古典神话）那伊阿得（住在河流、泉水和瀑布中的水泉女神）

2. glisten:*v.* (of something wet or greasy) shine; glitter （潮湿或油腻的东西）

闪闪发光；闪闪发亮 （e.g. His cheeks glistened with tears. 他的脸颊因流泪而闪闪发亮。）

3. marble: *n.* a hard crystalline metamorphic form of limestone, typically white with mottlings or streaks of colour, which is capable of taking a polish and is used in sculpture and architecture 大理石

4. drop: *n.* a small round or pear-shaped portion of liquid that hangs or falls or adheres to a surface （液体的）滴

◆ *A Lead-in Note* （简明导读）

据古希腊神话传说，那伊阿得是居于溪流和泉水中的水泽女神。此诗中，诗人赋予月亮以阴柔女性的形象。皎洁的月亮升起来，映在溪流中，犹如水泽女神那伊阿得“闪着湿漉漉的光，赤裸着白白的身躯”，肩膀一抖“将一滴一滴的星星抖落云中”。

◆ 那伊阿得

从溪流里
月亮升起，
闪着湿漉漉的光，
赤裸着白白的身躯。

湿漉漉的大理石纹理肩膀，
将一滴一滴的星星抖落云中。

031 James Joyce 詹姆斯·乔伊斯

◆ *The Poet's Profile* （诗人小档案）

詹姆斯·乔伊斯（1882—1941）：爱尔兰作家诗人，二十世纪最伟大的作家之一，后现代文学的奠基者之一，其作品及“意识流”思想对世界文坛影响巨大。其主要作品有短篇小说集《尤利西斯》，自传体小说《青年艺术家的自画像》，长篇小说《芬尼根的守灵夜》等。

◆ *What Counsel Has the Hooded Moon*

What counsel has the hooded moon
Put in thy heart, my shyly sweet,
Of Love in ancient plenilune,
Glory and stars beneath his feet—
A sage that is but kith and kin
With the comedian Capuchin?

Believe me rather that am wise
In disregard of the divine,
A glory kindles in those eyes,
Trembles to starlight. Mine, O Mine!
No more be tears in moon or mist
For thee, sweet sentimentalist.

◆ Annotations （原诗注释）

1. counsel: *n.* advice, especially that given formally （尤指正式的）建议；忠告

2. hooded: *adj.* (of an article of clothing) having a hood （衣服）带风帽的(e.g. a hooded cloak 一件带帽斗篷)

3. thy: *poss. adj.* (Also "thine" before a vowel) archaic or dialect form of your (元音前亦作"thine")(古旧用法或方言用法)你（您）的（同"your"）

4. shyly: *adv.* in a shy or timid or bashful manner 羞怯地；胆怯地；小心地

5. plenilune: *n.* (Astronomy) a full moon （天文学）望月；满月

6. glory: *n.* the splendour and bliss of heaven 天堂的荣耀（或福祉）(e.g. with the saints in glory 和沐浴在天堂荣耀中的圣人在一起)

7. sage: *n.* a profoundly wise man, especially one who features in ancient history or legend （尤指古代历史或传说中的）圣人；圣贤

8. kith: *n.* (in phrase "kith and kin"or "kith or kin") one's friends, acquaintances, and relations 朋友；相识；邻居

9. capuchin: a South American monkey with a cap of hair on the head which has the appearance of a cowl 卷尾猴；悬猴；僧帽猴

10. disregard: *n.* the action or state of disregarding or ignoring something 不顾；忽视

11. kindle: *v.* light or set on fire 点燃

12. thee: *pron.* [second person singular] archaic or dialect form of you, as the singular object of a verb or preposition （古英语"thou"的宾格，同"you"）你；汝

13. sentimentalist: *n.* someone who indulges in excessive sentimentality 多愁善感者；感伤主义者

◆ *A Lead-in Note*（简明导读）

此诗中，诗人认为月亮是圣贤老者的象征，只不过头上戴着一顶风帽——年轻人喜欢的装束。于是，他一下子联想到天主教圣方济会中嘉布遣会修士头戴尖顶风帽的滑稽形象。在此诗的第二节中，他以谦虚的口吻“自诩”为贤明的“圣贤”，借月抒发自己对身边情人的情感。

◆ 那头戴风帽的月亮给了你什么样的忠告

我羞涩的爱人啊，那头戴风帽的月亮
将什么样的忠告印到了你的心中？
忠告关乎他那自古就目睹的爱，
他脚下有荣光和星星——
他是传说中的圣贤，却只会
让人想起嘉布遣会修士的滑稽形象。

抛开那位圣贤不谈，请你相信：
我应算得上贤明。
荣光在眼中燃起，在星光里
闪烁。我的光！啊，我的星！
啊，爱人，你多愁善感，
月中再无泪水或泪滴为你而生。

Chapter 05

Moon and Feelings

第五章

月与情感

032 Robert Frost
罗伯特・弗罗斯特

◆ *The Poet's Profile* （诗人小档案）

罗伯特・弗罗斯特（1874—1963）：美国诗人，其以讽刺的笔触和朴实无华的语言风格著称。他的许多诗反映了他对新英格兰的亲密情感，包括诗集《波士顿以北》（1914）和《新罕布什尔州》（1923）等。他先后四次获得普利策奖。

◆ *The Freedom of the Moon*

I've tried the new moon tilted in the air
Above a hazy tree-and-farmhouse cluster
As you might try a jewel in your hair.
I've tried it fine with little breadth of luster,
Alone, or in one ornament combining
With one first-water start almost shining.

I put it shining anywhere I please.
By walking slowly on some evening later,
I've pulled it from a crate of crooked trees,
And brought it over glossy water, greater,
And dropped it in, and seen the image wallow,
The color run, all sorts of wonder follow.

◆ *Annotations* （原诗注释）

1. tilt: *v.* move or cause to move into a sloping position （使）倾斜；（使）侧倾 （e.g. The floor tilted slightly. 地板轻微倾斜。）

2. hazy: *adj.* vague, indistinct, or ill-defined 朦胧的；不清楚的；模糊的（e.g. hazy memories 朦胧的记忆）

3. cluster: *n.* a group of people or similar things positioned or occurring close together（人或物集中出现的）一群；一组 （e.g. a cluster of antique shops 古董店群）

4. jewel: *n.* an ornament or piece of jewellery containing such a stone or stones 宝石饰物；首饰

5. fine: *adj.* (of a thread, filament, or person's hair) thin （线、丝或头发）纤细的 （e.g. I have always had fine and dry hair. 我的头发总是又细又干。）

6. breadth: *n.* the distance of measurement from side to side of something; width 幅度；宽度

7. luster: *n.* a gentle sheen or soft glow, especially that of a partly reflective surface 光泽；光辉

8. ornament: *n.* a thing used or serving to adorn something but usually having no practical purpose, especially a small object such as a figurine 装饰品（尤指小雕像一类的小物件）

9. crate: *n.* a slatted wooden case used for transporting goods （运输货物的）板条箱 （e.g. a crate of banana s一箱香蕉）

10. crooked: *adj.* bent or twisted out of shape or out of place 弯曲的；歪曲的；扭曲的 （e.g. His teeth were yellow and crooked. 他的牙齿又黄又不整齐。）

11. glossy: *adj.* shiny and smooth 有光泽的；光滑的 （e.g. thick, glossy, manageable hair 浓密、光亮而又易梳理的头发）

12. wallow: *v.* (of a boat or aircraft) roll from side to side （船或航空器）颠簸；摇摆 （e.g. The small jet wallowed in the sky. 小型喷气式飞机在空中颠簸。）

◆ *A Lead-in Note* （简明导读）

此诗中，诗人将月亮如心爱之人佩戴珠宝首饰般佩戴到“一片朦胧的树木和农舍之上”。而且，诗人还说：“我喜欢哪里，就把月亮安放到哪里。”月亮仿佛可以随诗人所愿，被到处“佩戴”和“安放”。可以说，诗人弗罗斯特以月的自由来映衬人的自由，以月的自由度来象征人对自由的感受。

◆ 自由的月亮

新月斜挂天空中，我将其安放到
一片朦胧的树木和农舍之上佩戴好，
如同你在发间佩戴珠宝首饰般。
月亮细如一条银光带时，我将其佩戴好——
单独佩戴，或将其跟某饰品组合起来
佩戴，如同月亮迸出水面时，近乎闪耀。

我喜欢哪里，就把月亮安放到哪里。
后来某个晚上，悠闲漫步之际，
我把被缠入一排弯曲树间的月亮拽出，
将其带到更为开阔的光亮水域，
丢入水中，见其影像摇晃颠簸，
色随波散，各种惊叹随之而至。

033 Christina Georgina Rossetti
克里斯蒂娜·乔治娜·罗塞蒂

◆ *The Poet's Profile* （诗人小档案）

克里斯蒂娜·乔治娜·罗塞蒂（1830—1894）：英国女诗人，写了许多宗教诗（反映的是其作为高教会派英国圣公会教徒的信仰）、情诗、浪漫诗和儿童诗。她的著名作品当属《〈妖怪集市〉及其他诗集》(1862)。

◆ *Is the Moon Tired?*

Is the moon tired? She looks so pale
Within her misty veil:
She scales the sky from east to west,
And takes no rest.

Before the coming of the night
The moon shows papery white;
Before the dawning of the day
She fades away.

◆ *Annotations* （原诗注释）

1. misty: *adj.* full of, covered with, or accompanied by mist 笼罩着雾的；雾气覆盖的；有雾的 (e.g. The evening was cold and misty. 傍晚时天气寒冷，雾气迷蒙。)

2. scale: *v.* climb up or over (something high and steep) 攀登；翻越 (e.g. Thieves scaled an 8 feet high fence. 窃贼翻过了8英尺［约2.4米］高的栅栏。)

◆ *A Lead-in Note* （简明导读）

诗人克里斯蒂娜以简洁易懂的语言和拟人化的手法讲述了月儿的辛劳。全诗以问题开篇，自问自答。月儿很辛苦，却不为人知，因其“脸庞在雾纱后藏埋”。她来得很早，天还未黑就升起；她走的时候，不声不响，“她的踪影便无处寻找”。这其实就是一位辛劳母亲的真实写照，也是诗人的自我画像。诗人以月的辛劳，写出了人的辛劳，借月抒发情感。

◆ 月儿累了吗？

月儿累了吗？她面色如此苍白，
脸庞在雾纱后藏埋。
从东至西，她翻越天空，
一刻不停。

夜晚还未到来，
月儿的光如纸白。
天还未破晓，
她的踪影便无处寻找。

034 William Butler Yeats 威廉·巴特勒·叶芝

◆ *The Poet's Profile* （诗人小档案）

威廉·巴特勒·叶芝（1865—1939）：爱尔兰诗人和剧作家。叶芝的剧作《凯瑟琳伯爵夫人》（1892）和短篇故事集《凯尔特的黄昏》（1893）推动了爱尔兰的戏剧、文化和文学的复兴。他著名的诗歌作品包括《钟楼》《盘旋的楼梯》等。1923年，叶芝获诺贝尔文学奖。

◆ *The Crazed Moon*

Crazed through much child-bearing
The moon is staggering in the sky;
Moon-struck by the despairing
Glances of her wandering eye
We grope, and grope in vain,
For children born of her pain.

Children dazed or dead!
When she in all her virginal pride
First trod on the mountain's head
What stir ran through the countryside
Where every foot obeyed her glance!
What manhood led the dance!

Fly-catchers of the moon,

Our hands are blenched, our fingers seem
But slender needles of bone;
Blenched by that malicious dream
They are spread wide that each
May rend what comes in reach.

◆ *Annotations* （原诗注释）

1. craze: *v.* cause (someone) to be or appear to be wildly insane 使（某人）发狂；使（某人）变得发疯似的 （e.g. a crazed killer 疯狂的杀手）

2. bear: *v.* give birth to (a child) 生育（孩子）

3. stagger: *v.* walk or move unsteadily, as if about to fall 摇晃；踉跄；蹒跚（e.g. He staggered to his feet, swaying a little. 他摇摇晃晃地站起来，身体有点不稳。）

4. moon-struck: adj. unable to think or act normally, especially because of being in love （尤指因恋爱）迷乱的；茫然的；发呆的

5. grope: *v.* feel about or search blindly or uncertainly with the hands 摸索，暗中摸 （e.g. She got up and groped for her spectacles. 她起床摸索着找眼镜。）

6. dazed: *adj.* in a state of stunned confusion or shock 不清醒的；眩晕的

7. virginal: *adj.* being, relating to, or appropriate for a virgin （关于）处女的；童贞的

8. tread: *v.* (tread on) set one's foot down on top of （脚）踩；踏

9. stir: *n.* a commotion 骚动；骚乱（e.g. The event caused quite a stir. 那件事引起了很大的轰动。）

10. blench: *v.* (chiefly dialect) variant spelling of blanch（主要为方言用法）同“blanch”

blanch: *v.* make white or pale by extracting colour; bleach 使变白；漂白；使苍白 （e.g. The cold light blanched her face. 冷色的光使她的脸显得苍白。）

11. slender: *adj.* (of a person or part of the body) gracefully thin （人或身体部

位）苗条的；修长的；纤细的 （e.g. her slender neck 她修长的脖子）

12. malicious: *adj.* characterized by malice; intending or intended to do harm 恶意的；恶毒的；怀恨的 （e.g. malicious damage 恶意破坏）

13. rend: *v.* tear (something) into two or more pieces 撕裂；扯碎

◆ *A Lead-in Note* （简明导读）

诗人借“发了疯的月儿”来抒发人生情感。对这种情感的解读，则因人而异。有人认为，月儿是一个退化时代的象征；有人认为，月儿代表易变的幻象。另据分析，此诗中的“月儿”寓含了丰富的西方文化因素，涉及神话、宗教等层面。

◆ 发了疯的月儿

月儿生下很多孩子，发了疯，
踉踉跄跄穿行在天空。
此时，我们感到茫然，
而她的眼神绝望，游移不定。
我们摸来摸去，摸不到
一个孩子——降生于她疼痛中。

有些孩子昏迷，有些孩子死去！
遥想青春得意时，她玉洁冰清，
第一次踏上了大山最高处：
整个乡下多么喧嚣和沸腾！
每个人的步伐紧随着她的眼神！
多么阳刚之气将舞蹈引领！

我们用手将月儿捕捉，

手被染白，手指似乎变成
一根根修长的骨质细针。
将手染白的，是一场凶梦：
指间阔张，可碾碎所有
可及之物——力大无穷。

035 Sara Teasdale 萨拉·蒂斯代尔

◆ *The Poet's Profile* （诗人小档案）

萨拉·蒂斯代尔（1884—1933）：美国杰出的抒情诗人，她的诗收录于《〈特洛伊的海伦〉及其他诗歌集》（1911）、《江河入海》（1915）、《爱歌》（1917）、《火焰与影子》（1920）及《奇异的胜利》（1933）等中。萨拉·蒂斯代尔以具有浪漫色彩的抒情诗篇赢得了大众的钦佩，她的诗主要围绕一名女子对美、对爱情，以及对死亡不断变换的视角而展开。1918年，蒂斯代尔获得哥伦比亚大学诗歌学会奖，这一奖项就是普利策诗歌奖的前身。

◆ *The Kind Moon*

I think the moon is very kind
To take such trouble just for me.
He came along with me from home
To keep me company.

He went as fast as I could run;
I wonder how he crossed the sky?
I'm sure he hasn't legs and feet
Or any wings to fly.

Yet here he is above their roof;
Perhaps he thinks it isn't right
For me to go so far alone,

Tho' mother said I might.

◆ *Annotations* （原诗注释）

1. kind: *adj.* having or showing a friendly, generous, and considerate nature 亲切友好的 （e.g. She was a good, kind woman. 她是一个友善的好女人。）

2. company: *n.* the fact or condition of being with another or others, especially in a way that provides friendship and enjoyment 陪伴；伴随；交往 （e.g. I could do with some company. 陪我一会儿就行了。）

3. Tho' = Though

◆ *A Lead-in Note* （简明导读）

这首以孩童的口吻写成的小诗，充满了孩童的天真与好奇。诗中的情形，我们小时候也许都经历过："为了我，多大的麻烦他都不嫌。从我离家时起，紧紧跟随，一路与我为伴。"可是，月亮没长腿，没生脚，也没有翅膀，转眼间"他却悬在屋顶上方"。多么好心肠的月亮，无时无刻不与我为伴！可以说，月亮是孩子好奇心产生的源泉。

◆ 好心肠的月亮

我想，月亮心地和善，
为了我，劳心劳神。
从我离家时起，紧紧跟随，
一路与我为伴。

我跑起来有多快，他就有多快。
我纳闷：他如何将天空横穿？
我肯定：他没长腿，没长脚，

也没长翅膀可以飞翔。

可至此，他却悬在屋顶上方。
他或许认为：距离这么远，
不适合我一个人独行，
尽管母亲说，我可以不用陪伴。

036 Charlotte Smith
夏洛特·史密斯

◆ *The Poet's Profile* （诗人小档案）

夏洛特·史密斯（1749—1806）：英国浪漫主义女诗人及长篇小说家。夏洛特复兴了英国商籁体诗歌，为哥特式小说的规范作出了贡献，还写了一些政治感伤小说。夏洛特是一位成功的作家，在她一生的职业生涯中，出版过10部小说，3部诗集等作品。

◆ *To the Moon (Sonnet IV)*

Queen of the silver bow! —by thy pale beam,
Alone and pensive, I delight to stray,
And watch thy shadow trembling in the stream,
Or mark the floating clouds that cross thy way.
And while I gaze, thy mild and placid light
Sheds a soft calm upon my troubled breast;
And oft I think—fair planet of the night,
That in thy orb, the wretched may have rest:
The sufferers of the earth perhaps may go,
Released by death—to thy benignant sphere,
And the sad children of despair and woe
Forget in thee, their cup of sorrow here.
Oh! that I soon may reach thy world serene,
Poor wearied pilgrim—In this toiling scene!

◆ *Annotations* （原诗注释）

1. bow: *n.* a weapon for shooting arrows, typically made of a curved piece of wood joined at both ends by a taut string 弓

2. thy: *poss. adj.* (Also "thine" before a vowel) archaic or dialect form of your（元音前亦作"thine"）（古旧用法或方言用法）你（您）的（同"your"）

3. beam: *n.* a ray or shaft of light 光线；光柱（e.g. A beam of light flashed in front of her. 一柱光在她面前闪过。）

4. pensive: *adj.* engaged in, involving, or reflecting deep or serious thought; showing or expressing deep, often melancholy thought 沉思的；冥想的；忧虑的；忧郁的

5. delight: *v.* to take great pleasure or joy 感到高兴；以……为乐

6. stray: *v.* (poetic/literary) wander or roam in a specified direction（诗/文用法）漫步；徘徊；游荡（e.g. Over these mounds the Kurdish shepherd strays. 库尔德牧羊人游荡在这些土岗上。）

7. mark: *v.* notice or pay careful attention to 注意；留心（e.g. He'll leave you, you mark my words! 他会离开你的，你留意我的话！）

8. placid: *adj.* (especially of a place or stretch of water) calm and peaceful, with little movement or activity（尤指地方或水域）平静的；宁静的（e.g. the placid waters of a small lake 小湖平静的水面）

9. calm: *n.* the absence of nervousness, agitation, or excitement in a person 镇静；沉着；心平气和（e.g. His usual calm deserted him. 他不再如往日那样心平气和。）

10. oft = often

11. fair: *adj.* (archaic) beautiful; attractive（古旧用法）美丽的；动人的；有魅力的（e.g. the fairest of her daughters 她女儿中最漂亮的一位）

12. wretched: *adj.* (of a person) in a very unhappy or unfortunate state（人）不幸的；可怜的；苦恼的

13. benignant: *adj.* favorable; beneficial; kindly and benevolent 有利的；有益

的；慈祥的；善良的

14. sphere: *n.* (chiefly poetic/literary) a celestial body （主要为诗/文用法）天体

15. woe: *n.* (often humorous) great sorrow or distress （常用于幽默用法）悲哀；悲苦；苦恼 （e.g. The Everton tale of woe continued. 埃弗顿的悲哀故事还在延续。）

16. thee: *pron.* [second person singular] archaic or dialect form of you, as the singular object of a verb or preposition （古英语“thou”的宾格，同“you”）你；汝

17. cup: *n.* one's lot in life; something to be partaken of or endured; one's portion, as of joy or suffering 命运；经历；遭遇

18. serene: *adj.* calm, peaceful, and untroubled; tranquil 安详的；宁静的 （e.g. Her eyes were closed and she looked very serene. 她闭着眼，看上去很平静。）

19. pilgrim: *n.* (chiefly poetic/literary) a person whose life is compared to a journey （主要为诗/文用法）流浪者；旅客

◆ *A Lead-in Note* （简明导读）

诗人寄予月亮以“厚望”，称其为“银弓女王”。女王射出的箭，就是照亮夜晚天空的月光了。借助“银弓女王”的“亮箭”，诗人心中燃起了希望，认为月亮就是天堂一样的所在，是“悲惨者的温柔乡”，是“悲泣的孩子”的忘忧乡。在这个艰难的尘世，诗人是个可怜之人，是个倦怠的流浪者，月亮也是诗人的向往之地——“啊！我很快就抵达你那平静之所，世事艰难，可怜的我倦怠地流浪”。在此，月亮成了诗人希望寄托，承载了诗人一定的情感。

◆ 致月儿（商籁体第4首）

银弓女王！借着你那苍白的光亮，
我独自一个人沉思，喜悦地游荡，
看着你的影子摇晃在溪流之中，
或望着浮云在你必经之路流淌。
凝望之际，你的光线柔和而淡雅，
将舒适、宁静投进我烦乱的心房。
于是我常想，你是夜里皎洁球体，
你的眼或许是悲惨者的温柔乡：
他们是尘世的苦难人，免于一死，
或许可以去往你那怡人的地方。
悲泣的孩子，充满了绝望和烦忧，
到你那儿，会将此处的不幸遗忘。
啊！我很快就抵达你那平静之所，
世事艰难，可怜的我倦怠地流浪。

037 Thomas Hardy
托马斯·哈代

◆ *The Poet's Profile* （诗人小档案）

托马斯·哈代（1840—1928）：英国长篇小说家及诗人。他的作品多数描述了人们对苦难生活和命运作弄所施加的冷漠力量的抗争。其代表作有《卡斯特桥市长》（1866）、《德伯家的苔丝》（1891）和《无名的裘德》（1896）等。

◆ *The Moon Looks In*

I
I have risen again,
And awhile survey
By my chilly ray
Through your window-pane
Your upturned face,
As you think, "Ah—she
Now dreams of me
In her distant place!"

II
I pierce her blind
In her far-off home:
She fixes a comb,
And says in her mind,

"I start in an hour;
Whom shall I meet?
Won't the men be sweet,
And the women sour!"

◆ Annotations（原诗注释）

1. awhile: *adv.* for a short time 暂时；片刻 （e.g. Stand here awhile. 在这儿站一会儿。）

2. survey: *v.* (of a person or their eyes) look carefully and thoroughly at (someone or something), especially so as to appraise them 审视

3. chilly: *adj.* uncomfortably or unpleasantly cold 寒冷的

4. window pane of windowpane: n. a pane of glass in a window 窗玻璃

5. upturned: *adj.* (used of noses) turned up at the end; having been turned so that the bottom is no longer the bottom （鼻子）向上翘的；上下翻转过来的 （e.g. an upturned nose 翘鼻子）

6. ah: *exc.* used to express a range of emotions including surprise, pleasure, sympathy, and realization 啊；呀 （用于表示惊讶、喜悦、同情和意识到等一系列情绪）

7. pierce: *v.* (of a sharp pointed object) go into or through (something) （锋利尖锐物体）刺入；刺破；刺穿 （e.g. a splinter had pierced the skin 一根刺刺穿了皮肤）

8. far-off: *adj.* remote in time or space 久远的；遥远的 （e.g. a far-off country 遥远的国度）

9. fix: *v.* fasten (something) securely in a particular place or position 固定；缚紧；钉牢

10. sour: *adj.* having a rancid smell 恶臭的

◆ *A Lead-in Note* （简明导读）

此诗由两节构成，都是以“我”（月亮的化身）的视角展开的。月亮朝屋内看去，看到了远隔千里热恋男女截然不同的内心世界。男子想当然地认为，女子在睡梦中与自己相见，而女子却在梳妆打扮，想着一会儿出去会遇到什么样的人。

◆ 月亮朝屋内看去

一
我又升起，
用我寒冷的光线，
穿过你窗户的玻璃，
将你那张仰起的脸
扫视了一会儿。
你想：“哎呀，目前
在她那遥远之地，
她梦中与我相见！”

二
在她那遥远的家里，
我的光刺得她睁不开眼。
她抓紧一把梳子，
话语冒出心田：
“一小时后我出去，
什么人物我会遇见？
说不定，遇见的男子甜蜜，
遇到的女子臭气熏天！”

038 Emily Elizabeth Dickinson
埃米莉·伊丽莎白·狄更生

◆ *The Poet's Profile* （诗人小档案）

埃米莉·伊丽莎白·狄更生（1830—1886）：美国女诗人，她的诗独具一格：诗行短小，一般没有标题，经常使用近似押韵的方式和一些非常规的大写及标点，主题多与死亡和永生相关。

◆ *The Moon upon Her Fluent Route*

The Moon upon her fluent Route
Defiant of a Road—
The Star's Etruscan Argument
Substantiate a God—

If Aims impel these Astral Ones
The ones allowed to know
Know that which makes them as forgot
As Dawn forgets them—now—

◆ *Annotations* （原诗注释）

1. fluent: *adj.* (of speech, language, movement, or style) smoothly graceful and easy （讲话、语言、动作或风度）优美自如的 （e.g. His style of play was fast and fluent. 他的动作风格轻快优美。）

2. route: *n.* a way or course taken in getting from a starting point to a destination 路；路线；线路；航线

3. defiant: *adj.* showing defiance 挑衅的；蔑视的

4. Etruscan: *adj.* of or relating to ancient Etruria, its people, or their language. (与）伊特鲁里亚（有关）的；（与）伊特鲁里亚人（有关）的；（与）伊特鲁里亚语（有关）的

5. substantiate: *v.* provide evidence to support or prove the truth of 证实；证明 (e.g. They had found nothing to substantiate the allegations. 他们没有找到任何东西证实这些说法。)

6. impel: *v.* to push, drive, or force into motion 驱动；推动

7. astral: *adj.* of, relating to, or resembling the stars 星的；星形的

◆ *A Lead-in Note* （简明导读）

第一节中，诗人将月亮视作一位阴柔的女子。自古以来，她每天都重复着同样的路线，早已到了驾轻就熟的程度，以至于"下方的路，她没放在眼里边"。她通过自己长期的观察，找到了神灵存在的证据。第二节中，诗人认为包括月亮在内的整个宇宙中的天体，其存在都具有一定的"目的性"，都有"一些目标"驱动其昼夜不停地运行。但是，它们最终都会走向死亡——"被遗忘"，如同黎明到来，它们因失去光芒而被人遗忘。

◆ 月儿自如地踏上了自己的路线

月儿自如地踏上了自己的路线，
下方的路，她没放在眼里边——
这颗星对伊特鲁里亚文明的见证，
足以证明存在着神仙——

若有一些目标驱动这些星体，

它们的知情权得到允许，

它们就会弄清楚：谁令它们被遗忘，

就像黎明遗忘它们在——此时——

039 Robert Louis Stevenson
罗伯特·路易斯·史蒂文森

◆ *The Poet's Profile* （诗人小档案）

罗伯特·路易斯·史蒂文森（1850—1894）：苏格兰长篇小说家、诗人、散文家和游记作家。史蒂文森的成名作是冒险小说《金银岛》，其他著名作品包括《化身博士》和《绑架》。

◆ *The Moon*

The moon has a face like the clock in the hall;
She shines on thieves on the garden wall,
On streets and fields and harbour quays,
And birdies asleep in the forks of the trees.

The squalling cat and the squeaking mouse,
The howling dog by the door of the house,
The bat that lies in bed at noon,
All love to be out by the light of the moon.

But all of the things that belong to the day
Cuddle to sleep to be out of her way;
And flowers and children close their eyes
Till up in the morning the sun shall arise.

◆ *Annotations* （原诗注释）

1. quay: *n.* a stone or metal platform lying alongside or projecting into water for loading and unloading ships 码头；驳岸

2. birdie: *n.* (informal) a little bird （非正式用法）小鸟儿

3. squall: *v.* (of a baby or small child) cry noisily and continuously （婴儿或小孩子）号啕；啼哭 （e.g. Sarah was squalling in her crib. 莎拉在婴儿床上号啕大哭。）

4. squeak: *v.* make a high-pitched sound or cry 发出刺耳声；嘎吱作响；吱吱响 （e.g. He oiled the hinges to stop them squeaking. 他给合页上了些油，使它们不再嘎吱作响。）

5. howl: *v.* make a howling sound 号叫；怒吼；呼啸 （e.g. The wind howled around the house. 风在房屋周围怒号。）

6. cuddle: *v.* lie or sit close and snug 偎依 （e.g. They cuddled together to keep out the cold. 他们偎依在一起御寒。）

◆ *A Lead-in Note* （简明导读）

这是一个月圆之夜。大千世界中的百态，在月夜下呈现。月夜是夜行生物的乐园，有呜哇喊的猫，有吱吱叫的鼠，有狂吠的狗，有巢穴中的蝙蝠，甚至还有沿花园墙攀援的小偷。当然，月夜也是日行生物的避难所，使他们得以养精蓄锐，直至“到了早晨太阳升起，一切复原”。月儿犹如一位慈善、宽容的母亲，对所有生物都加以“关照”，几乎“包容”了一切。

◆ 月儿

月儿的脸如厅堂里那时钟的圆盘，
她的光照亮小偷沿花园墙攀援，
照亮大街、海港码头和田野，

还有熟睡在树杈间的小鸟。

呜哇喊的猫，吱吱叫的鼠，
狂吠的狗倚在房门的旁边，
巢穴中的蝙蝠在正午酣睡，
都爱凭借月光活动。

但是，所有白天行动的生物
都避开月儿不出，相依而眠。
花儿朵朵合拢，孩子闭眼入睡，
到了早晨太阳升起，一切复原。

040 Dylan Thomas
迪伦·托马斯

◆ *The Poet's Profile* （诗人小档案）

迪伦·托马斯（1914—1953）：威尔士诗人，作品包括《莫轻柔进入那美妙的夜晚》《死神将不会有统治权》等诗篇，被认为是20世纪威尔士最伟大的诗人之一。他以使用原创性的、有韵律的、巧妙的语言及意象而著名。

◆ *Clown in the Moon*

My tears are like the quiet drift
Of petals from some magic rose;
And all my grief flows from the rift
Of unremembered skies and snows.

I think, that if I touched the earth,
It would crumble;
It is so sad and beautiful,
So tremulously like a dream.

◆ *Annotations* （原诗注释）

1. clown: *n.* a comic entertainer, especially one in a circus, wearing a traditional costume and exaggerated make-up （尤指马戏团的）小丑；丑角

2. petal: *n.* each of the segments of the corolla of a flower, which are modified leaves and are typically coloured 花瓣

3. magic: *adj.* used in magic or working by magic; having or apparently having supernatural power s 魔法的；魔力的 （e.g. a magic wand 魔杖）

4. grief: *n.* deep or intense sorrow, especially caused by someone's death （尤指某人的亡故造成的）悲伤；悲痛

5. rift: *n.* a crack, split, or break in something 裂缝；裂口 （e.g. The wind had torn open a rift in the clouds. 风把云层吹开了一条裂缝。）

6. crumble: *v.* break or fall apart into small fragments, especially over a period of time as part of a process of deterioration 崩溃；瓦解 （e.g. their crumbling ancestral home 他们将要倒塌的祖屋）

◆ *A Lead-in Note* （简明导读）

整首诗以第一人称的视角展开；诗题中的“小丑”应是此诗的叙述者。我们知道，在西方文化中，小丑是孩子喜欢的角色。由此看来，此诗的内容可能与诗人的童年经历有关。诗人将童年的一些不幸经历诗歌化。换个角度看，小丑一般都是成年人扮演的，总是以那副一成不变的笑模样（化妆出来的笑脸）博得孩子甚至是大人的欢心。这样，此诗的内容就可能与诗人的人生状态有关了。

◆ 月亮上的小丑

我的滴滴泪水啊，如花瓣，
从某种魔力玫瑰上静静飘散。
我的一切忧伤流淌而出，
从我不记得的天空和积雪间。

我想，倘若我触碰到地球，
地球就会塌陷。
地球那么忧伤和美丽，
那么、那么似梦境一般。

041 Sir Philip Sidney
菲利浦·锡德尼爵士

◆ *The Poet's Profile* （诗人小档案）

菲利浦·锡德尼爵士（1554—1586）：英国作家、政治家及军人。其重要作品都是在他死后出版的。其中《阿尔卡迪亚》（Arcadia）（1590）是一部用散文和诗歌创作的田园般浪漫的传奇故事，其中的很多情节和人物都在后来斯宾塞、莎士比亚等人的作品中被借用过；《爱星者与星星》（1591）中有很多情感强烈的英语十四行诗，对莎士比亚的十四行诗影响极大；《诗辩》（1595）是英语文学批评中的第一个重要范本。

◆ *To the Sad Moon (Sonnet XXXI)*

With how sad steps, O Moon, thou climb'st the skies!
How silently, and with how wan a face!
What! May it be that even in heavenly place
That busy archer his sharp arrows tries?
Sure, if that long-with-love-acquainted eyes
Can judge of love, thou feel'st a lover's case:
I read it in thy looks; thy languished grace
To me, that feel the like, thy state descries.

Then, even of fellowship, O Moon, tell me,
Is constant love deemed there but want of wit?
Are beauties there as proud as here they be?
Do they above love to be loved, and yet

Those lovers scorn whom that love doth possess?
Do they call "virtue" there—ungratefulness?

◆ Annotations （原诗注释）

1. thou: *pron.* [second person singular] archaic or dialect form of you, as the singular subject of a verb （古旧用法或方言用法）（作动词的单数主语）你（同"you"）

2. climb'st = climbest = climbs

3. wan: *adj.* (of a person's complexion or appearance) pale and giving the impression of illness or exhaustion （人的脸色或外表）苍白的；病态的；疲倦的（e.g. She was looking wan and bleary-eyed. 她看上去脸色苍白，睡眼惺忪。）

4. heavenly: *adj.* of heaven; divine 天国的；神圣的

5. archer: *n.* a person who shoots with a bow and arrows, especially at a target as a sport 弓箭手；射箭运动员，这里的"archer"指的是罗马神话中的爱神丘比特（Cupid）。

6. acquaint: *v.* (acquaint someone with) make someone aware of or familiar with 使认识；使熟悉

7. feel'st = feelest = feels

8. thy: *poss. adj.* (Also "thine" before a vowel) archaic or dialect form of your（元音前亦作"thine"）（古旧用法或方言用法）你（您）的（同"your"）

9. languish: *v.* be forced to remain in an unpleasant place or situation 受苦；受折磨

10. descry: *v.* to discover by careful observation or scrutiny 观察出；探查出（e.g. He descried a message of hope in her words. 他从她的话语里觉察出一丝希望的信息。）

11. fellowship: *n.* a group of people meeting to pursue a shared interest or aim（志趣相同的）团体；协会；联谊会

12. o: *interj.* used to express surprise or strong emotion 哦；哟；啊；唉；哎

呀（表示惊讶或强烈的情感）

13. deem: *v.* (formal) regard or consider in a specified way （正式用法）认为；视为 （e.g. The event was deemed a great success. 大家认为该项活动很成功。）

14. want of: lacking

15. wit: *n.* mental sharpness and inventiveness; keen intelligence 颖悟力；聪颖；机智；才智

16. scorn: *v.* the feeling or belief that someone or something is worthless or despicable; contempt 鄙视；蔑视 （e.g. I do not wish to become the object of scorn. 我不希望成为鄙视的对象。）

17. doth = does

18. virtue: *n.* behaviour showing high moral standards 德行 （e.g. paragons of virtue 德行典范）

19. ungrateful: *adj.* not feeling or showing gratitude 不感激的；忘恩负义的；不领情的

◆ *A Lead-in Note* （简明导读）

诗人爱情受挫时仰望天空，看见了月亮，认为月亮那副模样跟自己十分相似。此诗前八行的最后，诗人推导出月亮跟自己同是天涯沦落人，同样受到爱情的折磨。此诗的后六行，诗人问了跟自己情感产生共鸣的月亮好几个问题。实际上是以问题代替答案，告诉读者诗人自己爱情失意的原因。

◆ 致伤心的月亮（商籁体第31首）

啊，月亮，你爬上天空，步履多么忧伤！
你默默无语，脸色多么难看似白霜！
什么？那个忙碌的弓箭手竟然朝你
射出利箭，在天空这么神圣的地方？
当然，若弓箭手那见惯爱情的眼睛

能鉴别爱，你感到的就是爱的境况：
你的表情和状态，让我了解了一切；
你优雅却受煎熬，因你我感受相像。

同在相思中的月亮啊，你能否告诉我吗，
永恒之爱注定，为何无法如愿以偿？
你那儿的美人是否跟这儿的一样傲慢？
是否喜欢被爱，而又
轻蔑真爱着她的人？
“不领你的情”难道是她们所说的“美德”？

042 Sylvia Plath
西尔维亚·普拉思

◆ *The Poet's Profile* （诗人小档案）

西尔维亚·普拉思（1932—1963）：美国诗人及小说家。1982年，她因《普拉思诗选》获得“普利策奖”。其代表作有诗集《精灵》（1965）和小说《钟形罐子》（1963）。

◆ *The Moon and the Yew Tree*

This is the light of the mind, cold and planetary.
The trees of the mind are black. The light is blue.
The grasses unload their griefs at my feet as if I were God,
Prickling my ankles and murmuring of their humility.
Fumy spiritous mists inhabit this place
Separated from my house by a row of headstones.
I simply cannot see where there is to get to.

The moon is no door. It is a face in its own right,
White as a knuckle and terribly upset.
It drags the sea after it like a dark crime; it is quiet
With the O-gape of complete despair. I live here.
Twice on Sunday, the bells startle the sky —
Eight great tongues affirming the Resurrection.
At the end, they soberly bong out their names.

The yew tree points up. It has a Gothic shape.
The eyes lift after it and find the moon.
The moon is my mother. She is not sweet like Mary.
Her blue garments unloose small bats and owls.
How I would like to believe in tenderness —
The face of the effigy, gentled by candles,
Bending, on me in particular, its mild eyes.

I have fallen a long way. Clouds are flowering
Blue and mystical over the face of the stars.
Inside the church, the saints will be all blue,
Floating on their delicate feet over cold pews,
Their hands and faces stiff with holiness.
The moon sees nothing of this. She is bald and wild.
And the message of the yew tree is blackness–blackness and silence.

◆ *Annotations* （原诗注释）

1. yew: *n.* a coniferous tree that has red berrylike fruits, and most parts of which are highly poisonous. 紫杉；红豆杉

2. planetary: *adj.* of, relating, or belonging to a planet or planets 行星的

3. unload: *v.* (chiefly US) give expression to (oppressive thoughts or feelings)（主要为美国用法）倾诉；吐露（思想或感情）（e.g. The meeting had been a chance for her to unload some of her feelings about her son. 这次见面为她提供了倾诉对儿子看法的机会。）

4. prickle: *v.* cause a tingling or mildly painful sensation in 引起刺痛 （e.g. I hate the way the fibres prickle your skin. 我讨厌纤维刺激皮肤的那种感觉。）

5. fumy: *adj.* full of fumes 冒烟的；多蒸汽的

6. inhabit: *v.* (of a person, animal, or group) live in or occupy (a place or environment)（人、动物或群体）居住于；栖息于 （e.g. a bird that inhabits North

America栖息于北美的一种鸟）

7. headstone: *n.* a slab of stone set up at the head of a grave, typically inscribed with the name of the dead person 墓碑

8. in one's own right: as a result of one's own claims, qualifications, or efforts, rather than an association with someone else 凭自身的权利（或资格、努力）而非凭借与他人的关系

9. knuckle: *n.* a part of a finger at a joint where the bone is near the surface, especially where the finger joins the hand 指关节；指节 （e.g. Charlotte rapped on the window with her knuckles. 夏洛特用指节轻敲着窗户。）

10. gape: *n.* a widely open mouth or beak 大张着的嘴（或喙）

10. resurrection: *n.* (the Resurrection) (in Christian belief) Christ's rising from the dead （基督教信仰）耶稣复活

11. bong: *v.* emit a low-pitched sound, as of a bell 发出当当声

12. Gothic: *adj.* of or in the style of Architecture prevalent in western

13. Mary: *n.* mother of Jesus; known as the (Blessed) Virgin Mary, or St Mary, or Our Lady. 玛利亚（耶稣的母亲，通称“圣母玛利亚”“圣玛利亚”或“圣母”

14. effigy: *n.* a sculpture or model of a person （某人的）雕像；模拟像

15. pew: *n.* a long bench with a back, placed in rows in the main part of some churches to seat the congregation 教堂长椅

◆ *A Lead-in Note* （简明导读）

从这首诗中可以看出，诗人的内心世界和外部世界之间发生了冲突。为平息这种冲突，诗人就以内心世界来影响外部世界。内心世界中的光“呈蓝色”，“寒冷且来自某个星球”，预示着这样的世界是死亡的世界，暗示着诗人的孤独。

◆ 月亮与紫杉树

这心灵之光，寒冷且飘忽不定。
心灵之树为黑色，心灵之光呈蓝色。
脚下的绿草向我倾诉悲痛，我似乎成了上帝；
它们刺痛我的脚踝，低声道出它们的卑微。
此处尽是如烟的迷雾，迷雾如精灵般浮现；
一排墓碑将此处与我的房子分隔开来。
我就是看不清我可到达何处。

月亮并非可出入的门。而是不折不扣的一张脸，
白如手指关节，极其心烦意乱。
月亮将大海拖在身后，似一种隐秘的罪恶行为；似在彻底
绝望中，月亮圆张大嘴却没声音发出。我居于此。
星期日，教堂的钟两次鸣响，打破了天空的沉寂——
教堂的钟伸出八只大舌头，宣告耶稣的复活。
最终，这些钟在叮当声中泰然报出各自的姓名。

紫杉树直指天空，如哥特式风格的外形。
循着紫杉树的指向，我望见了月亮。
月亮是我母亲，不如圣母玛利亚般甜美。
从她蓝色的外套中，小蝙蝠和猫头鹰纷飞而出。
我多么愿意相信柔情和体贴的存在啊——
圣母塑像的面孔，在烛光下显得温柔；
她俯视着我，特地为我投下温和的目光。

我早就堕落不去信奉了。云朵如花开放，
蓝色中带有神秘的色调，遮住了星星的脸。
教堂之内，各种神像都将变成蓝色，

以脆弱之脚支撑着悬浮在冷冷的长椅上，
手和脸僵直，以体现出神圣性。
这一切，月亮都看不到。她枯燥、荒凉。
而那紫杉树所能显示出来的，是黑暗——黑暗和寂静。

043 Amy Lowell
埃米·洛厄尔

◆ *The Poet's Profile* （诗人小档案）

埃米·洛厄尔（1874—1925）：美国女诗人，在她死后的第一年，即1926年，获得"普利策诗歌奖"。作为印象派中一位领军人物，洛厄尔以散文诗和令人愉悦的意象而闻名。

◆ *From China*

I thought:—
The moon,
Shining upon the many steps of the palace before me,
Shines also upon the chequered rice-fields
Of my native land.
And my tears fell
Like white rice grains
At my feet.

◆ *Annotations* （原诗注释）

1. palace: *n.* the official residence of a sovereign, president, archbishop, or bishop 宫殿；（总统的）官邸；（主教的）宅邸

2. chequered: *adj.* having a pattern consisting of alternating squares of different colours 多色方格图案的；有方格图案的

◆ *A Lead-in Note* （简明导读）

美国女诗人埃米·洛厄尔创作的这首《中国诗的灵感》，其灵感应该来自中国的古诗词作品，且极有可能是从“床前明月光，疑是地上霜。举头望明月，低头思故乡”（李白《静夜思》），“圆魄上寒空，皆言四海同。安知千里外，不有雨兼风”（李峤《中秋月二首》其二），以及“人有悲欢离合，月有阴晴圆缺，此事古难全。但愿人长久，千里共婵娟”（苏轼《水调歌头·明月几时有》片段）等有关月亮的诗歌作品中得到了启发，获得了灵感。

◆ 中国诗的灵感

我曾以为，
明亮的月光——
照在我眼前宫殿那一级级台阶之上，
也会照在我家乡
那一块块纵横交错的稻田之上。
至此，我的泪水啊，
如一粒粒白花花的大米，
滚落到脚下。

Chapter 06

Moon and Things

第六章

月与万物

044 Ella Wheeler Wilcox
埃拉·惠勒·威尔科克斯

◆ *The Poet's Profile* （诗人小档案）

埃拉·惠勒·威尔科克斯（1850—1919）：美国著名作家和诗人，写了许多部浪漫体诗集，其中以《激情诗集》最为成功。她最经久不衰的一首诗是《孤独》，里面有这样的诗行："你笑，全世界都跟着你笑；你哭，就你一人独自在哭。"

◆ *Moon and Sea*

You are the moon, dear love, and I the sea:
The tide of hope swells high within my breast,
And hides the rough dark rocks of life's unrest
When your fond eyes smile near in perigee.
But when that loving face is turned from me,
Low falls the tide, and the grim rocks appear,
And earth's dim coast-line seems a thing to fear.
You are the moon, dear one, and I the sea.

◆ *Annotations* （原诗注释）

1. swell: *v.* become or make greater in intensity, number, amount, or volume（在强度、数目、数量或体积方面）逐渐扩大（e.g. The murmur swelled to a roar. 窃窃私语的声音逐渐扩大形成一片喧哗。）

2. unrest: *n.* a feeling of disturbance and dissatisfaction in a person 不宁；

不安

3. perigee: *n.* (Astronomy) the point in the orbit of the moon or a satellite at which it is nearest to the earth （天文学）近地点

4. grim: *adj.* unrelentingly harsh; merciless or severe 无情的；残忍的；严酷的（e.g. Few creatures are able to thrive in this grim and hostile land. 很少有生命能在这片严酷的充满敌意的土地上生长繁衍。）

5. dim: *adj.* made difficult to see by darkness, shade, or distance （因为黑暗、阴影或距离）难以辨认的；不清楚的（e.g. a dim figure in the dark kitchen 黑暗厨房中隐约的身影）

◆ *A Lead-in Note* （简明导读）

诗人开篇就点明："亲密爱人，你是月，我是海。"月与海的关系显露无遗。大海受制于月亮而潮起潮落。潮起时，浪潮就是希望，不怕暗礁密布，起伏不平；潮落时，危险降临，就连地球隐约的海岸线，也俨然可怕的东西。

◆ 月与海

亲密爱人，你是月，我是海：
希望是浪潮，高高涌在我的胸怀，
掩住了动荡人生中起伏不平的暗礁，
此时你靠近近地点，眼含笑，惹人爱。
可当你布满爱意的脸扭转过去，
潮水低落，狰狞的礁石露了出来，
地球隐约的海岸线俨然可怕的东西。
亲密爱人，你是月，我是海。

045 Emily Elizabeth Dickinson
埃米莉·伊丽莎白·狄更生

◆ *The Poet's Profile* （诗人小档案）

埃米莉·伊丽莎白·狄更生（1830—1886）：美国女诗人，她的诗独具一格：诗行短小，一般没有标题，经常使用近似押韵的方式和一些非常规的大写及标点，主题多与死亡和永生相关。

◆ *Ah, Moon—and Star!*

Ah, Moon—and Star!
You are very far—
But were no one
Farther than you—
Do you think I'd stop
For a Firmament—
Or a Cubit—or so?

I could borrow a Bonnet
Of the Lark—
And a Chamois' Silver Boot—
And a stirrup of an Antelope—
And be with you—Tonight!

But, Moon, and Star,
Though you're very far—

There is one—farther than you—
He—Is more than a firmament—from Me—
So I can never go!

◆ Annotations （原诗注释）

1. ah: *exc.* used to express a range of emotions including surprise, pleasure, sympathy, and realization 啊；呀（用于表示惊讶、喜悦、同情和意识到等一系列情绪）

2. firmament: *n.* (poetic/literary) the heavens or the sky, especially when regarded as a tangible thing （诗/文用法）天空；太空；苍穹；苍天

3. cubit: *n.* an ancient measure of length, approximately equal to the length of a forearm 肘尺（一种古代长度单位）

4. bonnet: *n.* the ceremonial feathered headdress of an American Indian （美洲印第安人的）羽毛头饰

5. lark: *n.* a small ground-dwelling songbird with elongated hind claws and a song that is delivered on the wing, typically crested and with brown streaky plumage 百灵鸟；云雀

6. chamois: *n.* an agile goat-antelope with short hooked horns, found in mountainous areas of Europe from Spain to the Caucasus. (of the Pyrenees and Apennines, also called izard) 岩羚羊（见于阿尔卑斯山脉，欧洲东和东南部。)

7. boot: *n.* a sturdy item of footwear covering the foot and ankle, and sometimes also the leg below the knee 靴

8. stirrup or stirrup bone = stapes

stapes: *n.* (Anatomy) a small stirrup-shaped bone in the middle ear, transmitting vibrations from the incus to the inner ear （解剖学）镫骨

9. antelope: *n.* a swift-running deer-like ruminant with smooth hair and upward-pointing horns, native to Africa and Asia, and including the gazelles, impala, gnus, and elands 羚羊

◆ *A Lead-in Note* （简明导读）

此诗中，月亮和星星与“我”的距离，跟你与“我”的距离形成了对比。物理距离并不可怕，可怕的是心灵的距离，那是无法逾越的距离。月亮离我们很远，星星离我们更远，似乎都遥不可及。可如果有一个“他”离得比你们近一点，为了奔向“他”，一片苍天或者咫尺空间都一样，都阻止不了诗人的脚步。在诗的第二节，诗人更是表达了这种心愿。但在此诗的最后一节，诗人发出了感叹：“可是，月亮和星星啊”，你们和我只隔“一片苍天”，而“他——离我——超过一片苍天的距离——所以，我永远无法如愿！”此时，物理距离上升到了心灵距离的高度，是无法逾越的。

◆ 啊，月亮——还有星星！

啊，月亮——还有星星！
你们都很遥远——
可如果没有谁
比你们更遥远——
你们认为一片苍天，
或咫尺空间——
或类似距离——能阻止得了我？

我可以借到
云雀的羽饰——
还有岩羚羊的银靴子——
还有羚羊的镫骨——
奔向你，跟你在一起——就在今晚！

可是，月亮和星星啊，

尽管你们都很遥远——

有一个人，比你们更遥远——

他——离我——超过一片苍天的距离——

所以，我永远无法如愿！

046 Emily Elizabeth Dickinson
埃米莉·伊丽莎白·狄更生

◆ *The Poet's Profile* （诗人小档案）

埃米莉·伊丽莎白·狄更生（1830—1886）：美国女诗人，她的诗独具一格：诗行短小，一般没有标题，经常使用近似押韵的方式和一些非常规的大写及标点，主题多与死亡和永生相关。

◆ *The Moon is Distant from the Sea*

The Moon is distant from the Sea—
And yet, with Amber Hands—
She leads Him—docile as a Boy—
Along appointed Sands—

He never misses a Degree—
Obedient to Her Eye
He comes just so far—toward the Town—
Just so far—goes away—

Oh, Signor, Thine, the Amber Hand—
And mine—the distant Sea—
Obedient to the least command
Thine eye impose on me—

◆ Annotations （原诗注释）

1. epitaph: *n.* a phrase or form of words written in memory of a person who has died, especially as an inscription on a tombstone 纪念死者的文字；碑文

2. amber: *adj.* having the yellow colour of amber 琥珀色的 （e.g. her amber eyes 她那琥珀色的眸子）

3. docile: *adj.* ready to accept control or instruction; submissive 驯服的；顺从的 （e.g. a cheap and docile workforce 既廉价又听话的劳动力）

4. obedient: adj. complying or willing to comply with orders or requests; submissive to another's will 顺从的；服从的 （e.g. She was totally obedient to him. 她完全服从他。）

5. signor: *n.* a title or form of address used of or to an Italian-speaking man, corresponding to Mr. or sir 先生（对说意大利语男子的称呼）

6. thine: *poss. pron.* (form of "thy" used before a vowel) archaic form of yours; the thing or things belonging to or associated with thee （元音之前同"thy"）（古旧用法）你的（同"yours"）；（"thou"的物主代词）你（您）的东西

7. least: *det. & pron.* (usu. the least) smallest in amount, extent, or significance 最少的；最小的

8. impose: *v.* require (a duty, charge, or penalty) to be undertaken or paid 要求履行（义务）；要求付（费）；要求接受（惩罚）

◆ A Lead-in Note （简明导读）

此诗的前两节中，月亮具有女性的意象，大海则具有男性的意象。除了一些隐喻性的表述，诗人基本上向读者展示了一个科学道理——潮汐现象。当然，诗人借助科学道理作隐喻，旨在表达心中的情感。诗人借月亮与大海之间的关系作隐喻，喻指女子和男子之间的关系。这种关系的隐喻在此诗的最后一节中得以明朗化，只是叙述视角发生了转换，由第三人称的视角转向了第一人称的视角。诗人直呼对方为"绅士"，并说"你是，琥珀色的

手——”。这样，月亮就转而具有男子的意象，而前两节中大海的男子意象则转变成女诗人狄更生的意象：“而我是——遥远的大海——”。

◆ 月亮与大海相距遥远

月亮与大海相距遥远——
虽如此，她用琥珀色的手——
引领他——他像小男孩那样听话——
顺着约定的沙滩行走——

他寸步不离，紧紧跟随——
听从她眼眸的示意——
他跟随就这么远——离城镇——
就这么远——离去——

啊，绅士！你是，琥珀色的手——
而我是——遥远的大海——
听从每一个自你眼眸
发给我的号令，毫不倦怠——

047 Siegfried Sassoon 西格弗里德·沙逊

◆ *The Poet's Profile* （诗人小档案）

西格弗里德·沙逊（1886—1967）：英国诗人及小说家。在第一次世界大战服役期间，沙逊写了一些完全写实风格的诗歌，并以此闻名。

◆ *A Poplar and the Moon*

There stood a Poplar, tall and straight;
The fair, round Moon, uprisen late,
Made the long shadow on the grass
A ghostly bridge 'twixt heaven and me.
But May, with slumbrous nights, must pass;
And blustering winds will strip the tree.
And I've no magic to express
The moment of that loveliness;
So from these words you'll never guess
The stars and lilies I could see.

◆ *Annotations* （原诗注释）

1. poplar: *n.* a tall, fast-growing tree of north temperate regions, widely grown in shelter belts and for timber and pulp 白杨；杨树

2. fair: *adj.* (archaic) beautiful; attractive （古旧用法）美丽的；动人的；有魅力的（e.g. the fairest of her daughters 她女儿中最漂亮的一位）

3. ghostly: *adj.* of or like a ghost in appearance or sound; eerie and unnatural（外表或声音）似鬼的；古怪的；奇异的（e.g. a frightening, ghostly figure with a hood 戴着头巾如鬼魅般的可怕身影）

4. 'twixt = betwixt

betwixt: *prep.* archaic term for between （古旧用法）同“between”（在……之间）

5. slumbrous: *adj.* sleepy; drowsy 昏昏欲睡的；催眠的

6. blustering: *adj.* blowing in violent and abrupt bursts 狂风大作的；狂暴的

7. loveliness: *n.* the quality of being good looking and attractive; the qualities that give pleasure to the senses 可爱；漂亮；美好 （e.g. The loveliness of the scene was beyond compare. 景色之美无与伦比。）

8. lily: *n.* a bulbous plant with large trumpet-shaped, typically fragrant, flowers on a tall, slender stem. 百合花

◆ *A Lead-in Note* （简明导读）

此诗的大部分篇幅是以第三人称的客观性视角展开的，从倒数第三行起，角度转换到第一人称的视角，即身为战士的诗人自己的视角。月光皎洁，白杨挺拔，其影婆娑，构成了一幅优美的夜景图，以至于“我欲表达，却乏魔力”。但结尾两行，则预示着战争的惨烈，跟上述美景形成了强烈的对照而产生了反差。其实，这种预示在此诗的第三、四行已经有所显现：“草地上，白杨拉长影子，形似一座桥，幽灵般在我和天堂之间站立。”其中的“幽灵般”这一表述，预示着死亡的来临。

◆ 一棵白杨与月亮

一棵白杨立在那儿，高耸且笔直；
一轮皎洁的月，迟后升起。
草地上，白杨拉长影子，形似一座桥，

幽灵般在我和天堂之间站立。
可五月必定逝去，随着一个个昏睡的夜，
狂暴的风会剥光白杨的叶子。
那种美妙的时刻啊，
我欲表达，却乏魔力。
因此，从这些诗句中你永远都猜不出
我所看见的星星和百合的样子。

048 Vachel Lindsay
韦切尔·林赛

◆ *The Poet's Profile* （诗人小档案）

韦切尔·林赛（1879—1931）：美国诗人及现代歌唱诗歌的奠基人。林赛的作品收集在《〈威廉·布思将军进入了天堂〉及其他诗集》（1913）、《〈刚果河〉及其他诗集》（1914）、《每一个灵魂都是一个轮回》（1929）等中。

◆ *The Encyclopaedia*

"If I could set the moon upon
This table," said my friend,
"Among the standard poets
And brouchures without end,
And noble prints of old Japan,
How empty they would seem,
By that encyclopaedia
Of whim and glittering dream."

◆ *Annotations* （原诗注释）

1. encyclopaedia: *n.* a book or set of books giving information on many subjects or on many aspects of one subject and typically arranged alphabetically 百科全书；（某一学科的）专科全书；大全

2. standard: *adj.* (of a work, repertoire, or writer) viewed as authoritative or of

permanent value and so widely read or performed （作品、节目、作家）经典的；权威的 （e.g. His essays on the interpretation of reality became a standard text. 他诠释现实的短文已成了权威文本。）

3. brouchure = brochure

brochure: *n.* a small book or magazine containing pictures and information about a product or service 小册子

4. without end: without a limit or boundary 无止境地；无休止地 （e.g. a war without end 一场无休止的战争）

5. print: *n.* the text appearing in a book, newspaper, or other printed publication, especially with reference to its size, form, or style 印刷品；印出的文本

6. whim: *n.* a sudden desire or change of mind, especially one that is unusual or unexplained 突然产生的念头；一闪而过的念头；异想天开的念头；怪念头

7. glitter: *v.* shine with a bright, shimmering, reflected light （因反射而）闪闪发光 （e.g. Trees and grass glittered with dew. 树木和青草因晨露而闪闪发光。）

◆ *A Lead-in Note* （简明导读）

诗人林赛以儿童般奇幻而天真的想象，讲述了一个美妙的童话故事。故事中，月亮摇身一变，变成了一部百科全书，可能是因为月亮从古至今饱览人间冷暖，无所不知吧。要是在一张桌子上，将月亮摆在中间，周围尽管摆满了各类书籍，但“这些东西会露出多么空虚的模样”。这说明，月亮这本百科全书，让周围的一切变得暗淡。它照亮了人们的梦想，令梦想闪现出现实的光芒。

◆ 百科全书

我的朋友说：“倘若我将月亮
置于这张桌子之上，
置于经典诗人的作品间，

周围有数不尽的小册子摆放，
还有古日本非凡的印刷品作陪，
这些东西会露出多么空虚的模样！
因那本月亮百科全书
令人一闪念，想到了闪闪发光的梦想。”

049 William Butler Yeats
威廉·巴特勒·叶芝

◆ *The Poet's Profile* （诗人小档案）

威廉·巴特勒·叶芝（1865—1939）：爱尔兰诗人和剧作家。叶芝的剧作《凯瑟琳伯爵夫人》（1892）和短篇故事集《凯尔特的黄昏》（1893）推动了爱尔兰的戏剧、文化和文学的复兴。他著名的诗歌作品包括《钟楼》《盘旋的楼梯》等。1923年，叶芝获诺贝尔文学奖。

◆ *The Cat and the Moon*

The cat went here and there
And the moon spun round like a top,
And the nearest kin of the moon,
The creeping cat, looked up.
Black Minnaloushe stared at the moon,
For, wander and wail as he would,
The pure cold light in the sky
Troubled his animal blood.
Minnaloushe runs in the grass
Lifting his delicate feet.
Do you dance, Minnaloushe, do you dance?
When two close kindred meet.
What better than call a dance?
Maybe the moon may learn,
Tired of that courtly fashion,

A new dance turn.
Minnaloushe creeps through the grass
From moonlit place to place,
The sacred moon overhead
Has taken a new phase.
Does Minnaloushe know that his pupils
Will pass from change to change,
And that from round to crescent,
From crescent to round they range?
Minnaloushe creeps through the grass
Alone, important and wise,
And lifts to the changing moon
His changing eyes.

◆ *Annotations* （原诗注释）

1. spin: *v.* turn or cause to turn or whirl round quickly 旋转；使（快速）旋转（e.g. The girl spun round in alarm. 女孩惊慌地四处乱转。）

2. top: *n.* a conical, spherical, or pear-shaped toy that with a quick or vigorous twist may be set to spin 陀螺

3. kin: *n.* one's family and relations 亲戚（e.g. His kin are entrepreneurs. 他的亲戚是企业家。）

4. creep: *v.* move slowly and carefully, especially in order to avoid being heard or noticed 蹑手蹑脚地行走；轻悄悄地移动（e.g. He crept downstairs, hardly making any noise. 他蹑手蹑脚地下楼，几乎没发出什么声响。）

5. Minnaloushe: It refers to the name of the cat in the poem. 此处的“Minnaloushe”为专有名词，是诗中那只猫的名字，暂译成“明娜洛希”。

6. wail: *v.* give such a cry of pain, grief, or anger 恸哭；哀号；号啕

7. delicate: *adj.* skilful and finely judged; deft 灵巧的；灵敏的

8. kindred: *n.* one's family and relations 亲戚；亲属

9. courtly: *adj.* polished or refined, as befitting a royal court 有宫廷气派的；典雅的；高贵的 （e.g. He gave a courtly bow. 他非常文雅地鞠了个躬。）

10. sacred: *adj.* connected with God (or the gods) or dedicated to a religious purpose and so deserving veneration 与上帝（或神）相关的；奉献给上帝（或神）的；神圣的

11. pupil: *n.* the dark circular opening in the centre of the iris of the eye, which varies in size to regulate the amount of light reaching the retina 瞳孔

12. range: *v.* vary or extend between specified limits （在一定幅度或范围内）变动；变化；延伸 （e.g. patients whose ages ranged from 13 to 25 years 年龄在13到25岁之间的病人）

13. important: *adj.* (of a person) having high rank or status （人）位尊的；显要的

◆ *A Lead-in Note* （简明导读）

此诗中，月亮具有女性意象，喻指叶芝所追求的女神莫德·冈妮（Maud Gonne，1865—1953，爱尔兰女演员，女权运动者），而猫（具体来说，是黑猫，名字叫明娜洛希）则具有男性意象，喻指诗人自己。此诗中，明月与黑猫既形成鲜明的对照，又相辅相成。这首诗揭示了叶芝（猫）与莫德（月儿）之间无果的爱情。

◆ 猫与月儿

猫，走来又走去；
月儿，旋转似陀螺。
猫，月儿最近的亲戚，
蹑手蹑脚行走，举头仰视。
黑猫明娜洛希对月凝视。
他尽徘徊，他尽哀号，
因天空中这纯净的冷光

搅乱了他这种动物体内的血液。
明娜洛希在草地里奔跑，
举起了灵巧的爪子。
明娜洛希，你跳舞吗？你跳舞吗？
此时，两个关系亲密的人相遇。
跳舞，还有比这更好的叫法吗？
或许，月儿厌倦了自己高贵的样子，
就有可能学会
某种新式舞蹈旋转动作。
明娜洛希蹑手蹑脚穿过草地，
跨过一个又一个洒满月光的地方。
头顶上神圣的月儿，
换了副新相貌。
明娜洛希的瞳孔变化不已：
从圆月变成月牙，
从月牙变成圆月，
他知道这一系列变换吗？
明娜洛希蹑手蹑脚穿过草地，
尊贵，聪颖，无人陪伴。
明娜洛希向着变换的月，
抬起他变换的眼。

050 Vachel Lindsay
韦切尔·林赛

◆ *The Poet's Profile* （诗人小档案）

韦切尔·林赛（1879—1931）：美国诗人及现代歌唱诗歌的奠基人。林赛的作品收集在《〈威廉·布思将军进入了天堂〉及其他诗集》(1913)、《〈刚果河〉及其他诗集》(1914)、《每一个灵魂都是一个轮回》(1929)等中。

◆ *The Recreant Queens (To be tied to a pebble and thrown through a palace window)*

The Moon's a mirror where dim shades
Of queens are doomed to peer,
The beauteous queens that loved not love
Or faith or godly fear.
The night-wind makes their mirror grey.
The breath of Autumn drear,
And many mists of time and change
Have clouded it apace,
In mercy veiled it lest each queen
Too clearly see her face,
With long-past sins deep written there,
And ghostly rags she now must wear,
While slain men o'er her shoulders glare,
Leering at her disgrace.

◆ Annotations （原诗注释）

1. recreant: *adj.* unfaithful to a belief; apostate 不忠的；变节的

2. pebble: *n.* a small stone made smooth and round by the action of water or sand 卵石；砾石

3. dim: *adj.* (of a light, colour, or illuminated object) not shining brightly or clearly （光线、颜色或发光体）黯淡的；模糊的 （e.g. Her face was softened by the dim light. 在黯淡的灯光下，她脸部的线条变得柔和了。）

4. shade: *n.* (poetic/literary) a shadow or area of darkness （诗/文用法）阴影；阴暗处 （e.g. The shades of evening drew on. 夜幕降临。）

5. peer: *v.* look keenly or with difficulty at someone or something 凝视；盯着看；费力地看

6. beauteous: *adj.* (poetic/literary) beautiful （诗/文用法）漂亮的；美丽的

7. godly: *adj.* devoutly religious; pious 笃信宗教的；虔诚的

8. fear: *n.* (archaic) a mixed feeling of dread and reverence （古旧用法）敬畏（e.g. the love and fear of God 对上帝的热爱和敬畏）

9. breath: *n.* the air taken into or expelled from the lungs 气息；呼出（或吸入的）空气

10. drear: *adj.* (poetic/literary) term for dreary （诗/文用法）同 “dreary”

11. mist: *n.* used in reference to something that blurs one's perceptions or memory （使人感知或记忆模糊的）迷雾

12. cloud: *v.* make or become less clear or transparent （使）变模糊

13. apace: *adv.* (poetic/literary) swiftly; quickly （诗/文用法）飞快地；迅速地

14. veil: *v.* cover with or as though with a veil 以（似）面纱遮掩 （e.g. She veiled her face. 她用面纱遮着脸。）

15. ghostly: *adj.* of or like a ghost in appearance or sound; eerie and unnatural（外表或声音）似鬼的；古怪的；奇异的 （e.g. a frightening, ghostly figure with

a hood 戴着头巾如鬼魅般的可怕身影）

16. rag: *n.* old or tattered clothes 破旧衣服

17. slay: *v.* (archaic or poetic/literary) kill (a person or animal) in a violent way （古旧用法或诗/文用法）杀；杀戮；杀害 （e.g. St George slew the dragon. 圣乔治杀死了那条龙。）

18. glare: *v.* stare in an angry or fierce way 怒目而视；瞪眼看 （e.g. She glared at him, her cheeks flushing. 她瞪着他，两腮涨得通红。）

19. leer: *v.* look or gaze in an unpleasant, malign, or lascivious way 斜睨；讨厌（或恶意、挑逗）地看 （e.g. Bystanders were leering at the nude painting. 旁观者斜眼看着裸体画。）

20. disgrace: *n.* loss of reputation or the respect of others, especially as the result of a dishonourable action 丢脸；耻辱 （e.g. If he'd gone back it would have brought disgrace on the family. 如果他回来，会让他的家庭蒙羞。）

◆ A Lead-in Note （简明导读）

此诗中，月亮这面镜子在无形中被蒙上了一层面纱，对每一位不忠的王后网开一面："怜悯中唯恐每位王后的脸，过于清晰。"这正如题目所示，不忠的王后是要被绑上一块鹅卵石从宫殿窗户扔出去的。由于种种原因，月亮这面镜子不是很明亮的，它对不忠王后"脸上深深写着久远的罪过"加以模糊，成了不忠王后的"美颜镜"。

◆ 不忠的王后（要被绑上一块鹅卵石从宫殿窗户扔出去）

月亮是一面镜子，王后注定会往里
凝视她们模糊的影子。
亮丽的王后对爱情，对信念，
或对虔诚的敬畏，都不是一心一意。
夜晚的风将她们的镜子吹得灰白。

秋日倦怠的气息，以及
诸多时间和变化的迷雾，
让它快速变得模糊无比，
同时为它蒙上了一层面纱，
怜悯中唯恐每位王后的脸，过于清晰。
因她脸上深深写着久远的罪过，
她现在必须穿着幽灵般破旧之衣。
她的双肩之上，被害男子怒目圆睁，
睨视着她的耻辱行迹。

Chapter 07

Gentle and Charming Moon

第七章

月柔月媚

051 William Wordsworth 威廉·华兹华斯

◆ *The Poet's Profile* （诗人小档案）

威廉·华兹华斯（1770—1850）：英国浪漫主义诗人，其诗歌理论动摇了英国古典主义诗学的统治，有力地推动了英国诗歌的革新和浪漫主义运动的发展。其诗句“朴素生活，高尚思考（plain living and high thinking）”被作为牛津大学基布尔学院的格言。其代表作品有《抒情歌谣集》《丁登寺旁》《序曲》《她住在人迹罕至的地方》《水仙花》。

◆ *Strange Fits of Passion Have I Known*

Strange fits of passion have I known:
And I will dare to tell,
But in the lover's ear alone,
What once to me befell.

When she I loved looked every day
Fresh as a rose in June,
I to her cottage bent my way,
Beneath an evening-moon.

Upon the moon I fixed my eye,
All over the wide lea;
With quickening pace my horse drew nigh
Those paths so dear to me.

And now we reached the orchard-plot;
And, as we climbed the hill,
The sinking moon to Lucy's cot
Came near, and nearer still.

In one of those sweet dreams I slept,
Kind Nature's gentlest boon!
And all the while my eye I kept
On the descending moon.

My horse moved on; hoof after hoof
He raised, and never stopped:
When down behind the cottage roof,
At once, the bright moon dropped.

What fond and wayward thoughts will slide
Into a Lover's head!
"O mercy!" to myself I cried,
"If Lucy should be dead!"

◆ Annotations （原诗注释）

1. fit: *n.* a sudden uncontrollable outbreak of intense emotion, laughter, hysterics, coughing, or other action or activity （强烈的情感、笑声、歇斯底里、咳嗽等行为）突然一阵；突发；蓦地爆发 （e.g. in a fit of temper 一时性急）

2. passion: *n.* strong and barely controllable emotion 热情；激情 （e.g. a man of impetuous passion 一个极易冲动的人）

3. befall: *v.* (poetic/literary) (especially of something bad) happen to (someone) （诗/文用法） （尤指不幸的事）发生在（某人）身上；降临于 （e.g. A tragedy befell his daughter. 他女儿遭遇不幸。）

4. cottage: *n.* a small simple house, typically one in the country （尤指乡村的）小屋；村舍

5. lea: *n.* (poetic/literary) an open area of grassy or arable land （诗/文用法）草地；耕地 （e.g. The lowing herd winds slowly o'er the lea. 发出低沉叫声的牛群在草地上蜿蜒慢行。）

6. nigh: *adv. prep. & adj.* (archaic) near （古旧用法）（靠）近的（地）（e.g. They drew nigh unto the city. 他们朝城市走去。）

7. orchard: *n.* a piece of enclosed land planted with fruit trees （通常指围起来的）果园 （e.g. My orchard is bearing well this year. 今年我的果园果实累累。）

8. plot: *n.* a small piece of ground marked out for a purpose such as building or gardening （用于建筑或园林的）小块地；苗圃 （e.g. a vegetable plot 菜地）

9. cot: *n.* a type of bed, in particular （尤指一种类型的）床

10. boon: *n.* a thing that is helpful or beneficial 恩惠；裨益 （e.g. The route will be a boon to many travellers. 这条通道将方便许多游客。）

11. hoof: *n.* the horny part of the foot of an ungulate animal, especially a horse（有蹄动物，尤指马的）蹄 （e.g. There was a clatter of hoofs as a rider came up to them. 当一位骑手向他们骑来时，传来马蹄的得得声。）

12. fond: *adj.* affectionate; loving 深情的；爱慕的

13. wayward: *adj.* difficult to control or predict because of unusual or perverse behavior 任性的；难以捉摸的；反复无常的 （e.g. her wayward, difficult sister 她那个任性的、难于相处的妹妹）

14. o: *interj.* used to express surprise or strong emotion 哦；哟；啊；唉；哎呀（表示惊讶或强烈的情感）

15. mercy: *exc.* (archaic) used in expressions of surprise or fear （古旧用法）（表示惊愕或恐惧）哎呀

◆ *A Lead-in Note* （简明导读）

此诗是诗人华兹华斯《露西组诗》（共5首）中的一首，这组诗收录在

《抒情歌谣集》(Lyrical Ballads)中。此诗中，月亮这一意象反复出现，烘托出一种神秘的气氛，预示了诗人对露西的种种不祥之感，那是诗人所熟悉的奇特之情。从诗的最后两行，可以体会到诗人的悲哀和无奈，仿佛天要塌下来，但他却又无能为力。

◆ 我所熟悉的奇特之情阵阵闪现

我所熟悉的奇特之情阵阵闪现，
我要说出来，我有这个胆。
可是，我只对着情人的耳朵，
道出我曾经遭遇过的体验。

在爱她的季节里，她每日都
像六月里的玫瑰般新鲜。
我弯腰策马，赶往她住的小屋，
在一个有月亮的夜晚。

我凝视着月亮，
在一片宽阔的草地上面。
我策马加快了速度，
接近那些小路，有如此亲切之感。

现在，我策马奔至果园所在地，
接着开始骑马爬山。
此时，月下沉，沉向露西的小床，
越沉越低，一直沉到小床跟前。

我曾沉睡，沉入某个甜美的梦境，
梦见至高的恩惠来自仁慈大自然。

目前，自始至终，我一直
盯着持续下沉的月亮看。

我继续策马前行，马蹄从未
停歇：抬起又落下，往复循环。
明亮的月，沉到小屋后方，
便一下子跌落，消失不见。

啊，何等盲目而微妙的念头会滑到
情人的脑袋里面！
“噢，天呐！”我冲自己喊道，
“要是露西死了，我可怎么办！”

052 William Henry Davies
威廉·亨利·戴维斯

◆ *The Poet's Profile* （诗人小档案）

威廉·亨利·戴维斯（1871—1940）：英国诗人、作家，著有《超级流浪汉自传》《失业的滋味》《生活之歌》《在冬天》等。他写的《闲暇》《下雨》《快乐时光》等诗篇曾被谱成歌曲传唱。

◆ *The Moon*

Thy beauty haunts me heart and soul,
Oh, thou fair Moon, so close and bright;
Thy beauty makes me like the child
That cries aloud to own thy light:
The little child that lifts each arm
To press thee to her bosom warm.

Though there are birds that sing this night
With thy white beams across their throats,
Let my deep silence speak for me
More than for them their sweetest notes:
Who worships thee till music fails,
Is greater than thy nightingales.

◆ *Annotations* （原诗注释）

1. thy: *poss. adj.* (Also "thine" before a vowel) archaic or dialect form of your（元音前亦作"thine"）（古旧用法或方言用法）你（您）的（同"your"）

2. haunt: *v.* be persistently and disturbingly present, especially in someone's mind （尤指在脑际）萦绕 （e.g. cities haunted by the shadow of cholera 霍乱阴影笼罩之下的城市）

3. thou: *pron.* [second person singular] archaic or dialect form of you, as the singular subject of a verb （古旧用法或方言用法）（作动词的单数主语）你（同"you"）

4. thee: *pron.* [second person singular] archaic or dialect form of you, as the singular object of a verb or preposition （古英语"thou"的宾格，同"you"）你；汝

5. nightingale: *n.* a small migratory thrush with drab brownish plumage, noted for its rich melodious song which can often be heard at night 夜莺；歌鸲

◆ *A Lead-in Note* （简明导读）

诗人将月亮比作美人，一个令诗人痴迷得像个小女孩大声喊叫要拥有其所有光亮的"月美人"——"那个小女孩举起双臂，要将你揽进她温暖的怀抱"。由此可见月美人的美非比寻常！月美人有专属的鸟儿——夜莺为其歌唱。但是，诗人认为夜莺的音乐再甜美，也表达不出诗人对月美人的爱慕之情。于是，诗人笔锋一转，说"但还是让我用深沉的静默向你倾诉吧！鸟儿最甜美的音符也没有我的静默铿锵"。此时，也许沉默胜金，最深沉的爱不需言语，也许一个眼神足矣。

◆ 月美人

你的美，将我的身心萦绕。
啊，月美人！近在眼前，皓白外表。
你的美，令我痴迷得像个小女孩，
大声喊叫着，要让你照到：
那个小女孩举起双臂，
要将你揽进她温暖的怀抱。

今夜虽有鸟儿鸣唱，
鸟儿颈前有你白色的光亮，
但还是让我用深沉的静默向你倾诉吧！
鸟儿最甜美的音符也没有我的静默铿锵：
我对你的爱慕，音乐无法表达；
那种爱慕胜过夜莺对你的歌唱。

053 Ella Wheeler Wilcox
埃拉·惠勒·威尔科克斯

◆ *The Poet's Profile* （诗人小档案）

埃拉·惠勒·威尔科克斯（1850—1919）：美国著名作家和诗人，写了许多部浪漫体诗集，其中以《激情诗集》最为成功。她最经久不衰的一首诗是《孤独》，里面有这样的诗行："你笑，全世界都跟着你笑；你哭，就你一人独自在哭。"

◆ *The Old Moon in the New Moon's Arms*

The beautiful and slender young New Moon,
    In trailing robes of pink and palest blue,
Swept close to Venus, and breathed low: "A boon,
    A precious boon, I ask, dear friend, of you.

"O queen of light and beauty, you have known
    The pangs of love—its passions and alarms;
Then grant me this one favour, let my own—
    My lost Old Moon be once more in my arms."

Swift thro' the vapours and the golden mist—
    The Full Moon's shadowy shape shone on the night,
The New Moon reached out clasping arms and kissed
    Her phantom lover in the whole world's sight.

◆ *Annotations* （原诗注释）

1. slender: *adj.* (of a person or part of the body) gracefully thin （人或身体部位）苗条的；修长的；纤细的 （e.g. her slender neck 她修长的脖子）

2. robe: *n.* a long, loose outer garment reaching to the ankles worn, especially on formal or ceremonial occasions, as an indication of the wearer's rank, office, or profession（尤指在正式场合或礼仪场合穿的，标志穿衣者级别、职位或职业的）袍服；礼服

3. Venus: *n.* (Astronomy) the second planet from the sun in the solar system, the brightest celestial object after the sun and moon and frequently appearing in the twilight sky as the evening or morning star （天文学）金星；太白星

4. breathe: *v.* say something with quiet intensity （低声细气地）说出；吐露

5. boon: *n.* a thing that is helpful or beneficial 恩惠；裨益 （e.g. The route will be a boon to many travellers. 这条通道将方便许多游客。）

6. o: *interj.* used to express surprise or strong emotion 哦；哟；啊；唉；哎呀（表示惊讶或强烈的情感）

7: pang: *n.* a sudden sharp pain or painful emotion 一阵剧痛；一阵痛苦 （e.g. Lindsey experienced a sharp pang of guilt. 林赛经历了一阵极度痛苦的内疚。）

8. passion: *n.* an abandoned display of emotion, especially of anger 狂怒；盛怒

9. thro' = through

10. phantom: *n.* a figment of the imagination 幻象；幻觉 （e.g. The women suffered from phantom pain that no physician could ever find. 那些妇女有疼痛的幻觉，医生却一直无法确诊。）

◆ *A Lead-in Note* （简明导读）

此诗的题目（译法多种，其中包括"新旧双月争辉"）指的是一种比较奇特的天文现象，即新月时，月亮上处于夜晚的那一面为"地球返照"(earthshine)。也就是说，黑暗的那一面被地球光所照亮，也称作"月亮的灰

白辉光”（Moon's ashen glow）。“地球反照”是指从月球黑暗面反射出来的地球光。诗人被这一奇特的现象所吸引，以诗歌语言和拟人化手法创作了这首颇具故事情节的诗歌。

◆ 新月怀抱中的旧月

年轻的新月，美丽又苗条，
拖起粉中带有轻淡蓝色的长袍，
昂首移近金星，轻语："我恳请，
恳请好友你施贵恩，莫把头摇。

"啊，光与美的女王，你早已了解
爱的苦痛——有狂怒，有煎熬。
那你就行行好，让我将曾经的拥有——
我失去的旧月，再次抱牢。"

满月疾驰，穿越水汽和金色的迷雾——
其朦胧的外表泛着光，照亮夜霄。
新月伸出双臂拥抱，亲吻
她那幻影情人，任凭全世界都在观瞧。

054 William B. Tappan
威廉 · B. 塔潘

◆ *The Poet's Profile* （诗人小档案）

威廉 · B. 塔潘（1794—1849）：美国宗教诗人、制钟表匠、牧师及福音传道者。塔潘的创作娴熟流畅，很多作品令人爱不释手。其代表作有《〈新英格兰〉及其他诗集》《心灵之诗》《生命之诗》等。

◆ *Sweet Orb of Night*

Sweet orb of night! I saw thee rise
In cloudless lustre o'er the plain;
I saw thee climb the azure skies,
With radiant splendours in thy train:
I marked thy mildly pensive beam
At midnight's still and hallowed hour;
I watched the fitful, lonely gleam
That played on yonder ivied tower.

Sweet orb of night! I often love
When day with all its cares is o'er,
To wander in the silent grove,
And there the Source of Light adore:
O then, how false all else appears,
While wrapt in awe thy course I view,
And see thee mount the starry spheres,

And tread the fields of heavenly blue!

◆ Annotations （原诗注释）

1. orb: *n.* (poetic/literary) an eyeball; an eye （诗/文用法）眼球；眼睛

2. thee: *pron.* [second person singular] archaic or dialect form of you, as the singular object of a verb or preposition （古英语“thou”的宾格，同“you”）你；汝

3. luster: *n.* a gentle sheen or soft glow, especially that of a partly reflective surface 光泽；光辉

4. o'er = over

5. azure: *adj.* bright blue in colour like a cloudless sky 天蓝色的；蔚蓝色的

6. radiant: *adj.* sending out light; shining or glowing brightly 发光的；明亮的；光辉灿烂的

7. splendor: *n.* magnificent features or qualities 壮丽辉煌（的特色或格调）；华贵 （e.g. the splendours of the imperial court 皇家宫廷的壮丽辉煌）

8. thy: *poss. adj.* (Also "thine" before a vowel) archaic or dialect form of your （元音前亦作“thine”）（古旧用法或方言用法）你（您）的（同“your”）

9. in someone's train: following behind someone 跟随（某人或某事）

10. pensive: *adj.* engaged in, involving, or reflecting deep or serious thought 沉思的；冥想的；忧虑的；忧郁的

11. hallowed: *adj.* consecrated or holy 神圣的

12. fitful: *adj.* active or occurring spasmodically or intermittently; not regular or steady 阵发性的；间歇性的；不规律的；不稳定的 （e.g. Business was fitful. 生意时有时无。）

13. gleam: *n.* a faint or brief light, especially one reflected from something g （尤指反射的）微光（或短暂的光）

14. play: *v.* move lightly and quickly, so as to appear and disappear; flicker （轻快地）移动；显现；消逝；晃动；摇曳；变幻 （e.g. A smile played about

her lips. 她的嘴角露出一丝微笑。）

15. yonder: *adv.* (archaic or dialect) at some distance in the direction indicated; over there （古旧古或方言用法）在那边（指一定距离以外之处）

16. ivied: *adj.* covered in ivy 常青藤覆盖着的；爬满常青藤的 （e.g. the ivied rectory 爬满常青藤的教区长住宅）

17. grove: *n.* a small wood, orchard, or group of trees 树丛；小树林；果园（e.g. an olive grove 一小片橄榄树林）

18. adore: *v.* worship; venerate 崇拜；崇敬

19. o: *interj.* used to express surprise or strong emotion 哦；哟；啊；唉；哎呀（表示惊讶或强烈的情感）

20. wrapt = wrapped

21. awe: *n.* a feeling of reverential respect mixed with fear or wonder 敬畏；惊奇；惊叹 （e.g. They gazed in awe at the small mountain of diamonds. 他们惊奇地看着那一堆钻石。）

22. mount: *v.* climb up (stairs, a hill, or other rising surface) 登（楼梯、山或其他上升面）

23. sphere: *n.* (poetic/literary) the sky perceived as a vault upon or in which celestial bodies are represented as lying （诗/文用法）苍穹；天；天空

◆ A Lead-in Note （简明导读）

此诗中，诗人将月亮比作“黑夜迷人的眼”。这只眼令诗人敬畏不已，也仰慕不已。同时，这只眼极具争议性：或是柔媚的女子，或是万能的上帝。无论如何，对于这只眼，诗人是可望而不可即的，同时，这只眼又真实无比，令周围的一切显得虚无。

◆ 黑夜迷人的眼

黑夜迷人的眼！我看见你升起，
升到平原上无云遮掩的辉光里。
我看见你爬上湛蓝的天空，
紧随着你的，是四射的绚丽。
在午夜静谧而神圣的时间，
我将你略带忧思的光柱做了标记。
我看着你那间歇式孤独的微光，
在远处那座爬满常青藤的塔楼上消逝。

黑夜迷人的眼！白昼的一切烦忧
结束之后，我总是喜欢自己
在寂静的小树林中漫游——
在那里，光之源令我仰慕不已。
那时啊，你的行程令我深深敬畏，
其他一切看起来多么虚假无比。
我看见你登上布满星星的苍穹，
我看见你走在蓝蓝的空中区域。

055 Henry David Thoreau
亨利·大卫·梭罗

◆ *The Poet's Profile* （诗人小档案）

亨利·大卫·梭罗（1817—1862）：美国散文家、诗人、哲学家、废奴主义者及博物学家。梭罗是超验主义运动的关键人物。他最著名的作品是《瓦尔登湖》，又名《林中生活》。

◆ *The Moon*

Time wears her not; she doth his chariot guide;
Mortality below her orb is placed.
—Raleigh

The full-orbed moon with unchanged ray
Mounts up the eastern sky,
Not doomed to these short nights for aye,
But shining steadily.

She does not wane, but my fortune,
Which her rays do not bless,
My wayward path declineth soon,
But she shines not the less.

And if she faintly glimmers here,
And paled is her light,

Yet alway in her proper sphere
She's mistress of the night.

◆ Annotations （原诗注释）

1. doth = does

2. chariot: *n.* a horse-drawn wheeled vehicle, in particular （尤指）马车

3. mortality: *n.* the state of being subject to death 必死性 （e.g. The work is increasingly haunted by thoughts of mortality. 这工作越来越让人产生必死无疑的想法。）

4. Sir Walter Raleigh (c. 1552—1618), an English explorer, courtier, and writer. 沃尔特·罗利爵士（约1552—1618）：英国探险家、朝臣、作家。

5. orb: *n.* (poetic/literary) an eyeball; an eye （诗/文用法）眼球；眼睛

6. for aye: forever 永远

7. wane: *v.* (especially of a condition or feeling) decrease in vigour, power, or extent; become weaker （尤指状况、感觉）衰落；减少；减弱 （e.g. Confidence in the dollar waned. 对美元的信心减弱了。）

8. bless: *v.* (of a priest) pronounce words in a religious rite, to confer or invoke divine favour upon; ask God to look favourably on （牧师）为……祈神赐福；为……祈神保佑

9. wayward: *adj.* difficult to control or predict because of unusual or perverse behaviour 任性的；难以捉摸的；反复无常的 （e.g. his wayward emotions 他那无法预测的情绪）

10. declineth = declines

11. glimmer: *v.* shine faintly with a wavering light 发出闪烁的微光 （e.g. pools of glimmering light 发出荧荧微光的池塘）

12. alway = always

◆ *A Lead-in Note* （简明导读）

在诗人的心中，月亮是一个不老的传说，是美的化身，魅力无穷。柔媚的月儿“从未因夜晚短暂而感失望，而是闪着光亮，持之以恒”。诗人得不到这位女神的眷顾，但依然羡慕她的永恒：“我前路无常，很快消失，而她光亮丝毫未减。”她是一个奇迹，是诗人心中不灭的信仰。

◆ 月儿

时间无法将她磨蚀，她驾驭的是时间的马车。
她置死亡于眼底，毫不在意。
——罗利

圆圆的月儿，光亮不更，
登上了东方的天空。
从未因夜晚短暂而感失望，
而是闪着光亮，持之以恒。

她始终如一，但我命途多舛，
得不到她光线的偏袒。
我前路无常，很快消失，
而她光亮丝毫未减。

如果在这里她因暗淡而衰，
光线变得灰白，
那么，她球体上总会有一个地方
让她成为黑夜的主宰。

056 Walter de la Mare
沃尔特・德拉梅尔

◆ *The Poet's Profile* （诗人小档案）

沃尔特・德拉梅尔（1873—1956）：英国诗人、小说家，其代表作有《倾听者》等。

◆ *Silver*

Slowly, silently, now the moon
Walks the night in her silver shoon;
This way, and that, she peers, and sees
Silver fruit upon silver trees;
One by one the casements catch
Her beams beneath the silvery thatch;
Couched in his kennel, like a log,
With paws of silver sleeps the dog;
From their shadowy cote the white breasts peep
Of doves in silver feathered sleep
A harvest mouse goes scampering by,
With silver claws, and silver eye;
And moveless fish in the water gleam,
By silver reeds in a silver stream.

◆ *Annotations* （原诗注释）

1. shoon: *n.* (archaic) a plural of “shoe”（古旧用法）鞋 （“shoe”的复数形式）

2. peer: *v.* look keenly or with difficulty at someone or something 凝视；盯着看；费力地看

3. casement: *n.* (chiefly poetic/literary) a window （主要为主诗/文用法）窗户

4. thatch: *n.* a roof covering of straw, reeds, palm leaves, or a similar material 茅草屋顶

5. couch: *v.* (poetic/literary) lie down （诗/文用法）躺下；躺卧 （e.g. Two fair creatures, couched side by side in deepest grass. 两个美丽的生灵，并肩躺在草丛深处。）

6. kennel: *n.* a small shelter for a dog 狗屋；狗窝

7. cote: *n.* a shelter for mammals or birds, especially pigeons （养动物或鸟，尤其是鸽子的）窝；棚；栏

8. scamper: *v.* (especially of a small animal or child) run with quick light steps, especially through fear or excitement （尤指小动物、小孩）由于害怕或兴奋而蹦跳；奔逃 （e.g. He scampered in like an overgrown puppy. 他像一条长得超大的小狗一样蹦蹦跳跳地进来。）

9. reed: *n.* a tall, slender-leaved plant of the grass family, which grows in water or on marshy ground 芦苇

◆ *A Lead-in Note* （简明导读）

这首诗仿佛将我们带进一个童话般的世界。轻柔的月儿，在你浑然不觉间悄然地以她娇媚银色之光照耀着整个世界，令夜晚的一切具有了醉人的魅力。

◆ 银月

缓缓地，月儿穿着银鞋
在夜晚行走，一声不响。
一会儿这观观，一会儿那瞧瞧，
她所阅之处，都有银果结在银树上。
窗户将她的光线捉住，一束又一束
送进银色的茅草房。
狗趴在窝中熟睡，
爪子闪着银光。
暗影中的鸽舍，羽毛隐现，
身披银羽的白鸽进入了梦乡。
满载而归的小老鼠，银爪银眼，
匆匆而过，有些惊慌。
银色溪流中的银色芦苇边，
静静的鱼儿闪着银光。

057 Walt Whitman
沃尔特·惠特曼

◆ *The Poet's Profile* （诗人小档案）

沃尔特·惠特曼（1819—1892）：美国诗人、散文家及新闻记者，美国文坛从先验主义到现实主义过渡期的代表人物，被称作“自由体诗之父”。1855年，惠特曼出版了自由体诗集《草叶集》，集内收有《我对令人兴奋的躯体歌唱》和《自我之歌》这两首诗。在他有生之年，该诗集又出了八个增补及修订的版本。

◆ *Look Down, Fair Moon*

Look down, fair moon, and bathe this scene;
Pour softly down night's nimbus floods, on faces ghastly, swollen, purple;
On the dead, on their backs, with their arms toss'd wide,
Pour down your unstinted nimbus, sacred moon.

◆ *Annotations* （原诗注释）

1. bathe: *v.* soak or wipe gently with liquid to clean or soothe 浸洗；轻轻拭洗（e.g. She bathed and bandaged knee. 她把膝盖洗了洗，缠上绷带。）

2. nimbus: *n.* a light, aura, color, etc., that surrounds someone or something g（环绕人或物的）光（氛围或色彩）

3. ghastly: *adj.* causing great horror or fear; frightful or macabre 可怕的；可怖的；令人毛骨悚然的 （e.g. She was overcome with horror at the ghastly spectacle.

她被眼前可怕的景象吓倒了。）

4. swollen: *adj.* enlarged by or as if by swelling; tumid 膨胀的；肿起的

5. toss'd = tossed

toss: *v.* throw (something) somewhere lightly, easily, or casually 轻轻地（或随意地）扔；抛；掷

6. unstinted: *adj.* given without restraint; liberal 不吝啬的；慷慨的；无限制的（e.g. They received unstinted praise. 他们获得了大量赞誉。）

7 sacred: *adj.* made or declared or believed to be holy 神圣的

◆ *A Lead-in Note* （简明导读）

这是一首战争题材的自由体诗。诗中，柔媚月儿和壮烈阵亡的将士形成一种对照的效果。战争无情，战场残酷，将士阵亡，悲壮而惨烈，为护佑一方水土献出了宝贵的生命。此时，月亮升起，目睹了这一切。此时，能为死者带来一丝慰藉的，能够抚慰这些阵亡者的，恐怕只有那“娇柔的月儿”所带来的“夜晚的辉光洪流”了。于是，诗人呼喊：“倾倒你无穷无尽的辉光吧，神圣的月儿。”但是，不要太用力，不要太迅猛，而是“将夜晚的辉光洪流缓缓地倾倒吧”。

◆ 俯身看吧，娇柔的月儿

俯身看吧，娇柔的月儿，将此情此景浸润。
将夜晚的辉光洪流缓缓地倾倒吧：浸润那些恐怖、肿胀、紫色的面庞；
浸润那些死者，淹没死者的背，任其胳膊宽宽伸展。
倾倒你无穷无尽的辉光吧，神圣的月儿。

058 D. H. Lawrence
D. H. 劳伦斯

◆ *The Poet's Profile* （诗人小档案）

D. H. 劳伦斯（1885—1930）：英国小说家、诗人及散文家。他的代表作品有《儿子和情人》《虹》《恋爱中的女人》《查特莱夫人的情人》等。

◆ *A White Blossom*

A tiny moon as white and small as a single jasmine flower
Leans all alone above my window, on night's wintry bower,
Liquid as lime-tree blossom, soft as brilliant water or rain
She shines, the one white love of my youth, which all sin cannot stain.

◆ *Annotations* （原诗注释）

1. blossom: *n.* a flower or a mass of flowers, especially on a tree or bush （尤指树上的）花朵；花簇 （e.g. The slopes were ablaze with almond blossom. 山坡上盛开着扁桃树花。）

2. jasmine: *n.* an Old World shrub or climbing plant which bears fragrant flowers that are used in perfumery or tea and is popular as an ornamental 素馨；茉莉

3. wintry: *adj.* characteristic of winter, especially in feeling or looking very cold and bleak 冬天的；冬令的；（尤指感情、表情等）冷冰冰的；冷淡的；冷漠的 （e.g. a wintry landscape 冬日风景）

4. bower: *n.* a pleasant shady place under trees or climbing plants in a garden

or wood 树阴处

5. liquid: *adj.* having the translucence of water; clear 如水的；清澈的

6. lime: *n.* (also as lime-tree or lime tree) the evergreen citrus tree which produces this fruit, widely cultivated in warm climates 酸橙树（多产于温暖气候）

7. brilliant: *adj.* (of light) very bright and radiant 灿烂的；耀眼的 （e.g. Brilliant sunshine illuminated the scene. 灿烂的阳光照亮了整个场面。）

8. stain: *v.* (figurative) damage or bring disgrace to (the reputation or image of someone or something) （比喻用法）玷污；败坏（名声或形象）(e.g. The awful events would unfairly stain the city's reputation. 这些糟糕的事件会败坏这个城市的名声，这是不公平的。）

◆ *A Lead-in Note* （简明导读）

诗人将柔媚的月亮想象成一朵白色的茉莉花——白色纯洁，茉莉飘香，象征着诗人"青年时代的白色恋人"。这里，"白色"意味着纯真无邪。但是，"月亮甚微，又白又小"——相距甚远，但又是那么近在咫尺："在冬季夜晚的树阴处，独自靠在我的窗户上"。诗人跟这样"一朵白色的花"有缘无分。

◆ 一朵白色的花

月亮甚微，又白又小，像一朵茉莉花一样，
在冬季夜晚的树阴处，独自靠在我的窗户上。
她发出的光，如酸橙花般剔透，如耀眼的水和雨滴般绵柔；
她是我青年时代的白色恋人，所有罪过都无法玷污她的模样。

Chapter 08

Moonrise and Moonset

第八章

月升月落

059 Gerard Manley Hopkins
杰拉尔德·曼利·霍普金斯

◆ *The Poet's Profile* （诗人小档案）

杰拉尔德·曼利·霍普金斯（1844—1889）：英国诗人，最负盛名的维多利亚诗人。他探索性地在诗歌的韵律中使用跳韵及意象，给当时传统诗歌带来创新。其代表作有《德意志号的沉没》《风鹰》《斑驳的美丽》等。

◆ *Moonrise, June 19, 1876*

I awoke in the Midsummer not to call night, in the white and the walk of the morning:
The moon, dwindled and thinned to the fringe of a finger-nail held to the candle,
Or paring of paradisaical fruit, lovely in waning but lustreless,
Stepped from the stool, drew back from the barrow, of dark Maenefa the mountain;

A cusp still clasped him, a fluke yet fanged him, entangled him, not quite utterly.
This was the prized, the desirable sight, unsought, presented so easily,
Parted me leaf and leaf, divided me, eyelid and eyelid of slumber.

◆ Annotations （原诗注释）

1. dwindle: *v.* diminish gradually in size, amount, or strength （尺寸、数量或力量上）逐渐变小或缩小；减少；减弱，衰退 （e.g. Traffic has dwindled to a trickle. 来往车辆已减至涓涓细流了。）

2. fringe: *n.* an outer edge; margin; periphery 外缘；边沿；周边

3. paradisiacal: *adj.* of, like, or befitting paradise 天堂的；天堂似的；乐园的

4. paring: *n.* something, such as a skin or peel, that has been pared off 削下的皮等

5. wane: *v.* (of the moon) have a progressively smaller part of its visible surface illuminated, so that it appears to decrease in size （月亮）亏缺

6. stool: *n.* a plant crown from which shoots grow out; a root or stump of a tree or plant from which shoots spring （生长新芽的）根株；根孽；母株

7. barrow: *n.* hill or mound 小丘；土丘

8. Maenefa: *n.* Maenefa is a mountain in Wales, where Hopkins was living at the time. 迈内法山（英国威尔士境内一座山，是诗人霍普金斯当时生活的地方。）

9. cusp: *n.* each of the pointed ends of a crescent, especially of the moon 月角

10. clasp: *v.* (archaic) fasten (something) with a small device, typically a metal one （古旧用法）用（小装置，尤指金属装置）扣住 （e.g. One modest emerald clasped her robe. 一枚朴素的祖母绿扣住她的长袍。）

11. fluke: *n.* a broad triangular plate on the arm of an anchor; a barb on a harpoon or arrow 锚爪；（鱼叉、箭头等）倒钩

12. fang: *v.* (Archaic) grip; clutch （古旧用法）抓住；抓牢

13. entangle: *v.* cause to become twisted together with or caught in 缠住；使受到纠缠 （e.g. Fish attempt to swim through the mesh and become entangled. 鱼试图游过网眼，结果被网缠住。）

14. utterly: *adv.* completely; absolutely; entirely 全然；完全地；彻底地

15. prized: *adj.* highly valued 被看作最重要的；被看作最有价值的

16. unsought: *adj.* not searched for, requested, or desired 未经寻求（而得到）的；未经请求的；主动提供的

17. part: *v.* cause to divide or move apart, leaving a central space 使分开；使裂开（e.g. She parted the ferns and looked between them. 她拨开那些蕨类植物，朝中间看了看。）

18. divide: *v.* form a boundary between (two people or things) 隔开

19. eyelid: *n.* each of the upper and lower folds of skin which cover the eye when closed 眼皮；眼睑

20. slumber: *v.* sleep 沉睡 （e.g. Sleeping Beauty slumbered in her forest castle. 睡美人在森林城堡中沉睡。）

◆ *A Lead-in Note* （简明导读）

诗人霍普金斯是一位虔诚的耶稣会会士（罗马天主教修道会的神职人员），其大多数诗歌中的意象常常具有基督教方面的内涵，本诗便是其中的一首。这首诗中的月亮（残月）极有可能象征着上帝（例如，第五行让人想到了耶稣受难的画面）。但是，就此诗的字面意思而言，诗人纯粹是在描写一次残月升起时的景象，以及诗人对此次残月升起所发挥的想象。整首诗虽然不押韵，且具有散文诗的性质（但并非散文诗），但极富音乐性，是对霍普金斯本人提出的“弹跳韵式”的一次典型的尝试。

◆ *1876年6月19日，月亮升起*

我醒来，时值仲夏而非正值仲夏夜。四周一片白茫茫，清晨散步心舒畅：

月光渐弱，月体瘦成烛光映衬下的指甲；或者说，薄似
乐园之果剥下的皮。残月秀丽，但乏亮丽辉光。
月亮从暗色的迈内法山脚处迈开脚步，从迈内法山丘上退下山去。

但一枚尖角仍扣住他，一只钩爪似毒牙咬着他，缠着他，但并未死死咬缠不放。

此情此景弥足珍贵，渴为我属。未刻意去寻觅，得来却全不费工夫；

将我分割成一片又一片叶子，将我分裂为一个又一个沉睡的眼皮。

060 D. H. Lawrence
D. H. 劳伦斯

◆ *The Poet's Profile* （诗人小档案）

D. H. 劳伦斯（1885—1930）：英国小说家、诗人及散文家。他的代表作品有《儿子和情人》《虹》《恋爱中的女人》《查特莱夫人的情人》等。

◆ *Moonrise*

And who has seen the moon, who has not seen
Her rise from out the chamber of the deep,
Flushed and grand and naked, as from the chamber
Of finished bridegroom, seen her rise and throw
Confession of delight upon the wave,
Littering the waves with her own superscription
Of bliss, till all her lambent beauty shakes toward us
Spread out and known at last, and we are sure
That beauty is a thing beyond the grave,
That perfect, bright experience never falls
To nothingness, and time will dim the moon
Sooner than our full consummation here
In this odd life will tarnish or pass away.

◆ *Annotations* （原诗注释）

1. chamber: *n.* (poetic/literary or archaic) a private room, especially a bedroom

（诗/文用法或古旧用法）私室（尤指卧室）

2. deep: *n.* (poetic/literary) the sea （诗/文）海；海洋 （e.g. denizens of the deep 海中动物）

3. flushed: *adj.* (especially of the face) reddened or suffused with or as if with blood from emotion or exertion （脸）发红的；涨红的 （e.g. Her face was flushed with embarrassment. 她尴尬得满脸通红。）

4. grand: *adj.* (of a person) of high rank and with an appearance and manner appropriate to it 高贵的 （e.g. She was such a grand lady. 她是一位高雅的女士。）

5. bridegroom: *n.* a man on his wedding day or just before and after the event 新郎

6. confession: *n.* a statement of one's principles 信仰声明；行为准则的声明（e.g. His words are a political confession of faith. 他的话是一种政治信仰的声明。）

7. litter: *v.* make (a place) untidy with rubbish or a large number of objects left lying 使杂乱；使凌乱

8. superscription: *n.* something superscribed, esp. an address on a letter, parcel, etc.（信封等上的）姓名住址；题名

9. bliss: *n.* perfect happiness; great joy 完美的愉悦感；福分；欣喜 （e.g. She gave a sigh of bliss. 她幸福地长舒了一口气。）

10. lambent: *adj.* (poetic/literary) (of light or fire) glowing, gleaming, or flickering with a soft radiance （诗/文用法）（光或火）闪烁的；摇曳的；发柔光的（e.g. the magical, lambent light of the north 北方神秘、闪烁的光）

11. nothingness: *n.* the absence or cessation of life or existence （生命的）不存在（或终止）；死；虚无 （e.g. the fear of the total nothingness of death 对万事皆空的死亡所抱有的恐惧）

12. consummation: *n.* the action of making a marriage or relationship complete by having sexual intercourse 同房；圆房；完婚

13. tarnish: *v.* lose or cause to lose lustre, especially as a result of exposure to air or moisture （使）失去光泽 （e.g. Lemon juice would tarnish the gilded metal.

柠檬汁会使镀金金属失去光泽。)

◆ *A Lead-in Note* (简明导读)

劳伦斯将月亮拟人化成一位新娘。月升之时的这种美是永恒的，因为“那种美，坟墓里埋藏不住”，而且“永远不会化作/虚无”。但是，月升之时的这种美也是短暂的，是经不起时间考验的，因为“时间会更快地令月儿暗淡下来，快过我们奇特人生里，圆满婚姻失去光泽或消失殆尽的速度”。

◆ 月出

谁不曾见过明月，谁又曾见她
从深闺里起身，
裸裎、端庄、羞赧。仿佛
自那新婚的洞房里走出，谁又曾见她，升起将
身心愉悦的表白甩给波浪。
她用狂喜的笔触，令一波波浪涛凌空
乱舞，晃荡之中传来她柔和的美。
美散播开来，我们最终有了感受，于是敢肯定：
那种美，是不朽的；
那种完美、愉悦的体验，永远不会化作
虚无，但时间会更快地令月儿暗淡下来，
快过我们奇特人生里，圆满婚姻
失去光泽或消失殆尽的速度。

061 Thomas Hardy
托马斯·哈代

◆ *The Poet's Profile* （诗人小档案）

托马斯·哈代（1840—1928）：英国长篇小说家及诗人。他的作品多数描述了人们对苦难生活和命运作弄所施加的冷漠力量的抗争。其代表作有《卡斯特桥市长》（1866）、《德伯家的苔丝》（1891）和《无名的裘德》（1896）等。

◆ *Seeing the Moon Rise*

We used to go to Froom-hill Barrow
To see the round moon rise
Into the heath-rimmed skies,
Trudging thither by plough and harrow
Up the pathway, steep and narrow,
Singing a song.
Now we do not go there. Why?
Zest burns not so high!

Latterly we've only conned her
With a passing glance
From window or door by chance,
Hoping to go again, high yonder,
As we used, and gaze, and ponder,
Singing a song.

Thitherward we do not go:
Feet once quick are slow!

◆ Annotations （原诗注释）

1. heath: *n.* vegetation dominated by dwarf shrubs of the heather family 以杜鹃花科植物占优势的低矮灌木植物

2. rim: *v.* form or act as an outer edge or rim for 形成（或成为）……的边缘

3. trudge: *v.* walk slowly and with heavy steps, typically because of exhaustion or harsh conditions （尤指在疲劳状态或恶劣环境中）步履艰难地走

4. thither: *adv.* (archaic or poetic/literary) to or towards that place （古旧用法或诗/文用法）到（或向）那儿 （e.g. No trickery had been necessary to attract him thither. 引他到那边去根本不必设圈套。）

5. plough: *n.* a large farming implement with one or more blades fixed in a frame, drawn by a tractor or by animals and used for cutting furrows in the soil and turning it over, especially to prepare for the planting of seeds 犁

6. harrow: *n.* an implement consisting of a heavy frame set with teeth or tines which is dragged over ploughed land to break up clods, remove weeds, and cover seed 耙

7. pathway: *n.* a way that constitutes or serves as a path 小路；小径

8. steep: *adj.* (of a slope, flight of stairs, or angle) rising or falling sharply; almost perpendicular （斜面、楼梯、角度）陡的；陡峭的；陡直的

9. zest: *n.* great enthusiasm and energy 兴趣；兴味；热情 （e.g. They campaigned with zest and intelligence. 他们带着热情与才智投身运动。）

10. latterly: *adv.* recently 最近

11. con: *v.* to peruse or examine carefully 审阅；仔细查看

12. yonder: *adv.* (archaic or dialect) at some distance in the direction indicated; over there （古旧用法或方言用法）在那边（指一定距离以外之处）

13. ponder: *v.* to reflect or consider with thoroughness and care （仔细）考虑；

深思；默想

14. thitherward: *adv.* in that direction 在那边；向那边

◆ *A Lead-in Note* （简明导读）

当初，看月儿升起是情侣间凝聚力的体现。两个人手挽手、肩并肩，沿途哼着歌曲，不畏山路的狭窄和陡直，前去赏月。可是，“如今，我们不去那儿了，缘何？”因为激情岁月已过，剩下的只有平淡。如今，我们不再不辞辛苦去看月儿升起，只是“从窗户或门口偶尔瞥一眼，随意一瞥”。

◆ 看月儿升起

弗鲁姆希尔巴罗山，我们以前常去，
去看圆圆的月亮升起，
钻进灌木丛映衬下的天空。
我们艰难穿过犁、耙翻松的耕地，
踏上小径——狭窄、陡直，
沿途哼着歌曲。
如今，我们不去那儿了，缘何？
热情之火，不再高高燃起！

近来，我们只是远远看着月儿，
从窗户或门口偶尔
瞥一眼，随意一瞥。
我们希望再去那儿，高处站立，
跟以前一样，凝视和深思，
沿途哼着歌曲。
我们不再动身前往了：
曾经健步如飞，如今缓慢乏力！

062 E. Pauline Johnson
E・保利娜・约翰逊

◆ *The Poet's Profile* （诗人小档案）

E・保利娜・约翰逊（1861—1913）：加拿大女诗人、女作家及表演艺术家。约翰逊在19世纪后期负有盛名，很受欢迎。其主要诗作有《白色的贝壳数珠》《生于加拿大》《燧石和羽毛》。

◆ *Moonset*

Idles the night wind through the dreaming firs,
That waking murmur low,
As some lost melody returning stirs
The love of long ago;
And through the far, cool distance, zephyr fanned.
The moon is sinking into shadow-land.

The troubled night-bird, calling plaintively,
Wanders on restless wing;
The cedars, chanting vespers to the sea,
Await its answering,
That comes in wash of waves along the strand,
The while the moon slips into shadow-land.

O! soft responsive voices of the night
I join your minstrelsy,

And call across the fading silver light
As something calls to me;
I may not all your meaning understand,
But I have touched your soul in shadow-land.

◆ Annotations （原诗注释）

1. moonset: *n.* the setting or time of setting of the moon below the horizon 月落（时刻）（e.g. The best times to observe these meteors are after moonset. 观察这些流星的最佳时刻是月落之后。）

2. idle: *v.* move aimlessly or lazily 闲逛 （e.g. Robert idled along the pavement. 罗伯特沿着人行道闲逛。）

3. fir: *n.* an evergreen coniferous tree with upright cones and flat needle-shaped leaves, typically arranged in two rows. Firs are an important source of timber and resins 冷杉

4. wake: *v.* (figurative) cause (something) to stir or come to life （比喻用法）引起；激起；唤起 （e.g. It wakes desire in others. 这引起了他人的欲望。）

5. melody: *n.* a sequence of single notes that is musically satisfying 旋律 （e.g. He picked out an intricate melody on his guitar. 他用吉他一个音、一个音地慢慢奏出复杂的旋律。）

6. stir: *v.* arouse or prompt (a feeling or memory) or inspire (the imagination) 激起；引起（感情或回忆）；激发（想象力）（e.g. The story stirred many memories of my childhood. 故事勾起我童年的很多回忆。）

7. zephyr: *n.* (poetic/literary) a soft gentle breeze（诗/文用法）和风；微风

8. fan: *v.* (of breath or a breeze) blow gently on （呼吸或微风）轻拂；轻抚（e.g. His breath fanned her skin as he leant towards her. 他俯向她时，鼻息轻轻拂在她肌肤上。）

9. shadow-land or shadowland: n. (poetic/literary) a place in shadow （诗/文用法）阴暗处

10. plaintive: *adj.* sounding sad and mournful 伤心的；哀伤的 （e.g. a plaintive cry 悲号）

11. wander: *v.* walk or move in a leisurely, casual, or aimless way 漫游；漫步；闲逛 （e.g. He wandered aimlessly through the narrow streets. 他毫无目的地在狭窄的街道上溜达。）

12. restless: *adj.* (of a person or animal) unable to rest or relax as a result of anxiety or boredom （人或动物）焦躁不安的；不耐烦的 （e.g. The audience grew restless and inattentive. 观众变得焦躁不安，注意力不集中。）

13. cedar: *n.* a large tree of the pine family, in particular the cedar of Lebanon, with spreading branches 雪松

14. chant: *v.* say or shout repeatedly in a sing-song tone 反复说；反复喊

15. vespers: *n.* a service of evening prayer in the Divine Office of the Western Christian Church (sometimes said earlier in the day) （西派教会每天七段祈祷中的）晚课

16. strand: *n.* (poetic/literary) the shore of a sea, lake, or large river （诗/文用法）海滨；海滩；湖滨；河岸 （e.g. A heron glided to rest on a pebbly strand. 一只鹭轻轻地掠过天空，落在布满鹅卵石的岸边休息。）

17. while: *n.* (poetic/literary) during the time that （诗/文用法）在此期间 (e.g. Beseeching him, the while his hand she wrung. 她恳求他，并紧抓住他的手。)

18. o: *interj.* used to express surprise or strong emotion 哦；哟；啊；唉；哎呀（表示惊讶或强烈的情感）

19. minstrelsy: *n.* the practice of performing as a minstrel 吟游；游唱 （e.g. a long tradition of minstrelsy 悠久的吟游传统）

◆ *A Lead-in Note* （简明导读）

诗人约翰逊善于运用物象来抒发情感。此诗中，月亮是希望的象征，月落则代表希望的破灭。但是，月落时分各种物象的呈现，则给诗人带来了希

望，弥补了月落所带来的失望之情。

◆ 月落时分

夜风悠闲，掠过睡梦中的冷杉，
发出唤梦之声，低沉缠绵。
此时，某种失去的旋律复归，
勾起久远的爱恋。
从凉爽的远方，和煦的风轻拂而来，
月亮逐渐落至阴影地段。

夜鸟受惊，开始忧伤地啼叫不止，
煽动起焦躁的翅膀，徘徊难安。
虔诚的雪松对着大海，反复祷告着，
等待大海给出答案。
波涛洗刷着海滩，算是大海的回答，
此时月亮滑入阴影地段。

啊！夜晚吟唱出轻柔的应答之声，
我也要吟唱，与夜的声音相伴。
某种声音向我呼唤着，
我开始呼应，声音穿过银光，银光逐渐暗淡。
我或许不完全理解那声音的意思，
但我已触及其灵魂，就在那阴影地段。

063 Carl Sandburg
卡尔·桑德堡

◆ *The Poet's Profile* （诗人小档案）

卢·R. 萨雷特（1888—1954）：美国诗人、演讲家和教师。其代表诗集有《很多很多的月亮》（1920）、《上帝的盒子》（1922）、《徐升之烟》（1925）、《逆月飞行》（1931）以及《卢·萨雷特诗选》（1941）。

◆ *Moonset*

Leaves of poplars pick Japanese prints against the west.
Moon sand on the canal doubles the changing pictures.
The moon's good-by ends pictures.
The west is empty. All else is empty. No moon-talk at all now.
Only dark listening to dark.

◆ *Annotations* （原诗注释）

1. poplar: *n.* a tall, fast-growing tree of north temperate regions, widely grown in shelter belts and for timber and pulp 白杨；杨树

2. pick: *v.* make (a hole) in fabric by repeatedly pulling at something with one's fingers 在织物上挑（洞）

3. print: *n.* a piece of fabric or clothing with a decorative coloured pattern or design printed on it 印花布；印花布服装 （e.g. light summer print s 单薄的印花夏装）

4. canal: *n.* an artificial waterway constructed to allow the passage of boats or ships inland or to convey water for irrigation 运河；灌溉水渠

5. double: *v.* make twice as much or as many of (something) 使加倍；把……增加一倍 （e.g. Clare doubled her income overnight. 一夜之间克莱尔收入增加了一倍。）

◆ *A Lead-in Note* （简明导读）

这是一首自由体诗歌。有人认为，诗人桑德堡在这首诗中有意运用了“不具诗意的”（unpoetical）意象，写出了不一样的月落景象。此时月亮是希望的象征。月亮落下，“画面不再”，也“无处可闻月之语”。那么，空荡荡的黑暗之中，是否就没有希望了呢？在诗人桑德堡的眼里，未必如此——黑暗中也有希望存在。此时，“只有黑暗在听黑暗述说”。

◆ 月落

白杨叶刺破了日式印花布，花布映衬在西方。
月照运河沙流动，画面变换速倍增。
月亮道别，画面不再。
西方空荡荡。其他一切空荡荡。无处可闻月之语。
只有黑暗在听黑暗述说。

Chapter 09

Full Moon and Waning Moon

第九章

月圆月缺

064 Sara Teasdale
萨拉・蒂斯代尔

◆ *The Poet's Profile* （诗人小档案）

萨拉・蒂斯代尔（1884—1933）：美国杰出的抒情诗人，她的诗收录于《〈特洛伊的海伦〉及其他诗歌集》（1911）、《江河入海》（1915）、《爱歌》（1917）、《火焰与影子》（1920）及《奇异的胜利》（1933）等中。萨拉・蒂斯代尔以具有浪漫色彩的抒情诗篇赢得了大众的钦佩，她的诗主要围绕一名女子对美、对爱情，以及对死亡不断变换的视角而展开。1918年，蒂斯代尔获得哥伦比亚大学诗歌学会奖，这一奖项就是普利策诗歌奖的前身。

◆ *Moon's Ending*

Moon, worn thin to the width of a quill,
In the dawn clouds flying,
How good to go, light into light, and still,
Giving light, dying.

◆ *Annotations* （原诗注释）

1. quill: *v.* any of the main wing or tail feathers of a bird （鸟的翅膀或尾部的）大羽毛；翎

2. dawn: *n.* the first appearance of light in the sky before sunrise 黎明；拂晓；晨曦 （e.g. He set off at dawn. 他黎明时分出发。）

◆ *A Lead-in Note* （简明导读）

此诗中的月亮俨然一位不辞辛苦的勤劳之人，不分昼夜穿行于云层间。也许，在这样的辛勤劳作中，圆月磨成了残月，直至消失在夜空中。然后开始下一轮的辛勤劳作，永无休止。人的一生，也是如此。

◆ 月渐隐至无影踪

月亮在黎明的云层里穿行，
将自己磨得跟羽毛一样薄平。
月亮从黑夜穿行到白昼，多了不起！
仍放着光，渐隐至无影踪。

065 Vachel Lindsay
韦切尔・林赛

◆ *The Poet's Profile* （诗人小档案）

韦切尔・林赛（1879—1931）：美国诗人及现代歌唱诗歌的奠基人。林赛的作品收集在《〈威廉・布思将军进入了天堂〉及其他诗集》（1913）、《〈刚果河〉及其他诗集》（1914）、《每一个灵魂都是一个轮回》（1929）等中。

◆ *Euclid*

Old Euclid drew a circle
On a sand-beach, long ago.
He bounded and enclosed it
With angles thus and so.

His set of solemn greybeards
Nodded and argued much
Of arc and of circumference,
Diameter and such.

A silent child stood by them
From morning until noon,
Because they drew such charming
Round pictures of the moon.

◆ *Annotations* （原诗注释）

1. Euclid: *n.* (c.300 bc), Greek mathematician 欧几里得（约公元前300年），希腊数学家

2. bound: *v.* form the boundary of; enclose 形成界线；关；围入 （e.g. The ground was bounded by a main road on one side and a meadow on the other. 这块地一边是一条主干道，另一边是一块草地。）

3. enclose: *v.* surround or close off on all sides 围住；包围 （e.g. The entire estate was enclosed with walls. 整个庄园都用围墙围了起来。）

4. thus and so: of or relating to a particular way, manner, or arrangement 这样；这样那样；如此这般 （e.g. He told me that he had done thus and so in the matter. 他告诉我说他已这样处理了那件事。）

5. solemn: *adj.* characterized by deep sincerity 郑重的 （e.g. He swore a solemn oath to keep faith. 他郑重宣誓效忠。）

6. arc: *n.* a part of a curve, especially a part of the circumference of a circle 弧

7. circumference: *n.* the enclosing boundary of a curved geometric figure, especially a circle 周线（尤指圆周线）

8. diameter: *n.* a straight line passing from side to side through the centre of a body or figure, especially a circle or sphere （尤指圆或球体的）直径

9. draw: *v.* reach (a conclusion) by deduction or inference from a set of circumstances 推断出；形成（结论）

◆ *A Lead-in Note* （简明导读）

此诗中，一老一少形成了鲜明的对比。诗人以颇具调侃的口吻写出了大人物欧几里得的认真和旁观的小孩子的天真。在一个小孩子眼里，欧几里得画的那复杂的几何图形，像极了自己熟悉的圆圆的月亮，却不知道老爷爷做的是复杂的演算。

◆ 欧几里得

在一个沙滩上，在很久以前，
年迈的欧几里得画了一个圈。
他采用这样或那样的角度
将其限定并围拢了一番。

老人胡须灰白，郑重点着头，
论证了一遍又一遍：
圆弧多大，圆周多少，
直径多长，如此这般。

一个小孩默默不语，从早上
到中午一直站在旁边。
因为如此迷人的图画
形成了月亮的圆盘。

066 Walter de la Mare
沃尔特·德拉梅尔

◆ *The Poet's Profile* （诗人小档案）

沃尔特·德拉梅尔（1873—1956）：英国诗人、小说家，其代表作有《倾听者》等。

◆ *Full Moon*

One night as Dick lay half asleep,
Into his drowsy eyes
A great still light began to creep
From out the silent skies.
It was the lovely moon's, for when
He raised his dreamy head,
Her surge of silver filled the pane
And streamed across his bed.
So, for a while, each gazed at each—
Dick and the solemn moon—
Till, climbing slowly on her way,
She vanished, and was gone.

◆ *Annotations* （原诗注释）

1. drowsy: *adj.* sleepy and lethargic; half asleep 困倦的；瞌睡的；昏昏欲睡的；假寐的 （e.g. The wine had made her drowsy. 葡萄酒使她昏昏欲睡。）

2. creep: *v.* move slowly and carefully, especially in order to avoid being heard or noticed 蹑手蹑脚地行走；轻悄悄地移动（e.g. He crept downstairs, hardly making any noise. 他蹑手蹑脚地下楼，几乎没发出什么声响。）

3. surge: *n.* a sudden powerful forward or upward movement, especially by a crowd or by a natural force such as the waves or tide 汹涌（尤指人潮，波涛，潮汐等）（e.g. Flooding caused by tidal surges. 由潮汐猛涨而引起的洪水泛滥。）

4. pane: *n.* a single sheet of glass in a window or door 窗玻璃片；框格玻璃

5. vanish: *v.* gradually cease to exist 逐渐消失

◆ *A Lead-in Note*（简明导读）

诗人站在小男孩迪克的视角，以拟人的手法写出了孩子眼中光芒四射的满月形象。一天夜里，小迪克在半梦半醒之间睁开了眼睛："哇，原来是可爱的月光。"

◆ 满月

一天夜里，小迪克半梦半醒；
睡眼惺忪之时，
一缕皎洁的光，静静地从天空中
慢慢地爬进了屋子。
他睁开迷蒙的眼睛：
哇，原来是可爱的月光。
她银色的亮光注满了窗棂，
在床的周围流淌。
小迪克和庄严的月亮相互凝视，
持续了一段时间。
最终，月亮缓缓爬起，
从视线中消失不见。

067 Carl Sandburg
卡尔·桑德堡

◆ *The Poet's Profile* （诗人小档案）

卡尔·桑德堡（1878—1967）：美国诗人及传记作家。桑德堡的诗收录在《芝加哥诗集》（1915）、《烟与钢》（1920）、《桑德堡诗歌全集》（1950）、《蜜与盐》（1963）四部诗集中。桑德堡也因1926年至1939年间完成的亚伯拉罕·林肯的传记而闻名。此传记共分为六卷，包括《亚伯拉罕·林肯：北美大草原岁月》（共两卷）及《亚伯拉罕·林肯：战争岁月》（共四卷）。

◆ *Under the Harvest Moon*

Under the harvest moon,
When the soft silver
Drips shimmering
Over the garden nights,
Death, the gray mocker,
Comes and whispers to you
As a beautiful friend
Who remembers.

Under the summer roses
When the flagrant crimson
Lurks in the dusk
Of the wild red leaves,
Love, with little hands,

Comes and touches you
With a thousand memories,
And asks you
Beautiful, unanswerable questions.

◆ *Annotations* （原诗注释）

1. harvest moon: the full moon that is seen nearest to the time of the autumn equinox 获月 （最接近秋分时见到的满月）

2. drip: *v.* let fall or be so wet as to shed small drops of liquid 滴下液体；滴水；湿淋淋 （e.g. The tap won't stop dripping. 水龙头滴水不止。）

3. shimmer: *v.* shine with a soft tremulous light 发微光 （e.g. The sea shimmered in the sunlight. 大海在阳光下闪烁着。）

4. mocker: *n.* a person who mocks someone or something 嘲笑者；嘲弄者 （e.g. a mocker of authority 藐视权威的人）

5. flagrant: *adj.* conspicuously or obviously offensive 公然冒犯的

6. crimson: *n.* a rich deep red colour inclining to purple 深红色；绯红色

7. lurk: *v.* (of a person or animal) be or remain hidden so as to wait in ambush for someone or something 潜伏；埋伏 （e.g. A ruthless killer still lurked in the darkness. 一个残忍的杀手仍潜伏在黑暗中。）

8. dusk: *n.* semi-darkness 微暗；昏暗；幽暗

◆ *A Lead-in Note* （简明导读）

这是一首自由体诗，意象众多，内涵丰富。诗题中的“harvest moon”指的是最接近秋分时所能见到的满月，大致是公历的九月末和十月初之间的满月，相当于我们所说的金秋十月收获季节的满月，故称“收获月”。

月盈则亏，而收获则意味着一个季节的结束。鉴于此，此诗的第一节中，诗人主要以拟人的手法，借用“秋收季节的满月”这一主要意象来象征老年时光。与这个老年时光相对照的，就是人的“青年时代”了。本诗的第二节中，诗人也主要以拟人的手法，借用“夏季的玫瑰”这一主要意象来象征青年时代。

◆ 秋收季节的满月之下

秋收季节的满月之下，
月光笼罩着花园的夜晚。
轻淡的银色
亮闪闪地滴落下来。
此时，死神面色苍白，
扮成貌美的朋友，
念念不忘前来——嘲笑你，
对着你低声耳语。

夏季的玫瑰之下，
野生的红色叶子
所生长的幽暗之处，
埋伏着胆大妄为的深红色。
此时，爱神来到——
伸出小手触摸你，
给你带来成百上千的回忆。
而且，还问你
一些貌美的却无法回答的问题。

068 Elinor Morton Wylie
埃莉诺·莫顿·维利

◆ *The Poet's Profile* （诗人小档案）

埃莉诺·莫顿·维利（1885—1928）：美国女诗人及长篇小说家。1921年，其第一部商业性诗集《捕风的网》出版，而且很快取得了成功。1923年，《黑色装甲》出版，成为她的“另一部成功的诗集”。《纽约时报》对其赞不绝口：“书中无一词放置位置不当，也无一处节律失调，甚至没有一个多余的音节。”

◆ *Phases of the Moon*

Once upon a time I heard
That the flying moon was a Phoenix bird;
Thus she sails through windy skies,
Thus in the willow's arms she lies;
Turn to the East or turn to the West
In many trees she makes her nest.
When she's but a pearly thread
Look among birch leaves overhead;
When she dies in yellow smoke
Look in a thunder-smitten oak;
But in May when the moon is full,
Bright as water and white as wool,
Look for her where she loves to be,
Asleep in a high magnolia tree.

◆ Annotations （原诗注释）

1. phase: *n.* each of the aspects of the moon or a planet, according to the amount of its illumination, especially the new moon, the first quarter, the full moon, and the last quarter. 相（尤指新月、上弦月、满月和下弦月）

2. phoenix: *n.* (Mythology) a bird in Egyptian mythology that lived in the desert of Arab for 500 years and then consumed itself by fire, later to rise renewed from its ashes 长生鸟（埃及神话中的一种鸟，生活在阿拉伯沙漠中，活五百年后自焚，然后从灰烬中再生）；凤凰鸟

3. windy: *adj.* (of weather, a period of time, or a place) marked by or exposed to strong winds （天气、一段时间或地方）风大的；大风劲吹的

4. willow: *n.* a tree or shrub of temperate climates which typically has narrow leaves, bears catkins, and grows near water. Its pliant branches yield osiers for basketry, and the timber has various uses 柳树

5. arm: *n.* a large branch of a tree 大树枝

6. nest: *n.* a structure or place made or chosen by a bird for laying eggs and sheltering its young 鸟巢；鸟窝

7. pearly: *adj.* resembling a pearl in lustre or colour 有珍珠光泽的；珠色的（e.g. the pearly light of a clear, still dawn 晴朗、静谧清晨的珠灰色天光）

8. birch: *n.* a slender hardy tree which has thin peeling bark and bears catkins. Birch trees grow chiefly in northern temperate regions and yield hard, pale, fine-grained timber 桦；白桦

9. smite: *v.* (poetic/literary) strike with a firm blow （诗/文用法）重打；猛击（e.g. He smites the water with his sword. 他用剑猛击水。）

10. oak: *n.* a large tree which bears acorns and typically has lobed deciduous leaves 栎；橡树

11. wool: *n.* the fine soft curly or wavy hair forming the coat of a sheep, goat, or similar animal, especially when shorn and prepared for use in making cloth or yarn（尤指被剪下、待用于制布或纺纱的）羊毛

12. magnolia: *n.* a tree or shrub with large, typically creamy-pink, waxy flowers. 木兰

◆ *A Lead-in Note* （简明导读）

月相本来指不同阶段月亮所呈现出来的样子，如月圆、月缺等。此诗中，诗人发挥想象，写出了不同环境中月亮的形象，展示出月亮多变的形态。诗人或许希望借此来映射人或者人生的多变性。

◆ 月相

从前，有一个说法我听到：
月亮会飞，是一只凤凰鸟。
因此，她飞过狂风大作的天空；
因此，她栖息在柳树的怀抱。
有的朝向东方，有的朝向西方——
她筑的巢，很多树上都能见到。
从头顶桦树叶的缝隙间看去，
她不过是一根珠光闪耀的线条；
透过受雷击的橡树看她，
黄色的烟雾中不见了她的容貌。
可在五月，月儿盈满，
明亮如水，白如羊毛。
那就到她喜欢之所搜索——
她在高高的木兰树上睡着。

069 Christina Georgina Rossetti
克里斯蒂娜·乔治娜·罗塞蒂

◆ *The Poet's Profile* （诗人小档案）

克里斯蒂娜·乔治娜·罗塞蒂（1830—1894）：英国女诗人，写了许多宗教诗（反映的是其作为高教会派英国圣公会教徒的信仰）、情诗、浪漫诗和儿童诗。她的著名作品当属《〈妖怪集市〉及其他诗集》（1862）。

◆ *The Half Moon*

The half moon shows a face of plaintive sweetness
Ready and poised to wax or wane;
A fire of pale desire in incompleteness,
Tending to pleasure or to pain: —
Lo, while we gaze she rolleth on in fleetness
To perfect loss or perfect gain.

Half bitterness we know, we know half sweetness;
This world is all on wax, on wane:
When shall completeness round time's incompleteness,
Fulfilling joy, fulfilling pain? —
Lo, while we ask, life rolleth on in fleetness
To finished loss or finished gain.

◆ *Annotations* （原诗注释）

1. wax: *v.* (of the moon between new and full) have a progressively larger part of its visible surface illuminated, increasing its apparent size （月亮）渐满；变圆

2. wane: *v.* (of the moon) have a progressively smaller part of its visible surface illuminated, so that it appears to decrease in size （月亮）亏缺

3. lo: *exc.* (archaic) used to draw attention to an interesting or amazing event （古旧用法）（用以引起对有趣或惊奇之事的注意）嗟夫；看；瞧

4. rolleth = rolls

5. round: *v.* pass and go round (something) so as to move on in a changed direction 绕过；拐过 （e.g. The ship rounded the cape and sailed north. 船绕过海角，向北航行。）

◆ *A Lead-in Note* （简明导读）

这首诗中，“半月”象征着一种不稳定的“中间”状态。这样的中间状态不会持久，总是会向两个方向转变：或逐渐亏缺至“新月”，或逐渐圆满至“盈月”。究竟向哪个方向转变，我们不能坐以待毙，也不能只问不做。命运最终的走向，全在你自己的把握，命运掌握在你自己的手中。

◆ 半月

半月的面孔，亦哀伤亦欢愉，
时刻准备着去亏缺，或变圆满。
苍白的欲望之火，不完整之中有所趋：
或趋于快乐，或趋于不欢。
瞧啊，我们凝视着她，她却飞速移：
移向彻底亏损，或彻底盈满。

一半苦痛我们懂，一半欢愉我们知——
这个世界亦如此：亦亏缺亦圆满。
何时从完整体过渡到不完整体，
从快乐无比转变为倍感不欢？
瞧啊，我们在发问，生活却在飞速移：
移向最终的亏损，或最终的盈满。

070 Sara Teasdale
萨拉·蒂斯代尔

◆ *The Poet's Profile* （诗人小档案）

萨拉·蒂斯代尔（1884—1933）：美国杰出的抒情诗人，她的诗收录于《〈特洛伊的海伦〉及其他诗歌集》（1911）、《江河入海》（1915）、《爱歌》（1917）、《火焰与影子》（1920）及《奇异的胜利》（1933）等中。萨拉·蒂斯代尔以具有浪漫色彩的抒情诗篇赢得了大众的钦佩，她的诗主要围绕一名女子对美、对爱情，以及对死亡不断变换的视角而展开。1918年，蒂斯代尔获得哥伦比亚大学诗歌学会奖，这一奖项就是普利策诗歌奖的前身。

◆ *The New Moon*

Day, you have bruised and beaten me,
As rain beats down the bright, proud sea,
Beaten my body, bruised my soul,
Left me nothing lovely or whole—

Yet I have wrested a gift from you,
Day that dies in dusky blue:
For suddenly over the factories
I saw a moon in the cloudy seas—

A wisp of beauty all alone
In a world as hard and gray as stone—
Oh who could be bitter and want to die

When a maiden moon wakes up in the sky?

◆ Annotations （原诗注释）

1. bruise: *v.* inflict such an injury on (someone or something) 使瘀伤；打青（e.g. a bruised knee 撞青了的膝盖）

2. beat down: (of rain) fall hard and continuously （雨）不停地倾盆而下

3. proud: *adj.* imposing; splendid 雄伟的；壮丽的 （e.g. Bulrushes emerge tall and proud from the middle of the pond. 水烛壮观地挺立于池塘中央。）

4. wrest: *v.* take (something, especially power or control) from someone or something else after considerable effort or difficulty 辛苦谋求；费力抢得 （e.g. They wanted to allow people to wrest control of their lives from impersonal bureaucracies. 他们希望允许人们从没有人情味的官僚主义官员手中夺回自己生命的主宰权。）

5. dusky: *adj.* (poetic/literary) dim （诗/文用法）暗淡的；昏暗的；幽暗的（e.g. Dusky light came from a small window. 从一扇小窗中透出昏暗灯光。）

6. cloudy: *adj.* (of a liquid) not transparent or clear （液体）混浊的 （e.g. The pond water is slightly cloudy. 池塘的水有点混浊。）

7. wisp: *n.* a small thin or twisted bunch, piece, or amount of something 小把；小束；小捆；缕；绺 （e.g. Wisps of smoke rose into the air. 缕缕轻烟袅袅升起。）

8. gray = grey

9. oh: *exc.* used to express a range of emotions including surprise, anger, disappointment, or joy, or when reacting to something that has just been said （表示惊讶、愤怒、失望、高兴等感情）噢；啊；哦；唉；哎呀

10. bitter: *adj.* feeling or showing anger, hurt, or resentment because of bad experiences or a sense of unjust treatment 愤怒的；委屈的；受伤害的；怨恨的

◆ *A Lead-in Note* （简明导读）

此诗中，诗人以拟人化手法赋予“新月”一定的象征意义。可以说，新月宛如冰清玉洁、出淤泥而不染的荷花。这朵荷花为诗人带来了希望和光明。

◆ 新月

白昼，你将我打青，把我打垮，
如同雨在明亮、壮观的大海上倾盆而下。
你打垮我身体，打青我灵魂，
耗尽我的可爱和完整才作罢。

我却从你手中抢得一份礼，
而暗蓝中，你消失无踪——
因陡然间视线越过座座工厂，
我看见月亮浸润在浑浊的大海中。

那娇弱的美独一无二，
周围的世界如石头般坚硬和灰青。
啊！看到空中苏醒的初生洁月，
还能有谁愿意在怨恨中了结此生？

071 George Gordon Byron
乔治·戈登·拜伦

乔治·戈登·拜伦（1788—1824）：英国19世纪初期伟大的浪漫主义诗人。其代表作品有《恰尔德·哈罗尔德游记》《唐璜》《她走在美丽的光彩里》。

◆ *So We'll Go No More A-roving*

So, we'll go no more a-roving
So late into the night,
Though the heart be still as loving,
And the moon be still as bright.

For the sword outwears its sheath,
And the soul wears out the breast,
And the heart must pause to breathe,
And love itself have rest.

Though the night was made for loving,
And the day returns too soon,
Yet we'll go no more a-roving
By the light of the moon.

◆ *Annotations* （原诗注释）

1. rove: *v.* travel constantly without a fixed destination; wander 流浪；漫游

2. outwear: *v.* last longer than 比……耐久 (e.g. a material that will outwear any other waterproof sheeting 比其他任何防水布都耐用的材料)

3. sheath: *n.* a cover for the blade of a knife or sword （刀或剑的）鞘

◆ *A Lead-in Note* （简明导读）

诗人拜伦以月亮（多半为圆月前后的月相）"明亮依然"与爱情的倦怠形成了对比。在诗人眼里，月亮是永恒的象征，但实际上月有圆缺之变，月光也有明暗之分。在明亮依然的月亮的衬托下，虽心里仍怀有爱意，但"我们不再漫游缠绵"了。

◆ 我们不再漫游缠绵

没错，我们不再漫游缠绵，
在这个夜已深深的时间——
尽管心里一直怀有爱意，
尽管月亮还是明亮依然。

剑未损，剑鞘已蹭破；
魂犹在，胸膛已磨穿；
一呼一吸间，心须短停顿——
爱本身则需休息一番。

尽管这个夜适合表达爱意，
尽管天亮就在眨眼间，
但在月光的照耀下，
我们不再漫游缠绵。

072 Christina Georgina Rossetti
克里斯蒂娜·乔治娜·罗塞蒂

◆ *The Poet's Profile* （诗人小档案）

克里斯蒂娜·乔治娜·罗塞蒂（1830—1894）：英国女诗人，写了许多宗教诗（反映的是其作为高教会派英国圣公会教徒的信仰）、情诗、浪漫诗和儿童诗。她的著名作品当属《〈妖怪集市〉及其他诗集》（1862）。

◆ *Lady Moon*

O Lady Moon, your horns point toward the east:
Shine, be increased;
O Lady Moon, your horns point toward the west:
Wane, be at rest.

◆ *Annotations* （原诗注释）

1. o: *interj.* used to express surprise or strong emotion 哦；哟；啊；唉；哎呀（表示惊讶或强烈的情感）

2. horn: *n.* the extremity of the moon or other crescent （弯月的）钩尖；月牙钩

3. wane: *v.* (of the moon) have a progressively smaller part of its visible surface illuminated, so that it appears to decrease in size （月亮）亏缺

◆ *A Lead-in Note* （简明导读）

诗人罗塞蒂以儿童的视角，写出了对月亮心存的天真和好奇。在儿童的眼中，那缺了又圆、圆了又缺的月亮，宛如一位尊贵的女士，魔力无限。

◆ 月亮女士

啊，月亮女士！你的尖钩指向东方：
照耀，逐渐增强。
啊，月亮女士！你的尖钩指向西面：
亏缺，消失无光。

073 Emily Elizabeth Dickinson
埃米莉·伊丽莎白·狄更生

◆ *The Poet's Profile* （诗人小档案）

埃米莉·伊丽莎白·狄更生（1830—1886）：美国女诗人，她的诗独具一格：诗行短小，一般没有标题，经常使用近似押韵的方式和一些非常规的大写及标点，主题多与死亡和永生相关。

◆ *Which is the Best—the Moon or the Crescent?*

Which is the best—the Moon or the Crescent?
Neither—said the Moon—
That is best which is not—Achieve it—
You efface the Sheen.

Not of detention is Fruition—
Shudder to attain.
Transport's decomposition follows—
He is Prism born.

◆ *Annotations* （原诗注释）

1. crescent: *n.* the curved sickle shape of the waxing or waning moon 月牙形；新月形；弦月形；（月亮）镰刀形

2. achieve: *v.* reach, attain, or successfully bring about (a desired objective, level, or result) by effort, skill, or courage （通过努力、技术或勇气）达到；取

得；获得；实现（目标、水平、结果）

3. efface: *v.* erase (a mark) from a surface 擦掉；抹去（痕迹） (e.g. With time, the words are effaced by the frost and the rain. 时光流逝，霜冻和雨水将字迹抹去了。)

4. sheen: *n.* a soft lustre on a surface 光泽；光辉

5. detention: *n.* the withholding of something belonging to or claimed by another r 扣留（属于他人之物）；强留

6. fruition: *n.* the realization of a plan or project （计划、方案的）实现；完成 (e.g. New methods will come with the fruition of that research. 随着那个研究的完成，新的方法即将产生。)

7. shudder: *n.* an act of shuddering 震动；颤动；战栗；打颤 (e.g. The elevator rose with a shudder. 电梯震动一下向上升起。)

8. transport: *n.* the act of transporting or the state of being transported 运送；运输；移动

9. decomposition: *n.* the act or result of decomposing; disintegration 分解；腐烂

10. prism: *n.* (Optics) a glass or other transparent object in this form, especially one that is triangular with refracting surfaces at an acute angle with each other and that separates white light into a spectrum of colours （光学）棱镜；折光物

◆ *A Lead-in Note* （简明导读）

"盈月或新月——哪个最佳?"这其实是一个哲学问题。月亮盈满则亏，月亏后则渐渐盈满。月盈月亏，月亏月盈，周而复始。即便你得到了"盈月"，也不会停留多久，"其辉光即遭抹杀"。所以，"强留不是如愿以偿"：这样的拥有，并非圆满。因为月亮"随后，在游移中分解"。每一次的月升月落，月亮都得以重生："他生而为棱镜，折光而发。"这里，诗人运用了拟人的手法，称月亮为"他"，应该也带有爱情方面的寓意。

◆ 盈月或新月——哪个最佳?

盈月或新月——哪个最佳?
没有最佳——盈月回答——
最佳的，不符实——得之——
其辉光即遭抹杀。

强留不是如愿以偿——
获得中担惊受怕。
随后，在游移中分解——
他生而为棱镜，折光而发。

074 Percy Bysshe Shelley
珀西·比希·雪莱

◆ *The Poet's Profile* （诗人小档案）

珀西·比希·雪莱（1792—1822）：英国文学史上最有才华的抒情诗人之一，被誉为“诗人中的诗人”，与乔治·戈登·拜伦一起被称为英国浪漫主义诗歌的“双子星座”。他的著名作品包括政治诗歌《麦布女王》（1813年），诗剧《解放了的普罗米修斯》（1820），论文《诗辩》（1821），以及悼念济慈的挽诗《阿东尼斯》（1821）。

◆ *The Waning Moon*

And like a dying lady lean and pale,
Who totters forth, wrapt in a gauzy veil,
Out of her chamber, led by the insane
And feeble wanderings of her fading brain,
The moon arose up in the murky east,
A white and shapeless mass.

◆ *Annotations* （原诗注释）

1. wane: *v.* (especially of a condition or feeling) decrease in vigour, power, or extent; become weaker （尤指状况或感觉）衰落；减少；减弱 （e.g. Confidence in the dollar waned. 对美元的信心减弱了。）

2. lean: *adj.* (of a person or animal) thin, especially healthily so; having no su-

perfluous fat （人或动物）瘦的 （e.g. his lean, muscular body 他精瘦刚健的身体）

3. totter: *v.* move in a feeble or unsteady way 蹒跚；跌跌撞撞；踉跄 （e.g. a hunched figure tottering down the path 一个一路踉跄的驼背身影）

4. wrapt = wrapped: archaic or poetic form of wrapped （“wrapped”一词的古旧形式或其在诗歌中的用法）

5. gauzy: *adj.* resembling gauze; thin and translucent 薄纱似的；薄而透明的 (e.g. a gauzy dress 一件薄纱衣服）

6. veil: *n.* a piece of fine material worn by women to protect or conceal the face 面纱；面罩 （e.g. a white bridal veil 新娘的白色面纱）

7. chamber: *n.* (poetic/literary or archaic) a private room, especially a bedroom (诗/文用法或古旧用法）私室（尤指卧室）

8. feeble: *adj.* lacking physical strength, especially as a result of age or illness (尤指因年老或疾病而）虚弱的；衰弱的；乏力的 （e.g. My legs are very feeble after the flu. 患了流感之后，我的腿虚弱乏力。）

9. murky: *adj.* dark and gloomy, especially due to thick mist 阴暗的；昏暗的；漆黑的 （e.g. The sky was murky and a thin drizzle was falling. 天色晦暗，细雨蒙蒙。）

10. shapeless: *adj.* (especially of a garment) lacking a distinctive or attractive shape （尤指衣服）难看的；样子不好的 （She wore a shapeless frock and no make-up. 她穿一件没有样子的连衣裙，也没有化装。）

◆ *A Lead-in Note* （简明导读）

此诗中，雪莱以拟人化的手法，将“减渐亏之月”比作一位“奄奄一息的女士”。给人的感觉是，“亏月”已到了“穷途末路”的地步，因其逐渐亏损而“骨瘦面白”，大不如从前盈月之时的模样。她在“昏暗的东方”升起，那里已经没有了太阳的光辉，再加上“一层薄薄的面纱”，渐亏的月儿就成了“不成形的一团白，清辉不再”。

◆ 渐亏之月

月儿如奄奄一息的女士，骨瘦面白，
蹒跚向前，一层薄薄的面纱裹缠于外。
她自寝宫而出，精神失常；
她游走乏力，大脑日趋衰败。
月儿升起在昏暗的东方——
不成形的一团白，清辉不再。

075 Amy Lowell
埃米·洛厄尔

◆ *The Poet's Profile* （诗人小档案）

埃米·洛厄尔（1874—1925）：美国女诗人。在她死后的第一年，即1926年，获得“普利策诗歌奖”。作为印象派中一位领军人物，洛厄尔以散文诗和令人愉悦的意象而闻名。

◆ *The Crescent Moon*

Slipping softly through the sky
Little horned, happy moon,
Can you hear me up so high?
Will you come down soon?

On my nursery window-sill
Will you stay your steady flight?
And then float away with me
Through the summer night?

Brushing over tops of trees,
Playing hide and seek with stars,
Peeping up through shiny clouds
At Jupiter or Mars.

I shall fill my lap with roses

Gathered in the Milky Way,
All to carry home to mother.
Oh! What will she say!

Little rocking, sailing moon,
Do you hear me shout—Ahoy!
Just a little nearer, moon,
To please a little boy.

◆ *Annotations* （原诗注释）

1. crescent: *n.* the curved sickle shape of the waxing or waning moon 月牙形；新月形；弦月形；（月亮）镰刀形

2. horned: *adj.* (poetic/literary) crescent-shaped （诗/文用法）新月形的；弯月形的 （e.g. the horned moon 弦月）

3. nursery: *n.* a room in a house for the special use of young children （家庭中的）幼儿房

4. window-sill: a ledge or sill forming the bottom part of a window 窗沿；窗台

5. peep: *v.* look quickly and furtively at something, especially through a narrow opening （尤指从缝隙中）偷看；窥探 （e.g. His door was ajar and she couldn't resist peeping in. 他的门半开着，因此她忍不住向里偷看。）

6. shiny: *adj.* (of a smooth surface) reflecting light, typically because very clean or polished （光滑表面）发亮的；闪光的 （e.g. shiny hair 有光泽的头发）

7. Jupiter: *n.* (Astronomy) the largest planet in the solar system, a gas giant which is the fifth in order from the sun and one of the brightest objects in the night sky （天文学）木星（太阳系中最大的行星，靠近太阳的第五颗气态巨星，为夜空中最明亮的星体之一）

9. Mars: *n.* (Astronomy) a small reddish planet which is the fourth in order from the sun and is periodically visible to the naked eye （天文学）火星

10. Milky Way: a faint band of light crossing the sky, made up of vast numbers of faint stars. It corresponds to the plane of our Galaxy, in which most of its stars are located 银河（系）

11. ahoy: *exc.* (Nautical or humorous) a call used in hailing （航海语或幽默用法）喂；啊嗬

◆ *A Lead-in Note* （简明导读）

诗人以丰富的想象写出了一个小男孩儿天真的想象。在诗中小男孩儿的眼里，那“两端长角的小月牙儿”无疑一个“高高在上”的小女孩儿。小男孩儿想跟这个小女孩儿拉近距离，问她：“把高度降下来，你可否愿意?”小男孩儿羡慕小女孩能够“掠过树梢，跟星星/一起玩着捉迷藏的游戏”。小男孩儿想要小女孩儿靠近一点点，听到自己的呼喊。这样，小男孩就会欢快无比。

◆ 小月牙儿

两端长角的小月牙儿，
轻柔滑过天空，欢快无比。
你高高在上，能否听见我的声音?
把高度降下来，你可否愿意?

我的小房间里有个窗台，
你能否飞到上面稳稳停止?
然后，穿过夏夜的天空，
你能否带上我漂浮着远去?

掠过树梢，跟星星
一起玩着捉迷藏的游戏。

透过亮晶晶的云层，
仰头把木星和火星窥视。

我要在大腿面上摆满玫瑰——
这些花儿采集自银河系。
统统拿回家送给妈妈——
啊！她会说出什么话语！

小月牙儿摇呀摇，飘呀飘，
一定听听我的喊声——嘿，你！
小月牙儿啊，只需再靠近一点儿，
好让一个小男孩儿欢快无比。

076 Rose Terry Cooke
罗斯·特里·库克

◆ *The Poet's Profile* （诗人小档案）

罗斯·特里·库克（1827—1892）：美国女诗人及作家。她的第一首诗歌1851年发表于《纽约每日论坛报》，并得到其编辑查尔斯·A. 达娜的盛赞。1860年，罗斯出版了第一部诗集，其中有许多韵诗。

◆ *New Moon*

Once, when the new moon glittered
So slender in the West,
I looked across my shoulder,
And a wild wish stirred my breast.

Over my white, right shoulder
I looked at the silver horn,
And wished a wish at even
To come to pass in the morn.

Whenever the new moon glittered,
So slender and so fine,
I looked across my shoulder,
And wished that wish of mine!

Now, when the West is rosy,

And the snow-wreaths blush below,
And I see the light white crescent
Float downward, soft and slow;

I never look over my shoulder,
As I used to look before;
For my heart is older and colder,
And now I wish no more!

◆ *Annotations* （原诗注释）

1. glitter: *v.* shine with a bright, shimmering, reflected light （因反射而）闪闪发光 （e.g. Trees and grass glittered with dew. 树木和青草因晨露而闪闪发光。）

2. slender: *adj.* (of a person or part of the body) gracefully thin （人或身体部位）苗条的；修长的；纤细的

3. wild: *adj.* extravagant or unreasonable; fanciful 荒诞的；不合常理的；异想天开的 （e.g. Who, even in their wildest dreams, could have anticipated such a victory? 再怎么异想天开，谁能想到会取得这样一个大胜利？）

4. horn: *n.* the extremity of the moon or other crescent （弯月的）钩尖；月牙钩

5. come to pass: to happen; to occur; to come true 发生；实现

6. even: *n.* (archaic or poetic/literary) the end of the day; evening （古旧用法或诗/文用法）黄昏；傍晚 （e.g. Bring it to my house this even. 今晚把它带到我家里来。）

7. morn = morning

8. fine: *adj.* of imposing and dignified appearance or size 气势宏伟的；堂皇的 （e.g. a very fine Elizabethan mansion 一座气势不凡的伊丽莎白时代的豪宅）

9. rosy: *adj.* (especially of a person's skin) coloured like a pink or red rose, typically as an indication of health, youth, or embarrassment （尤指人的皮肤）玫瑰色

的；（浅）玫瑰红的；肤色红润的；脸红的（尤指作为健康、年轻或尴尬的标志）

10. blush: *v.* show shyness, embarrassment, or shame by becoming red in the face （因害羞、尴尬或羞耻）脸红

11. crescent: *n.* the curved sickle shape of the waxing or waning moon 月牙形；新月形；弦月形；（月亮）镰刀形

◆ *A Lead-in Note* （简明导读）

曾经，夜晚的“新月”给诗人带来了希望，诗人不禁异想天开，许下了“希望在早晨变成现实”的愿望。那是什么样的愿望？那个愿望变成现实了吗？答案不得而知。

如今，那弯给诗人带来希望的“新月”，已经变得“浅白”，且“轻柔、缓慢，向下飘去。”岁月不饶人，诗人已老，而且“如今也没有什么愿望可许”了。最终，愿望难以实现，虽然“新月”依然挂在夜晚的天空中。

◆ 新月

曾经，在西部天空里
新月闪亮，如此纤细。
我回头而望，
异想天开的愿望在胸中燃起。

右肩之上洒满月光，
我顺着右肩看了眼弯月，银光熠熠。
我在夜晚许了个愿，
希望在早晨变成现实。

无论新月何时闪亮，

如此纤细，如此有气势，
我都回头而望，
许下那个愿——我自己的期许！

如今，西方露出玫瑰色，
下方环状积雪上，红晕泛起。
我看见那浅白的新月——
轻柔、缓慢，向下飘去。

我再也不像从前那般，
回头望去。
因我的心已变老，已变寒，
如今也没有什么愿望可许。

077 D. H. Lawrence D. H. 劳伦斯

◆ *The Poet's Profile* （诗人小档案）

D. H. 劳伦斯（1885—1930）：英国小说家、诗人及散文家。其代表作品有《儿子和情人》《虹》《恋爱中的女人》《查特莱夫人的情人》等。

◆ *New Moon*

The new moon, of no importance
lingers behind as the yellow sun glares
and is gone beyond the sea's edge;
earth smokes blue;
the new moon, in cool height above the blushes,
brings a fresh fragrance of heaven to our senses.

◆ *Annotations* （原诗注释）

1. linger: *v.* stay in a place longer than necessary, typically because of a reluctance to leave （不愿离开而）逗留；多停留

2. glare: *v.* (of the sun or an electric light) shine with a strong or dazzling light （太阳或电灯）发出强光（或刺眼的光）(e.g. The sun glared out of a clear blue sky. 晴空里，太阳白花花的，很刺眼。)

3. cool: *adj.* of, relating to, or characteristic of colors, such as blue and green, that produce the impression of coolness （颜色）素净的，冷色的

4. blush: *n.* a pink or pale red tinge 粉红；淡红（e.g. The roses were white with a lovely pink blush. 那些玫瑰白色中带有漂亮的粉红色。）

◆ *A Lead-in Note*（简明导读）

一个普通的“新月”升起、夕阳落下的景致，在诗人的笔下，仿佛具有了一定的象征意义。这是一个新旧交替的时刻。新月初生，当然“微不足道”，有所畏惧才“逗留不前”。但是，大势已去，太阳“消失在大海的边际”。此时，“大地冒着蓝色的烟气”预示着交替时刻的到来。新月高挂，一切素净起来，新月为我们带来了“天空的芬芳”，那是“清新的味道”。

◆ 新月

新月逗留不前，微不足道，
黄澄澄的太阳闪耀，
消失在大海的边际，
大地冒着蓝色的烟气。
素净的新月高挂，下方一片淡红色调，
给我们感官带来天空的芬芳，清新的味道。

Chapter 10

What Different Creatures and Inanimate Objects Said about the Moon

第十章

月因物异

078 Vachel Lindsay
韦切尔·林赛

◆ *The Poet's Profile* （诗人小档案）

韦切尔·林赛（1879—1931）：美国诗人及现代歌唱诗歌的奠基人。林赛的作品收集在《〈威廉·布思将军进入了天堂〉及其他诗集》（1913）、《〈刚果河〉及其他诗集》（1914）、《每一个灵魂都是一个轮回》（1929）等中。

◆ *The Old Horse in the City*

The moon's a peck of corn. It lies
Heaped up for me to eat.
I wish that I might climb the path
And taste that supper sweet.

Men feed me straw and scanty grain
And beat me till I'm sore.
Some day I'll break the halter-rope
And smash the stable-door,

Run down the street and mount the hill
Just as the corn appears.
I've seen it rise at certain times
For years and years and years.

◆ Annotations （原诗注释）

1. peck: *n.* (archaic) a large number or amount of something （古旧用法）许多；大量（e.g. a peck of dirt 一大堆污物）

2. scanty: *adj.* small or insufficient in quantity or amount 少量的；不足的（e.g. They paid whatever they could out of their scanty wages to their families. 他们尽己所能地从微薄的工资里拿出钱来补贴家里。）

3. sore: *adj.* (of a part of one's body) painful or aching （身体某部位）疼痛的（e.g. My feet were sore and my head ached. 我的脚和头都很痛。）

4. halter: *n.* a rope or strap placed around the head of a horse or other animal, used for leading or tethering it （马等动物的）笼头；缰绳；系索

5. smash: *v.* violently knock down or crush inwards 猛力撞倒（e.g. Soldiers smashed down doors. 士兵们用力把门撞倒。）

6. stable: *n.* a building set apart and adapted for keeping horses 马厩

7. mount: *v.* climb up (stairs, a hill, or other rising surface) 登（楼梯、山或其他上升面）

◆ A Lead-in Note （简明导读）

诗人以城中老马的视角，写出了老马眼中的月亮。在城中老马的眼中，月亮成了自由的象征，给了老马奋争的勇气：只要挣脱缰绳，爬上那月光小径，吃到那一大堆苞米——月亮，老马就获得了自由，不再忍受人类的痛打。

◆ 城里老马眼中的月亮

月亮是一大堆苞米，在那里
堆砌起来，等着我去吃。
我多希望爬上那月光小径，

品尝那味道——超级甜蜜。

人类喂我草，还有少许谷物，
却打我，打得我疼痛不止。
有那么一天，我要扯断缰绳，
撞碎厩舍的门——猛然用力。

跑过大街，登上小山，
就在那堆苞米浮现之际。
在很多、很多、很多年中
某些时段，我看到月亮升起。

079 Vachel Lindsay
韦切尔·林赛

◆ *The Poet's Profile* （诗人小档案）

韦切尔·林赛（1879—1931）：美国诗人及现代歌唱诗歌的奠基人。林赛的作品收集在《〈威廉·布思将军进入了天堂〉及其他诗集》(1913)、《〈刚果河〉及其他诗集》(1914)、《每一个灵魂都是一个轮回》(1929)等中。

◆ *What the Hyena Said*

The moon is but a golden skull,
She mounts the heavens now,
And Moon-Worms, mighty Moon-Worms
Are wreathed around her brow.

The Moon-Worms are a doughty race:
They eat her gray and golden face.
Her eye-sockets dead, and molding head:
These caverns are their dwelling-place.

The Moon-Worms, serpents of the skies,
From the great hollows of her eyes
Behold all souls, and they are wise:
With tiny, keen and icy eyes,
Behold how each man sins and dies.

When Earth in gold-corruption lies
Long dead, the moon-worm butterflies
On cyclone wings will reach this place—
Yea, rear their brood on earth's dead face.

◆ *Annotations* （原诗注释）

1. hyena: *n.* a doglike African mammal with forelimbs that are longer than the hindlimbs and an erect mane. Hyenas are noted as scavengers but most are also effective hunters 鬣狗

2. skull: *n.* a bone framework enclosing the brain of a vertebrate; the skeleton of a person's or animal's head 颅骨；头骨

3. mount: *v.* climb up (stairs, a hill, or other rising surface) 登（楼梯、山或其他上升面）

4. heaven: *n.* (often heavens) (poetic/literary) the sky, esp. perceived as a vault in which the sun, moon, stars, and planets are situated （诗/文用法）天空

5. mighty: *adj.* possessing great and impressive power or strength, especially on account of size 强大的；强有力的

6. wreathe: *v.* (poetic/literary) twist or entwine (something flexible) round or over something （诗/文用法）把……绕成一圈；盘绕；缠绕

7. brow: *n.* a person's forehead 额；脑门

8. doughty: *adj.* (archaic or humorous) brave and persistent （古旧用法或幽默用法）勇敢而坚忍的；强韧的（e.g. His doughty spirit kept him going. 他勇敢坚忍的精神使他能够坚持下来。）

9. socket: *n.* a natural or artificial hollow into which something fits or in which something revolves 窝；槽；臼（e.g. the eye socket 眼窝）

10. dead: *adj.* (of a part of the body) having lost sensation; numb （身体部位）无知觉的；麻木的

11. mold: *v.* to become overgrown with minute fungi forming on vegetable or animal matter, commonly as a downy or furry coating, and associated with decay or dampness 长出真菌或霉菌

12. cavern: *n.* a cave, or a chamber in a cave, typically a large one （尤指大的）洞穴；山洞；（洞穴的）深凹处；深处

13. serpent: *n.* (chiefly poetic/literary) a large snake （主要为诗/文用法）巨蛇

14. hollow: *n.* a hole or depression in something 凹陷处；洞 （e.g. a hollow at the base of a large tree 大树底部的一个洞）

15. behold: *v.* (archaic or poetic/literary) see or observe (someone or something, especially of remarkable or impressive nature) （古旧用法或诗/文用法）看；观看（尤指看非凡的或感人的人或事物）(e.g. The botanical gardens were a wonder to behold. 植物园是值得一看的奇观。)

16. corruption: *n.* (archaic) decay; putrefaction （古旧用法）腐坏；腐烂 （e.g. The potato turned black and rotten with corruption. 土豆变黑腐烂了。)

17. cyclone: *n.* (Meteorology) a system of winds rotating inwards to an area of low barometric pressure, with an anticlockwise (northern hemisphere) or clockwise (southern hemisphere) circulation; a depression （气象学）旋风；龙卷风

18. yea: *adv.* used for emphasis, especially to introduce a stronger or more accurate word than one just used （用于强调）的确；诚然 （e.g. He was full, yea, crammed with anxieties. 的确，他忧心忡忡。)

19. rear: *v.* (of an animal) care for (its young) until they are fully grown （动物）喂养（幼崽）

20. brood: *n.* a family of young animals, typically birds, produced at one hatching or birth 一窝（小动物，尤指小鸟）

◆ *A Lead-in Note* （简明导读）

诗人借鬣狗之口，以丰富的想象道出了鬣狗眼中月亮的形象，对月亮的

意象做了另一番超乎寻常的呈现。月亮呈现出一位女子的形象，但却只剩下一个“金色头骨……升上天空飘浮”。月亮的这一命运要“归功”于“月亮蠕虫”这个坚韧的族群——蠕虫化作月光，洒向地球，从而照亮了地球。蠕虫的生死轮回导致了月亮的圆缺。

◆ 鬣狗眼中的月亮

月亮只是女子的金色头骨，
她现已升上天空飘浮。
月亮蠕虫，强大的月亮蠕虫，
缠绕在她的额部。

月亮蠕虫是个坚韧的族群，
吃的是她金灰色的面部。
她眼窝暗淡，脑袋生了霉，
蠕虫就地凿洞而居。

月亮蠕虫是天空的巨蛇，
从她眼睛的大洞钻出。
它们睿智，看着凡尘众生——
转动冰冷、敏锐的小眼珠，
看着每个人如何犯错和入墓。

地球腐烂成一堆金色而躺下
长眠之时，它们化虫成蝶，扇动
翅膀，旋风般到达此所——
对，用地球死去的面部喂养其幼虫。

080 Vachel Lindsay
韦切尔·林赛

◆ *The Poet's Profile* （诗人小档案）

韦切尔·林赛（1879—1931）：美国诗人及现代歌唱诗歌的奠基人。林赛的作品收集在《〈威廉·布思将军进入了天堂〉及其他诗集》（1913）、《〈刚果河〉及其他诗集》（1914）、《每一个灵魂都是一个轮回》（1929）等中。

◆ *What the Snow Man Said*

The Moon's a snowball. See the drifts
Of white that cross the sphere.
The Moon's a snowball, melted down
A dozen times a year.

Yet rolled again in hot July
When all my days are done
And cool to greet the weary eye
After the scorching sun.

The moon's a piece of winter fair
Renewed the year around,
Behold it, deathless and unstained,
Above the grimy ground!

It rolls on high so brave and white
Where the clear air-rivers flow,
Proclaiming Christmas all the time
And the glory of the snow!

◆ *Annotations* （原诗注释）

1. drift: *n.* a large mass of snow, leaves, or other material piled up or carried along by the wind （雪、树叶等大量的）吹积物；吹飘

2. sphere: *n.* (poetic/literary) the sky perceived as a vault upon or in which celestial bodies are represented as lying （诗/文用法）苍穹；天；天空

3. weary: *adj.* feeling or showing tiredness, especially as a result of excessive exertion or lack of sleep （尤指过度劳累或睡眠不足）疲劳的；疲倦的 （e.g. He gave a long, weary sigh. 他发出了一声疲倦的长叹。）

4. scorching: *adj.* very hot 炎热的

5. piece: *n.* a coin of specified value 硬币 （e.g. a 10p piece 一枚十便士的硬币）

6. fair: *adj.* (of weather) fine and dry （天气）晴朗干爽的；宜人的

7. renew: *v.* give fresh life or strength to 使获得新生；使复活 （e.g. She would face the future with renewed determination. 她将以百倍的决心面对未来。）

8. behold: *v.* (past and past participle beheld) [often in imperative] (archaic or poetic/literary) see or observe (someone or something, especially of remarkable or impressive nature) （古旧用法或诗/文用法）看；观看 （尤指看非凡的或感人的人或事物） （e.g. The botanical gardens were a wonder to behold. 植物园是值得一看的奇观。）

9. unstained: *adj.* not stained 未被玷污的；无污点 （或斑点）的

10. grimy: *adj.* covered with or characterized by grime 满是污垢的；肮脏的 （e.g. the grimy industrial city 肮脏的工业城市）

11. proclaim: *v.* announce officially or publicly （正式）宣告；（公开）声明

(e.g. Army commanders proclaimed a state of emergency. 陆军指挥官宣布进入紧急状态。)

◆ *A Lead-in Note* （简明导读）

诗人以拟人的手法，写出了雪人眼中的月亮意象。雪人眼中的月亮跟雪有着千丝万缕的联系。月亮是白色的："白色堆积，穿越天空旋转。月亮是个雪球，一年之中/历经十二次融化之变。"夏日炎热，雪人"我的日子一去不复返"了，但"月亮清凉，仍又转动，慰藉疲惫的眼"。因此，雪人羡慕"洁白而恒久的月亮"。

◆ 雪人眼中的月亮

月亮是个雪球。我看见
白色堆积，穿越天空旋转。
月亮是个雪球，一年之中
历经十二次融化之变。

就在七月炎热之时，
我的日子一去不复返。
当烈日落下，月亮清凉，
仍又转动，慰藉疲惫的眼。

月亮融入怡人的冬日，
将整年都更新了一番。
看看吧，洁白而恒久的月亮，
悬在肮脏的大地上边。

皎洁的月亮高悬，勇敢地翻转

在清澈流淌的气流之河上边，
时刻都在宣布圣诞来到，
还展示出白雪的壮观。

081 Vachel Lindsay
韦切尔·林赛

◆ *The Poet's Profile* （诗人小档案）

韦切尔·林赛（1879—1931）：美国诗人及现代歌唱诗歌的奠基人。林赛的作品收集在《〈威廉·布思将军进入了天堂〉及其他诗集》（1913）、《〈刚果河〉及其他诗集》（1914）、《每一个灵魂都是一个轮回》（1929）等中。

◆ *What the Scare-crow Said*

The dim-winged spirits of the night
Do fear and serve me well.
They creep from out the hedges of
The garden where I dwell.

I wave my arms across the walk.
The troops obey the sign,
And bring me shimmering shadow-robes
And cups of cowslip-wine.

Then dig a treasure called the moon,
A very precious thing,
And keep it in the air for me
Because I am a King.

◆ *Annotations* （原诗注释）

1. scare-crow: *n.* an object made to resemble a human figure, set up to scare birds away from a field where crops are growing 稻草人

2. dim: *adj.* (of a light, colour, or illuminated object) not shining brightly or clearly （光线、颜色或发光体）黯淡的；模糊的 （e.g. Her face was softened by the dim light. 在黯淡的灯光下，她脸部的线条变得柔和了。）

3. spirit: *n.* a fairy or sprite; a supernatural being 鬼怪；妖精；幽灵；神灵

4. creep: *v.* move slowly and carefully, especially in order to avoid being heard or noticed 蹑手蹑脚地行走；轻悄悄地移动 （e.g. He crept downstairs, hardly making any noise. 他蹑手蹑脚地下楼，几乎没发出什么声响。）

5. hedge: *n.* a fence or boundary formed by closely growing bushes or shrubs （矮树）树篱

6. dwell: *v.* live in or at a specified place （正式用法）居住；生活 （e.g. Groups of gypsies still dwell in these caves. 一些吉卜赛部落仍然住在这些山洞里。）

7. walk: *n.* a path 小路

8. troop: *n.* a group of people or animals of a particular kind 一群 （或一批）人（或动物） （e.g. a troop of musicians 一群音乐家）

9. shimmer: *v.* shine with a soft tremulous light 发微光 （e.g. The sea shimmered in the sunlight. 阳光照射下，海水闪着微光。）

10. robe: *n.* a long, loose outer garment worn, especially on formal or ceremonial occasions, as an indication of the wearer's rank, office, or profession （尤指在正式场合或礼仪场合穿的、标志穿衣者级别、职位或职业的）袍服；礼服

11. cowslip: *n.* a European primula with clusters of drooping fragrant yellow flowers in spring, growing on dry grassy banks and in pasture 黄花九轮草；立金花；报春花

◆ *A Lead-in Note* （简明导读）

诗人以拟人的手法，写出了稻草人眼中的月亮意象。唯我独尊的稻草人，想象力如孩子般丰富多彩。诗中的故事也许发生在一个万圣节的夜晚，月亮还没有完全发出光芒，居于花园之中的稻草人看不清黑夜精灵的翅膀，但这些精灵无疑都是稻草人的侍从，听从稻草人的指挥。吓“人”的稻草人，白昼驱鸟，为人所造，受人指使，却成了夜晚的主宰——精灵对其臣服，就算是悬空的月亮也成了稻草人的陪衬。

◆ 稻草人眼中的月亮

翅膀隐约的黑夜精灵，
惧怕我，服侍我，很周到。
精灵悄悄从花园树篱外
进入，花园是我的老巢。

我正对着小路挥动手臂，
精灵一行领会了这种信号，
为我带来微微发亮的影子礼服，
还端上一杯杯酒，黄花九轮草酿造。

接着，他们挖出一个宝贝
叫月亮，很珍贵，很稀少。
他们将之悬空，算是给了我，
因我是王，一切归我领导。

082 Vachel Lindsay
韦切尔·林赛

◆ *The Poet's Profile* （诗人小档案）

韦切尔·林赛（1879—1931）：美国诗人及现代歌唱诗歌的奠基人。林赛的作品收集在《〈威廉·布思将军进入了天堂〉及其他诗集》（1913）、《〈刚果河〉及其他诗集》（1914）、《每一个灵魂都是一个轮回》（1929）等中。

◆ *What Grandpa Mouse Said*

The moon's a holy owl-queen.
She keeps them in a jar
Under her arm till evening,
Then sallies forth to war.

She pours the owls upon us.
They hoot with horrid noise
And eat the naughty mousie-girls
And wicked mousie-boys.

So climb the moonvine every night
And to the owl-queen pray:
Leave good green cheese by moonlit trees
For her to take away.

And never squeak, my children,

Nor gnaw the smoke-house door:
The owl-queen then will love us
And send her birds no more.

◆ *Annotations* （原诗注释）

1. holy: *adj.* dedicated or consecrated to God or a religious purpose; sacred 献身于上帝（或宗教）的；尊崇上帝（或宗教）的；神圣的

2. owl: *n.* a nocturnal bird of prey with large eyes, a facial disc, a hooked beak, and typically a loud hooting call 鸱鸮；枭；猫头鹰

3. jar: *n.* a wide–mouthed cylindrical container made of glass or pottery, especially one used for storing food the contents of such a container 罐子，坛子；广口瓶

4. sally: *v.* (formal or humorous) set out from a place to do something （正式用法或幽默用法）动身；外出 （e.g. I made myself presentable and sallied forth. 我把自己打扮得像模像样出发了。）

5. hoot: *v.* (of an owl) utter a hoot （猫头鹰）叫

6. horrid: *adj.* causing horror 恐怖的；可怕的 （e.g. a horrid nightmare 可怕的梦魇）

7. naughty: *adj.* (especially of children) disobedient; badly behaved （尤指孩童）顽皮的；淘气的；不听话的

8. mousie: *n.* diminutive for mouse 小老鼠

9. wicked: *adj.* playfully mischievous 恶作剧的；淘气的；调皮的 （e.g. Ben has a wicked sense of humour. 本有一种恶作剧似的幽默感。）

10. vine: *n.* the slender stem of a trailing or climbing plant （蔓生植物或攀缘植物）藤；蔓

11. pray: *v.* wish or hope strongly for a particular outcome or situation 祈望；祈求

12. gnaw: *v.* bite at or nibble something persistently 咬；啃；啮

13. smoke-house: n. (chiefly N. Amer.) a shed or room for curing food by exposure to smoke （主要为北美用法）（熏制食品的）烟熏室

◆ *A Lead-in Note* （简明导读）

此诗中，鼠爷爷眼中的月亮是神圣的猫头鹰女王——世代与老鼠为敌的猫头鹰女王，以此吓唬那些不听话的淘气包：“鼠女孩”和“鼠男童”——那些吱吱叫、不停啃咬的小老鼠，俨然人类世界中大人以“恐吓”来哄小孩时的场景。在鼠爷爷的眼中，那猫头鹰女王胳膊下的坛子中藏匿的众鹰，就是月亮发出的光芒。月光一倾泻，鼠辈就遭殃。因此，鼠爷爷说：“在洒满月光的树旁放美味绿奶酪，让她带走，以保太平。”

◆ 鼠爷爷眼中的月亮

月亮是猫头鹰女王，很神圣，
将众鹰藏到胳膊下的坛子中，
一直藏到夜晚来临，
才开始动身出征。

她向我们将那些猫头鹰倾倒，
众鹰齐下，发出可怕的叫声，
吃掉了不听话的鼠女孩，
吃掉了顽皮的鼠男童。

因此，月亮藤每晚都爬上去，
祈求鹰女王手下留情：
在洒满月光的树旁放美味绿奶酪，
让她带走，以保太平。

好了，我的孩子，切莫吱吱叫，
也莫将烟熏食品屋的房门啃咬。
这样，鹰女王就会喜爱我们，
不再将她的鹰倾倒。

083 Vachel Lindsay
韦切尔·林赛

◆ *The Poet's Profile* （诗人小档案）

韦切尔·林赛（1879—1931）：美国诗人及现代歌唱诗歌的奠基人。林赛的作品收集在《〈威廉·布思将军进入了天堂〉及其他诗集》(1913)、《〈刚果河〉及其他诗集》(1914)、《每一个灵魂都是一个轮回》(1929)等中。

◆ *What the Rattlesnake Said*

The Moon's a little prairie-dog.
He shivers through the night.
He sits upon his hill and cries
For fear that I will bite.

The Sun's a broncho. He's afraid
Like every other thing,
And trembles morning, noon and night
Lest I should spring and sting.

◆ *Annotations* （原诗注释）

1. rattlesnake: *n.* a heavy-bodied American pit viper with a series of horny rings on the tail that produce a characteristic rattling sound when vibrated as a warn-

ing 响尾蛇

2. prairie: *n.* (American) a large open area of grassland, esp. in the Mississippi River valley （美国用法）大草原（尤其指密西西比河河谷一带）

3. shiver: *v.* (of a person or animal) shake slightly and uncontrollably as a result of being cold, frightened, or excited （人或动物因寒冷、惊吓或兴奋而）颤抖；哆嗦 （e.g. They shivered in the damp foggy cold. 他们在湿冷的雾天直哆嗦。）

4. broncho or bronco: *n.* a wild or half-tamed horse of the western US （美国西部地区的）野马；半驯化的马

◆ *A Lead-in Note* （简明导读）

此诗中，剧毒在身的响尾蛇，其眼中的月亮只不过是一只体形矮小的草原狗。月上枝头，在响尾蛇看来，是“他坐在自家山头哭号，怕我咬他一口”。别说月亮这只草原狗了，就算是大显神威的太阳这匹响尾蛇眼中的“野马”，也对响尾蛇恐惧有加。日升日落，在响尾蛇的眼中不过是“战栗不止”。之所以这样，响尾蛇认为太阳“唯恐我跳起，将他咬疼”。月亮是一面镜子，照到了响尾蛇的内心世界，那是一个“目中无人”的自我境地。

◆ 响尾蛇眼中的月亮

月亮是只矮小的草原狗，
走过黑夜，浑身颤抖。
他坐在自家山头哭嚎，
怕我咬他一口。

太阳是匹野马，但心存恐惧，
跟其他东西一样惊恐。
早晨、中午、晚上他都战栗不止，
唯恐我跳起，将他咬疼。

Chapter 11

What Different People Said about the Moon

第十一章

月因人异

084 Vachel Lindsay
韦切尔·林赛

◆ *The Poet's Profile* （诗人小档案）

韦切尔·林赛（1879—1931）：美国诗人及现代歌唱诗歌的奠基人。林赛的作品收集在《〈威廉·布思将军进入了天堂〉及其他诗集》（1913）、《〈刚果河〉及其他诗集》（1914）、《每一个灵魂都是一个轮回》（1929）等中。

◆ *What the Forester Said*

The moon is but a candle-glow
That flickers thro' the gloom:
The starry space, a castle hall:
And Earth, the children's room,
Where all night long the old trees stand
To watch the streams asleep:
Grandmothers guarding trundle-beds:
Good shepherds guarding sheep.

◆ *Annotations* （原诗注释）

1. forester: *n.* a person in charge of a forest or skilled in planting, managing, or caring for trees 林务员；林务官

2. glow: *n.* a steady radiance of light or heat 发出光（或热）（e.g. The setting sun cast a deep red glow over the city. 落日给城市上空投下一道深红色的霞光。）

3. flicker: *v.* (of a flame) burn fitfully, alternately flaring up and dying down（火焰）摇曳；忽隐忽现 （e.g. the flickering flames of the fire 闪烁不定的火焰）

4. thro' = through

5. gloom: *n.* (poetic/literary) a dark or shady place （诗/文用法）阴暗处

6. starry: *adj.* full of or lit by stars 布满星星的；星光照耀的 （e.g. a starry sky 繁星点点的天空）

7. castle: *n.* a large building or group of buildings fortified against attack with thick walls, battlements, towers, and in many cases a moat 城堡；堡垒

8. stream: *n.* a small, narrow river 小河；小溪

9. trundle–bed: *n.* a truckle bed 装有脚轮的床

10. shepherd: *n.* a person who tends and rears sheep 牧羊人

◆ *A Lead–in Note* （简明导读）

此诗中，护林员眼中的月亮就是“一支蜡烛在发光，摇曳的烛光穿过了黑暗”，照亮了星空，照亮了地球。地球上有护林员守护的树林，树林中“有古老的树整夜站岗，看着条条小溪入眠”。地球上还有“老奶奶守护着孩子的滚轮床，好羊倌守护着羊群的安全”。从护林员眼中的月亮意象，可见护林员的胸怀非同寻常。

◆ 护林员眼中的月亮

月亮不过是一支蜡烛在发光，
摇曳的烛光穿过了黑暗。
星空浩瀚，是城堡里的厅堂；
地球是孩子们的房间——
那里有古老的树整夜站岗，

看着条条小溪入眠。
老奶奶守护着孩子的滚轮床，
好羊倌守护着羊群的安全。

085 Vachel Lindsay
韦切尔·林赛

◆ *The Poet's Profile* （诗人小档案）

韦切尔·林赛（1879—1931）：美国诗人及现代歌唱诗歌的奠基人。林赛的作品收集在《〈威廉·布思将军进入了天堂〉及其他诗集》（1913）、《〈刚果河〉及其他诗集》（1914）、《每一个灵魂都是一个轮回》（1929）等中。

◆ *A Sense of Humor (Spoken by the Author in his own person)*

No man should stand before the moon,
To make sweet song thereon,
With dandified importance,
His sense of humor gone.

Nay, let him don the motley cap,
The jester's chastened mien,
If he would woo that looking-glass
And see what should be seen.

O mirror on fair Heaven's wall!
We find there what we bring;
So let us smile in honest part,
And deck our souls, and sing.

Yea, by the chastened jest alone
Will ghosts and terrors pass;
And fays, and merry friendly things
Throw kisses through the glass.

◆ *Annotations* （原诗注释）

1. thereon: *adv.* (formal) on or following from the thing just mentioned （正式用法）在其上；随即 （e.g. The order of the court and the taxation consequent thereon 法院的决议及其诉讼费用审定结果）

2. dandified: *adj.* self-consciously sophisticated or elaborate 精心制作；详细阐述的 （e.g. He writes a dandified prose. 他写一种华美的散文。）

3. nay: *adv.* (archaic or dialect) no （古旧用法或方言用法）不 （e.g. Nay, I must not think thus. 不，我可不能那样想。）

4. don: *v.* put on (an item of clothing) 穿上（一件衣服）(e.g. In the dressing room the players donned their football shirts. 在更衣室，队员们穿上了球衣。）

5. motley: *adj.* having many colors; variegated; parti-colored 杂色的；五颜六色的

6. jester: *n.* (historical) a professional joker or 'fool' at a medieval court, typically wearing a cap with bells on it and carrying a mock sceptre （历史上的用法）（中世纪宫廷）逗乐小丑

7. chastened: *adj.* subdued; humbled; refined or purified 缓和的；有节制的；精练的；经磨炼的

8. mien: *n.* a person's look or manner, especially one of a particular kind indicating their character or mood 风度；态度 （e.g. He has a cautious, academic mien. 他有谨慎的学者风度。）

9. woo: *v.* try to gain the love of (someone, typically a woman), especially with a view to marriage 向（女子）求爱；求婚

10. o: *interj.* used to express surprise or strong emotion 哦；哟；啊；唉；哎

呀 （表示惊讶或强烈的情感）

11. fair: *adj.* (of weather) fine and dry （天气）晴朗干爽的；宜人的

12. deck: *v.* decorate or adorn brightly or festively 装饰；打扮

13. yea: *adv.* used for emphasis, especially to introduce a stronger or more accurate word than one just used （用于强调）的确；诚然 （e.g. He was full, yea, crammed with anxieties. 的确，他忧心忡忡。）

14. fay: *n.* (poetic/literary) a fairy （诗/文用法）仙子；仙女

15. merry: *adj.* cheerful and lively 欢快的；兴高采烈的 （e.g. The narrow streets were dense with merry throngs of students. 狭窄的街道挤满了欢快的学生。）

◆ *A Lead-in Note* （简明导读）

诗人林赛以幽默的语气写出了诗人自己眼中的月亮意象，没有借助任何其他人或物的视角来述说，算是“名副其实”了。

月亮是一面镜子，在月亮面前，我们应装扮一番，表现出一丝幽默之感。

◆ 一丝幽默之感（诗人自己眼中的月亮）

谁都不应一站到月亮前，
就随即甜蜜地歌唱。
他若那样刻意自我突出，
则幽默之感尽丧。

行不通。若他向那面镜子求婚，
就会看到镜中自己的长相。
那样就给他戴顶杂色帽子吧，
那是逗乐小丑历经磨炼的模样。

啊，宜人的镜子！挂在天堂的墙壁，
那墙壁是我们找到随身之物的地方。
因此，让我们真诚地微笑吧，
装扮起灵魂，开始歌唱。

就这样。幽灵和恐惧都会经过
历经磨炼的逗乐小丑身旁。
仙女以及欢愉而友好的东西，
都向镜中飞吻，不受镜子的阻挡。

086 Vachel Lindsay
韦切尔·林赛

◆ *The Poet's Profile*（诗人小档案）

韦切尔·林赛（1879—1931）：美国诗人及现代歌唱诗歌的奠基人。林赛的作品收集在《〈威廉·布思将军进入了天堂〉及其他诗集》（1913）、《〈刚果河〉及其他诗集》（1914）、《每一个灵魂都是一个轮回》（1929）等中。

◆ *The Soul of the Gambler (What the Ghost of the Gambler Said)*

Where now the huts are empty,
Where never a camp-fire glows,
In an abandoned canyon
A gambler's ghost arose.

He muttered there, "The moon's a sack
Of dust." His voice rose thin:
"I wish I knew the miner man;
I'd play, and play to win.

"In every game in Cripple Creek
Of old, when stakes were high,
I held my own. Now I would play
For that sack in the sky.

"The sport would not be ended there.
'Twould rather be begun.
I'd bet my moon against His stars,
And gamble for the Sun."

◆ *Annotations* （原诗注释）

1. gambler: *n.* a person who wagers money on the outcome of games or sporting events 赌博者；赌徒 （e.g. The gambler bought off the police and thus was able to operate freely. 赌徒贿赂了警察，于是便可以毫无顾忌地赌博。）

2. hut: *n.* a small single-storey building of simple or crude construction, serving as a poor, rough, or temporary house or shelter （简陋的）小屋

3. glow: *v.* give out steady light without flame （没有火焰地）发光 （e.g. The tips of their cigarettes glowed in the dark. 他们的烟头在黑暗中闪光。）

4. canyon: *n.* a deep gorge, typically one with a river flowing through it, as found in North America （尤指北美有河流流过的）峡谷

5. mutter: *v.* say something in a low or barely audible voice, especially in dissatisfaction or irritation （尤指不满或愤怒时）小声地说；嘟哝；咕哝

6. thin: *adj.* (of a sound) faint and high-pitched （声音）细的；尖的 （e.g. a thin, reedy little voice 尖 细的微弱声音）

7. miner: *n.* a person who works in a mine 矿工

8. cripple: *n.* (archaic or offensive) a person who is unable to walk or move properly through disability or because of injury to their back or legs （古旧用法，含有冒犯之意）残疾人；跛子

9. creek: *n.* a stream, brook, or minor tributary of a river 小溪；小河；（河）小支流

10. of old: in or belonging to the past 过去的 （e.g. He was more reticent than of old. 他比过去更加沉默。）

11. stake: *n.* a sum of money or something else of value gambled on the out-

come of a risky game or venture 赌本；赌注

12. hold one's own: retain a position of strength in a challenging situation 坚守住；不退让

13. sport: *n.* (dated) entertainment; fun （古旧用法）娱乐；消遣；乐趣（e.g. It was considered great sport to catch him out. 抓出他的错误被认为是一大快事。）

14. 'Twould = It would

◆ *A Lead-in Note* （简明导读）

此诗中，月亮这面镜子照到了赌徒死后的世界，那是一个不减生前赌性甚至强过生前赌性的世界。在这个世界里，赌徒的鬼魂眼中的月亮是一袋尘埃，但这个赌博成性的家伙还是要赌，一袋尘埃也不放过，要"赢下空中那一袋子"。最后，贪得无厌的赌徒的鬼魂"要拿赢到手的月亮赌他那些星星，再为赢到太阳，赌上一局"。

◆ 赌徒的灵魂（赌徒的鬼魂眼中的月亮）

在一个遗弃的峡谷里，
一座座小屋现已空置，
营火也从未燃起来，
一个赌徒的鬼魂爬起。

他原地嘟囔："月亮是尘埃
一袋。"他的声音尖细：
"但愿我认识那位挖矿的家伙；
我要玩，玩赢全局。

"当时在跛河区每一场

赌局中，赌金很高之时，
我也不退让。眼下我要玩，
赢下空中那一袋子。

“乐趣不会就此而止，
而是刚刚才开始。
要拿赢的月亮赌他那些星星，
再为赢到太阳，赌上一局。”

087 Vachel Lindsay
韦切尔·林赛

◆ *The Poet's Profile* （诗人小档案）

韦切尔·林赛（1879—1931）：美国诗人及现代歌唱诗歌的奠基人。林赛的作品收集在《〈威廉·布思将军进入了天堂〉及其他诗集》（1913）、《〈刚果河〉及其他诗集》（1914）、《每一个灵魂都是一个轮回》（1929）等中。

◆ *What the Miner in the Desert Said*

The moon's a brazen water-keg,
A wondrous water-feast.
If I could climb the sands and drink
And give drink to my beast,

If I could drain that keg, the flies
Would not be biting so,
My burning feet be spry again,
My mule no longer slow,

And I could rise and dig for ore
And reach my fatherland,
And not be food for ants and hawks,
And perish in the sand.

◆ Annotations （原诗注释）

1. miner: *n.* a person who works in a mine 矿工

2. brazen: *adj.* (chiefly poetic/literary) made of brass （主要为诗/文用法）黄铜制的

3. keg: *n.* a small barrel, especially one of less than 10 gallons or (in the US) 30 gallons （尤指小于10加仑或美制30加仑的）小桶

4. wondrous: *adj.* (poetic/literary) inspiring a feeling of wonder or delight; marvelous （诗/文用法）令人惊奇的；奇妙的

5. feast: *n.* a large meal, typically one in celebration of something 庆宴；宴会

6. beast: (usu. beasts) a domestic animal, especially a bovine farm animal 家畜；耕牛

7. drain: *v.* (of a person) drink the entire contents of (a glass or other container) 喝干：喝光（杯子等）中的液体 (e.g. He seized the Scotch set before him and drained it. 他抓起面前的苏格兰威士忌一饮而尽。

8. spry: *adj.* (especially of an old person) active: lively （尤指老人）充满活力的；活跃的；精力充沛的

9. mule: *n.* the offspring of a donkey and a horse (strictly, a male donkey and a female horse), typically sterile and used as a beast of burden 骡；马骡

10. ore: *n.* a naturally occurring solid material from which a metal or valuable mineral can be extracted profitably 矿；矿石；矿砂

11. fatherland: *n.* a person's native country, especially when referred to in patriotic terms 祖国

12. hawk: *n.* a diurnal bird of prey with broad rounded wings and a long tail, typically taking prey by surprise with a short chase 鹰

13. perish: *v.* suffer death, typically in a violent, sudden, or untimely way 死亡（尤指暴死、猝死、夭折） (e.g. A great part of his army perished of hunger and disease. 他的大部分军队死于饥饿和疾病。)

◆ *A Lead-in Note* （简明导读）

此诗中，矿工奋战在干燥而炎热沙漠里，挥汗如雨，其眼中的月亮具有实用主义色彩：是一只小水桶，而且具有黄铜质地。在这位矿工的眼里，月亮不亚于是一场水的盛宴，引人入胜。赴完这场盛宴，一切都会不同。其中，“我灼痛的双脚又将恢复活力，我的那头骡子就不会再慢腾腾”。在矿工的眼里，月亮就是希望，就是力量的源泉，也是活下去的理由。

◆ 沙漠矿工眼中的月亮

月亮是黄铜质小水桶，
是一场水的盛宴，引人入胜。
要是我能爬上沙丘去喝，
让我家畜也喝尽兴，

我再将小桶喝干，就不会有
如此叮咬的飞蝇，
我灼痛的双脚又将恢复活力，
我的那头骡子就不会再慢腾腾。

那么，我就可起身挖完矿而归，
从此不再离乡背井；
那么，我就不会沦为蚁和鹰的口中物，
而猝死在沙漠之中。

088 Vachel Lindsay
韦切尔·林赛

◆ *The Poet's Profile* （诗人小档案）

韦切尔·林赛（1879—1931）：美国诗人及现代歌唱诗歌的奠基人。林赛的作品收集在《〈威廉·布思将军进入了天堂〉及其他诗集》(1913)、《〈刚果河〉及其他诗集》(1914)、《每一个灵魂都是一个轮回》(1929)等中。

◆ *The Moon Is Compared to a City (What the Tired Reformer Said)*

The moon's a perfect city, with
Curved walls encompassed round;
With yellow palaces upreared
Upon a glittering ground.

Sometimes a disk, a planet dead;
But on this splendid night,
When all the sky is shining clear,
When my whole heart is light,

I think it is a place for friends.
My soul is there in mirth,
With golden-robed good-citizens,
Far from the dusty earth.

Hail to the perfect city then!
I love your doors and domes,
Your turrets and your palaces,
Your terraces, your homes.

◆ *Annotations* （原诗注释）

1. reformer: *n.* a person who brings about reform, as in politics （政治）改良者；改革者

2. encompass: *v.* surround and have or hold within 环绕；围绕

3. uprear: *v.* to raise up; lift; to build; erect 举起；竖起；建起

4. glittering: *adj.* shining with a shimmering or sparkling light 发出微光的；闪烁的

5. mirth: *n.* amusement, especially as expressed in laughter 欢乐；欢笑 （e.g. His six-foot frame shook with mirth. 他那六英尺身躯乐得直抖。）

6. hail: *v.* to fall or shower like hai l 像冰雹一样落下

7. dome: *n.* (poetic/literary) a stately building （诗/文用法）雄伟的建筑物

8. turret: *n.* a small tower on top of a larger tower or at the corner of a building or wall, typically of a castle （尤指城堡的）角楼；塔楼

9. terrace: *n.* a level paved area next to a building; a patio （与建筑物相连的）露台；平台

◆ *A Lead-in Note* （简明导读）

诗人以第一人称的视角展示了改革家眼中的月亮意象。地球上的改革家在疲惫不堪之际，抬头看见了月亮。此时，在这样的改革家眼中月亮是一方净土，是一座完美的城。此时，这个“无生机的星球，有时似碟”，但在这个夜晚却不一般，因为“那里远离尘土飞扬的地球，公民守法，穿着金色长袍”，那是改革家的理想之地啊！此诗最后一节中，诗人转向了第二人称的

视角，如同月亮就在眼前，对其诉说衷肠："我爱你那里的门，还有建筑的壮观，我爱你那里的宫殿和塔楼，我爱你那里的露台和家中房间。"

◆ 月亮被比作一座城（疲惫的改革家眼中的月亮）

月亮是一座完美的城，周围
有弯弯曲曲的城墙环绕，
还有黄色的宫殿竖立于
闪着微光的地表。

无生机的星球，有时似碟，
但这个夜晚很奇妙：
闪闪发亮，天空清澈，
我的心轻松飘摇。

我想那座城里有朋友聚集，
在那儿我的心充满欢笑。
那里远离尘土飞扬的地球，
公民守法，穿着金色长袍。

那就奔向那座完美之城吧！
我爱你那里的门，还有建筑的壮观，
我爱你那里的宫殿和塔楼，
我爱你那里的露台和家中房间。

089 Vachel Lindsay
韦切尔·林赛

◆ *The Poet's Profile* （诗人小档案）

韦切尔·林赛（1879—1931）：美国诗人及现代歌唱诗歌的奠基人。林赛的作品收集在《〈威廉·布思将军进入了天堂〉及其他诗集》（1913）、《〈刚果河〉及其他诗集》（1914）、《每一个灵魂都是一个轮回》（1929）等中。

◆ *The Moon Is a Knight in Armor (What the Soldier Said)*

Oh, see the knight in armor,
Who keeps his visor down
And charges with a moon-beam spear
On hard hearts of the town;

Who makes the shabby fountain-square
A flowering, glimmering park,
Who pierces with a sharp-sweet dream
The crabbed minds and dark;

Who conquers those who see him not,
Their brooding heads bent down;
The knight whose scarcely-heeded strokes
Have cleansed and cleared the town!

◆ *Annotations* （原诗注释）

1. knight: *n.* (in the Middle Ages) a man raised by a sovereign to honourable military rank after service as a page and squire （中世纪的）骑士

2. armor: *n.* the metal coverings formerly worn by soldiers or warriors to protect the body in battle 盔甲

3. visor: *n.* a movable part of a helmet that can be pulled down to cover the face （头盔的）面甲；面罩

4. charge: *v.* rush forward in attack 冲锋 （e.g. The plan is to charge headlong at the enemy. 计划是向敌人猛烈冲锋。）

5. shabby: *adj.* in poor condition through long use or lack of care 破旧的；破烂的

6. fountain: *n.* an ornamental structure in a pool or lake from which one or more jets of water are pumped into the ai r 喷泉

7. glimmer: *v.* shine faintly with a wavering light 发出闪烁的微光 （e.g. pools of glimmering light 发出荧荧微光的池塘）

8. pierce: *v.* (of a sharp pointed object) go into or through (something) （锋利尖锐物体）刺入；刺破；刺穿

9. crabbed: *adj.* ill-humoured 乖戾的；易怒的

10. dark: *n.* nightfall 黄昏；夜幕 （e.g. I'll be home before dark. 我黄昏前会到家。）

11. brooding: *adj.* showing deep unhappiness of though t 忧思的；哀思的 （e.g. He stared with brooding eyes. 他用一双沉思的眼睛盯着看。）

12. heed: *v.* pay attention to; take notice of 注意；留心；关注；理会 （e.g. He should have heeded the warnings. 他本应听从警告才是。）

13. stroke: *n.* an act of hitting or striking someone or something; a blow 敲；打；击；打击

14. cleanse: *v.* make (something, especially the skin) thoroughly clean 彻底清洁（某物，尤指皮肤）；使（某物，尤指皮肤）清洁 （e.g. This preparation will cleanse and tighten the skin. 这种制剂会彻底清洁收紧肌肤。）

◆ A Lead-in Note（简明导读）

此诗中，月亮在士兵的眼中成了一名骁勇善战的骑士，只见“他将面部盔甲一拉到底，手持月光长矛，冲向城市坚固的中心区域”。征战之中的士兵，抬头望见月亮，月亮就成了士兵理想的寄托。月亮这位骑士所向披靡，战无不胜，就连其美梦也颇具攻击性：“他用尖尖的美梦/刺破黑暗和易怒的心地。”谁敢对月亮骑士视而不见，月亮骑士就将谁征服，并“令其将沉思的头颅放低”——因思考问题而忽视了月亮骑士的存在，也不行。月亮骑士的月光长矛，杀伤力惊人：“骑士的攻击几乎无人察觉，却彻底清理了整座城市。”

◆ 月亮是穿戴盔甲的骑士（士兵眼中的月亮）

啊，看那位穿戴盔甲的骑士：
他将面部盔甲一拉到底，
手持月光长矛，
冲向城市坚固的中心区域。

他将破败的喷泉广场变成
闪光的花园——花开遍地。
他用尖尖的美梦
刺破黑暗和易怒的心地。

他征服那些对他视而不见之辈，
令其将沉思的头颅放低。
骑士的攻击几乎无人察觉，
却彻底清理了整座城市。

090 Vachel Lindsay
韦切尔·林赛

◆ *The Poet's Profile* （诗人小档案）

韦切尔·林赛（1879—1931）：美国诗人及现代歌唱诗歌的奠基人。林赛的作品收集在《〈威廉·布思将军进入了天堂〉及其他诗集》(1913)、《〈刚果河〉及其他诗集》(1914)、《每一个灵魂都是一个轮回》(1929)等中。

◆ *Drying Their Wings (What the Carpenter Said)*

The moon's a cottage with a door—
Some folk can see it plain.
Look! You may catch a glint of light
A-sparkle through the pane,
Showing the place is brighter still
Within, though bright without.
There at a cosy open fire
Strange babes are grouped about:
The children of the Wind and Tide,
The urchins of the sky,
Drying their wings from storms and things
So they again can fly.

◆ Annotations （原诗注释）

1. carpenter: *n.* a person who makes and repairs wooden objects and structure s 木匠

2. cottage: *n.* a small simple house, typically one in the country （尤指乡村的）小屋；村舍

3. plain: *adj.* easy to perceive or understand; clear 明显的；明白的；清晰的；清楚的 （e.g. The advantages were plain to see. 优势显而易见。）

4. glint: *n.* a small flash of light, especially as reflected from a shiny surface （尤指光亮的表面等所发出的）微光 （e.g. the glint of gold in his teeth 他的金牙闪闪发光）

5. pane: *n.* a single sheet of glass in a window or door 窗玻璃片；框格玻璃

6. within: *adv.* inside; indoors 在里面；户内 （e.g. Enquire within. 请入内询洽。）

7. without: *adv.* (archaic or poetic/literary) outside （古旧用法或诗/文用法）在外面；在外部 （e.g. the enemy without 外面的敌人）

8. cosy: *adj.* giving a feeling of comfort, warmth, and relaxation 舒适的；温暖的；安逸的 （e.g. The flickering lamp gave the room a cosy lived-in air. 摇曳的灯光给房间一种温暖而有人气的感觉。）

9. group: *v.* put together or place in a group or groups 把……聚集到一起；使形成 （一个或多个）组（群、团体等）（e.g. Three wooden chairs were grouped around a dining table. 三把木椅子被放在餐桌周围。）

10. urchin: *n.* (archaic) a goblin （古旧用法）小精灵；小妖精

◆ A Lead-in Note （简明导读）

此诗中，月亮的意象是装有一扇门的村舍。这是木匠眼中的月亮意象，月亮仿佛是这位木匠的杰作。所以，木匠给孩子讲月亮的故事时，如数家珍。

月亮是一面镜子，照到了木匠的理想世界，照到了木匠那颗童真之心。

◆ 晾晒翅膀（木匠对孩子述说自己眼中的月亮）

月亮是座村舍，装门一扇，
有些乡亲能清楚看得见。
看呐！可瞥见一缕微光，
透过框格玻璃闪现。
这表明，村舍里面更加
明亮，尽管外面明亮一片。
那里，在一堆温馨的明火旁，
怪婴这里一组，那里一团。
他们是大风和海潮之子；
他们是天空的小精灵，成百上千。
暴风雨之类过后，他们晾晒翅膀，
期待能再次飞上天。

091 Vachel Lindsay
韦切尔·林赛

◆ *The Poet's Profile* （诗人小档案）

韦切尔·林赛（1879—1931）：美国诗人及现代歌唱诗歌的奠基人。林赛的作品收集在《〈威廉·布思将军进入了天堂〉及其他诗集》（1913）、《〈刚果河〉及其他诗集》（1914）、《每一个灵魂都是一个轮回》（1929）等中。

◆ *Yet Gentle Will the Griffin Be (What Grandpa Told the Children)*

The Moon? It is a griffin's egg,
Hatching tomorrow night;
And how the little boys will watch
With shouting and delight
To see him break the shell and stretch
And creep across the sky.
The boys will laugh, the little girls,
I fear, may hide and cry.
Yet gentle will the griffin be,
Most decorous and fat;
And walk up to the Milky Way
And lap it like a cat.

◆ *Annotations* （原诗注释）

1. griffin: *n.* a mythical creature with the head and wings of an eagle and the body of a lion, typically depicted with pointed ears and with the eagle's legs taking the place of the forelegs （神话中的）狮身鹰首兽

2. hatch: *v.* (of an egg) open and produce a young animal （蛋）孵化 （e.g. Eggs need to be put in a warm place to hatch. 蛋要放在温暖的地方孵化。）

3. creep: *v.* move slowly and carefully, especially in order to avoid being heard or noticed 蹑手蹑脚地行走；轻悄悄地移动 （e.g. He crept downstairs, hardly making any noise. 他蹑手蹑脚地下楼，几乎没发出什么声响。）

4. decorous: *adj.* in keeping with good taste and propriety; polite and restrained 得体的；有礼貌的；庄重的 （e.g. Charlotte gave David a decorous kiss. 夏洛特礼节性地吻了戴维一下。）

5. Milky Way: a faint band of light crossing the sky, made up of vast numbers of faint stars. It corresponds to the plane of our Galaxy, in which most of its stars are located 银河（系）

6. lap: *v.* (of an animal) take up (liquid) with the tongue in order to drink （动物）舔食（流体）

◆ *A Lead-in Note* （简明导读）

此诗中，老爷爷以孩子般童真，对孩子道出了他自己眼中的月亮意象。孩子们问老爷爷："月亮是啥?"老爷爷答："是狮身鹰首兽的卵，孵化时间是明天夜晚。"于是，孩子们就产生了好奇之心。小男孩会专心地看狮身鹰首兽这只神兽如何将卵孵化——月升的过程；"小女孩呢——我想，会躲藏，会大喊"说明小女孩或羞于观看，或者对这只神兽心存畏惧，"但狮身鹰首兽也很温柔"——这只神兽不总是凶猛恐怖的，有时还是"极其温文尔雅，肥胖饱满"的。不信你瞧："神兽踏上天河，如猫舔食——那里似乎有奶洒在路面。"

月亮是一面镜子，照到了老爷爷的童心，也照到了孩子们的好奇之心。

◆ 但狮身鹰首兽也很温柔（爷爷对孩子们讲他眼中的月亮）

月亮是啥？是狮身鹰首兽的卵，
孵化时间是明天夜晚。
在喊叫和喜悦之中，
小男孩会专心观看——
看着神兽破壳而出，肢体伸开，
然后穿越天空，行动缓慢。
小男孩放声大笑，小女孩呢——
我想，会躲藏，会大喊。
但狮身鹰首兽也很温柔，
极其温文尔雅，肥胖饱满。
神兽踏上天河，如猫舔食——
那里似乎有奶洒在路面。

092 Vachel Lindsay
韦切尔·林赛

◆ *The Poet's Profile* （诗人小档案）

韦切尔·林赛（1879—1931）：美国诗人及现代歌唱诗歌的奠基人。林赛的作品收集在《〈威廉·布思将军进入了天堂〉及其他诗集》(1913)、《〈刚果河〉及其他诗集》(1914)、《每一个灵魂都是一个轮回》(1929)等中。

◆ *The Beggar Speaks*

("What Mister Moon Said to Me.")

Come, eat the bread of idleness,
Come, sit beside the spring:
Some of the flowers will keep awake,
Some of the birds will sing.

Come, eat the bread no man has sought
For half a hundred years:
Men hurry so they have no griefs,
Nor even idle tears:

They hurry so they have no loves:
They cannot curse nor laugh —

Their hearts die in their youth with neither
Grave nor epitaph.

My bread would make them careless,
And never quite on time—
Their eyelids would be heavy,
Their fancies full of rhyme:

Each soul a mystic rose-tree,
Or a curious incense tree:
Come, eat the bread of idleness,
Said Mister Moon to me.

◆ *Annotations* （原诗注释）

1. beggar: *n.* a person, typically a homeless one, who lives by asking for money or food （尤指无家可归的）乞丐；叫花子

2. idleness: *n.* the trait of being idle out of a reluctance to work 懒惰；闲散；安逸

3. spring: *n.* a place where water or oil wells up from an underground source, or the basin or flow formed in such a way 泉

4. grief: *n.* trouble or difficulty, or an instance of this 烦恼；难事；悲伤的事

5. idle: *adj.* without purpose or effect; pointless 无目的的；无用的；无意义的 （e.g. He did not want to waste valuable time in idle chatter. 他不想把宝贵的时间浪费在毫无意义的闲聊上。）

6. grave: *n.* a place of burial for a dead body, typically a hole dug in the ground and marked by a stone or mound 墓穴；坟墓

7. epitaph: *n.* a phrase or form of words written in memory of a person who has died, especially as an inscription on a tombstone 纪念死者的文字；碑文

8. careless: *adj.* showing no interest or effort; casual 不感兴趣的，不做努力的；随意的 （e.g. She gave a careless shrug. 她随意地耸耸肩。）

9. eyelid: *n.* each of the upper and lower folds of skin which cover the eye when closed 眼皮；眼睑

10. fancy: *n.* a thing that one supposes or imagines, typically an unfounded or tentative belief or idea 想象出来的事物 （尤指无根据或不成熟的看法、观点）（e.g. I've a fancy they want to be alone. 我猜他们不想被打扰。）

11. mystic: *adj.* of or relating to religious mysteries or occult rites and practices 神秘的；玄妙的 （e.g. He is interested in mystic rites and ceremonies. 他对神秘的仪式感兴趣。）

12. curious: *adj.* strange; unusual 奇特的；离奇古怪的 （e.g. a curious sensation overwhelmed her. 一种奇怪的感觉笼罩了她。）

13. incense: *n.* a gum, spice, or other substance that is burned for the sweet smell it produces 香（树脂、香料等燃烧可得香气的物质）

◆ *A Lead-in Note* （简明导读）

在乞丐眼里，月亮就是一块圆面包，可以不劳而获。但这块面包却是夜晚泉水中的月亮，是一块“半个世纪时光里/没有谁成功得到过的面包”。乞丐透过月亮这块面包，窥见了尘世的炎凉。

◆ 乞丐眼中的月亮

（“是月亮先生对我说的。”）

来吧，不劳而获吃面包；
来吧，在泉水边坐好：
有些花儿会继续开，
有些鸟儿会鸣叫。

来吧，吃半个世纪时光里
没有谁成功得到过的面包：
人人来去匆匆，故无悲伤，
也不无缘无故把泪掉。

人人来去匆匆，故无爱可言：
他们无脏话，更无欢笑；
年纪轻轻，他们的心就死去，
无坟墓筑起，更无碑文可考。

我的面包，他们毫无关心，
我也从未按时吃到——
他们的眼皮沉重起来，
幻觉中充满了韵律的味道：

每个人都是玫瑰树，都很神秘；
抑或散香的树，都很了不起。
来吧，不劳而获吃面包，
月亮先生这样对我说道。

093 Vachel Lindsay
韦切尔·林赛

◆ *The Poet's Profile* （诗人小档案）

韦切尔·林赛（1879—1931）：美国诗人及现代歌唱诗歌的奠基人。林赛的作品收集在《〈威廉·布思将军进入了天堂〉及其他诗集》(1913)、《〈刚果河〉及其他诗集》(1914)、《每一个灵魂都是一个轮回》(1929)等中。

◆ *The Scissors-grinder (What the Tramp Said)*

The old man had his box and wheel
For grinding knives and shears.
No doubt his bell in village streets
Was joy to children's ears.

And I bethought me of my youth
When such men came around,
And times I asked them in, quite sure
The scissors should be ground.

The old man turned and spoke to me,
His face at last in view.
And then I thought those curious eyes
Were eyes that once I knew.

"The moon is but an emery-wheel
To whet the sword of God,"
He said, "and here beside my fire
I stretch upon the sod

"Each night, and dream, and watch the stars
And watch the ghost-clouds go,
And see the sword of God in Heaven
A-waving to and fro.

"I see that sword each century, friend.
It means the world-war comes,
With all its bloody wicked chiefs
And hate-inflaming drums.

"Men talk of Peace, but I have seen
That emery-wheel turn round.
The voice of Abel cries again
To God from out the ground.

"The ditches must flow red, the Plague
Go stark and screaming by,
Each time the sword of God takes edge
Within the midnight sky.

"And those that scorned their brothers here
And sowed a wind of shame
Will reap the whirlwind as of old,
And face relentless flame."

And thus the scissors-grinder spoke,
His face at last in view.

And there beside the railroad-bridge
I saw the Wandering Jew.

◆ *Annotations* （原诗注释）

1. grinder: *n.* a person employed to grind cutlery, tools, or cereals （磨刀剪、工具、谷物等的）磨工

2. tramp: *n.* a person who travels from place to place on foot in search of work or as a vagrant or beggar 漂泊者；流浪汉；乞丐

3. grind: *v.* sharpen, smooth, or produce (something) by crushing or by friction 打磨；磨快；磨光 （e.g. Power from a waterwheel was used to grind cutlery. 水轮产生的动力用来磨刀。）

4. shear: *n.* (often shears) a pair of scissors （大）剪刀

5. bethink: *v.* (bethink oneself) (formal or archaic) come to think （正式用法或古旧用法）想起；思考；考虑 （e.g. He bethought himself of the verse from the Book of Proverbs. 他想起了《圣经》中《箴言》篇里的诗节。）

6. emery: *n.* denoting materials coated with emery for polishing, smoothing, or grinding （打磨材料）涂金刚砂的 （e.g. emery paper 砂纸）

6. whet: *v.* sharpen the blade of (a tool or weapon) 磨快；磨 （工具或武器）

7. fire: *n.* a collection of fuel, especially coal or wood, burnt in a controlled way to provide heat or a means for cooking （尤指烧煤或木柴的）炉火；灶火

8. sod: *n.* (the sod) the surface of the ground, with the grass growing on it 草皮

9. to and fro: in a constant movement backwards and forwards or from side to side 来来往往地；往复地 （e.g. She cradled him, rocking him to and fro. 她把他放在摇篮里，不停地摇着。）

10. chief: *n.* a leader or ruler of a people or clan （民族或部落）首领；酋长

11. inflame: *v.* provoke (someone) to strong feelings 激起……的强烈感情 （e.g. Her sister was inflamed with jealousy. 她姐姐因忌妒而发怒了。）

12. Abel: *n.* (in the Bible) the second son of Adam and Eve, murdered by his

brother Cain 《圣经》中的亚伯（亚当和夏娃的第二子，被其兄该隐所杀）

13. ditch: *n.* a narrow channel dug in the ground, typically used for drainage alongside a road or the edge of a field 沟；壕

14. plague: *n.* a contagious disease that spreads rapidly and kills many people 瘟疫

15. stark: *adj.* unpleasantly or sharply clear; impossible to avoid 光秃的；空荡荡的；明显的；无掩饰的

16. scream: *v.* give a long, loud, piercing cry or cries expressing extreme emotion or pain 尖叫

17. sow: *v.* verb plant (seed) by scattering it on or in the earth 播（种）

18. reap: *v.* (figurative) receive (a reward or benefit) as a consequence of one's own or other people's actions （比喻用法）获得；收到；得到（报答或好处）

19. whirlwind: *n.* a column of air moving rapidly round and round in a cylindrical or funnel shape 旋风

20. of old: in or belonging to the past 过去的 （e.g. He was more reticent than of old. 他比过去更加沉默。）

21. relentless: *adj.* never ending; oppressively constant 不间断的；持续的

22. Jew: *n.* a member of the people and cultural community whose traditional religion is Judaism and who trace their origins to the ancient Hebrew people of Israel 犹太人

◆ *A Lead-in Note* （简明导读）

此诗中，流浪汉跟走街串巷磨剪刀的匠人有着基本相同的人生境遇：四处游荡以谋生。因此，流浪汉看到磨剪刀老者的到来，给孩子们的童年带来欢乐时，不由得想起了自己的年轻时光。从跟老者的交谈中，流浪汉得知磨剪刀匠人眼中的月亮意象，以及这种意象的象征意义。月亮是一面镜子，照到了战争的残酷，照到了流浪汉、磨剪刀匠人等普通人的渴望，那就是和平。

◆ 磨剪刀匠人（流浪汉的述说）

老者在车轮子上架起箱子，
四处磨刀、磨剪子去。
乡村的街道上，他的铃声
无疑是孩童耳中的乐趣。

就此，我想起自己年轻时，
这样的匠人绕行而至。
多次请他们进屋，我清楚：
需要他们来磨剪子。

老者转过身，跟我交谈，
他的脸最终显现。
我想，在哪里我曾经
见过他那双好奇的眼。

“月亮不过是只砂轮，
用来打磨上帝之剑。”
他接着说：“在这儿的炉火旁，
在这块草皮上，我每晚

“都舒展四肢而卧，做梦，看星星，
看着幽灵一样的云飘远。
还看见在天空之中来回
舞动的那把上帝之剑。

“朋友，每世纪中我见到那把剑时，
都意味着世界战争的开场。

首领个个都邪恶之极，
憎恨之火激起，战鼓阵阵敲响。

“人们谈论和平，但我已看见
那只砂轮变圆的样子。
亚伯又向上帝呼喊，
声音传来——从大地那里。

“壕沟里一定有鲜血流淌，瘟疫
肆虐，呼啸着来袭。
上帝之剑每次在午夜的天空
磨得锋利，都会如此。

“那些蔑视自家兄弟之人，在此
埋下了耻辱之风的种子。
像过往一样，收获的果实将是旋风，
面临的大火也将无休止。”

就这样，磨剪刀匠人跟我交谈，
他的脸最终显现。
就在那儿的铁路桥旁，
那个游荡的犹太人进入我的视线。

094 Vachel Lindsay
韦切尔·林赛

◆ *The Poet's Profile* （诗人小档案）

韦切尔·林赛（1879—1931）：美国诗人及现代歌唱诗歌的奠基人。林赛的作品收集在《〈威廉·布思将军进入了天堂〉及其他诗集》(1913)、《〈刚果河〉及其他诗集》(1914)、《每一个灵魂都是一个轮回》(1929)等中。

◆ *What the Young Rhymer Said*

No poet spent with visions,
Bit by the City's teeth,
Laughing at fortune, seeking
Fame and the singer's wreath,
But must grow brave this evening,
Humming a wilder tune,
Armed against men and nations.
Why? He beholds the moon!

◆ *Annotations* （原诗注释）

1. rhymer: *n.* a writer who composes rhymes; a maker of poor verses (usually used as terms of contempt for minor or inferior poets) 作诗者；打油诗人

2. spent: *adj.* having no power or energy left 耗尽的；精疲力竭的 (e.g. The

movement has become a spent force. 这场运动势头已尽，再无作为了。)

3. vision: *n.* (often visions) a vivid mental image, especially a fanciful one of the future （尤指对未来的）幻想；梦想

4. bite: *v.* (of an animal or a person) use the teeth in order to inflict injury （动物或人）咬伤

5. wreath: *n.* an arrangement of flowers, leaves, or stems fastened in a ring and used for decoration or for laying on a grave 花圈；花环；花冠

6. hum: *v.* sing with closed lips 哼曲子 （e.g. She was humming a cheerful tune. 她哼着一首快乐的曲子。）

7. behold: *v.* (archaic or poetic/literary) see or observe (someone or something, especially of remarkable or impressive nature) （古旧用法或诗/文用法）看；观看（尤指看非凡的或感人的人或事物） （e.g. The botanical gardens were a wonder to behold. 植物园是值得一看的奇观。）

◆ *A Lead-in Note* （简明导读）

此诗中，年轻诗人眼中的月亮意象跟磨剪刀匠人眼中的月亮意象如出一辙：月亮是磨刀石，在月圆之时将上帝之剑磨得锋利。月圆之时是“世界战争”开场之际，是生灵涂炭之时。年轻的诗人血气方刚，年轻气盛。他们嘲笑命运，追求声望，充满幻想。他们不会被“城市的牙齿”咬伤。这里的“城市的牙齿”可能是指文明社会中的各种艰难险阻和荆棘坎坷。但是，今晚月圆，年轻的诗人要丢掉幻想，放弃名誉，武装起来去对抗士兵和强敌，以捍卫家园。要放下“靡靡之音”般的诗句，转而“将更狂野的曲调哼唱”，因为他们“看见了月亮”。

◆ 年轻诗人眼中的月亮

没有哪位诗人会垮下，因为幻想；
没有哪位诗人会被城市的牙齿咬伤。
不会的，哪怕他嘲笑命运，追求
诗人的桂冠称号和声望。
可今晚，他必须勇敢起来，
将更狂野的曲调哼唱；
武装起来，对抗士兵和民族。
为什么？他看见了月亮。

095 Vachel Lindsay 韦切尔·林赛

◆ *The Poet's Profile* （诗人小档案）

韦切尔·林赛（1879—1931）：美国诗人及现代歌唱诗歌的奠基人。林赛的作品收集在《〈威廉·布思将军进入了天堂〉及其他诗集》（1913）、《〈刚果河〉及其他诗集》（1914）、《每一个灵魂都是一个轮回》（1929）等中。

◆ *The Strength of the Lonely (What the Mendicant Said)*

The moon's a monk, unmated,
Who walks his cell, the sky.
His strength is that of heaven-vowed men
Who all life's flames defy.

They turn to stars or shadows,
They go like snow or dew—
Leaving behind no sorrow—
Only the arching blue.

◆ *Annotations* （原诗注释）

1. strength: *n.* the number of people comprising a group, typically a team or army（团体的，尤指球队或军队的）实力；人数 （e.g. The peacetime strength of the army

was 415,000. 那支军队和平时期的人数是415000。)

2. mendicant: *n.* a member of a mendicant order 托钵修士

3. monk: *n.* a member of a religious community of men typically living under vows of poverty, chastity, and obedience 修道士；僧侣

4. walk: *v.* travel along or over (a route or area) on foot 沿（某线路）行走；走过（某地区）(e.g. The police department has encouraged officers to walk the beat. 警察局鼓励警官沿划定路线步行巡逻。)

5. cell: *n.* a small room in which a prisoner is locked up or in which a monk or nun sleeps 单人牢房；（修士、修女睡的）单人小室

6. defy: *v.* openly resist or refuse to obey 公然反抗；藐视 （e.g. a woman who defies convention 反传统的女子）

7. dew: *n.* tiny drops of water that form on cool surfaces at night, when atmospheric vapour condenses 露；露滴；露水 （e.g. The grass was wet with dew. 草地被露水打湿了。)

8. blue: *n.* (poetic/literary) the sky or sea, or the unknown （诗/文用法）天空；大海；未知世界 （e.g. Far out upon the blue were many sails. 大海远处有许多帆船。)

◆ *A Lead-in Note* （简明导读）

托钵修士（mendicant或mendicant friar），也译作“化缘修士”“乞食修士”等，属“托钵修会”或“乞食修会”（基督教的一大派别天主教的一个分支）的成员。他们号召人民要安于贫困，忠于上帝，以托钵乞食为生。他们眼中的月亮，俨然具有他们自身的特点：终身不娶的独行僧，其居室是辽阔的天空，供其自由自在地游荡。

◆ 孤独者的实力（托钵修士眼中的月亮）

月亮是独行僧，一妻未娶，
行走于天空——他的居室。

有些人藐视人生烈焰，誓忠于神，
他集这些人的实力于一体。

他们转向阴影或星星，
最终消失，似雪或似露。
身后不留半点悲哀，
唯有苍穹映入眼目。

096 Vachel Lindsay
韦切尔·林赛

◆ *The Poet's Profile* （诗人小档案）

韦切尔·林赛（1879—1931）：美国诗人及现代歌唱诗歌的奠基人。林赛的作品收集在《〈威廉·布思将军进入了天堂〉及其他诗集》（1913）、《〈刚果河〉及其他诗集》（1914）、《每一个灵魂都是一个轮回》（1929）等中。

◆ *What the Sexton Said*

Our dust will be upon the wind
Within some certain years,
Though you be sealed in lead to-day
Amid the country's tears.

When this idyllic churchyard
Becomes the heart of town,
The place to build garage or inn,
They'll throw your tombstone down.

Your name so dim, so long outworn,
Your bones so near to earth,
Your sturdy kindred dead and gone,
How should men know your worth?

So read upon the runic moon
Man's epitaph, deep-writ.
It says the world is one great grave.
For names it cares no whit.

It tells the folk to live in peace,
And still, in peace, to die.
At least, so speaks the moon to me,
The tombstone of the sky.

◆ *Annotations* （原诗注释）

1. dust: *n.* (poetic/literary) a dead person's remains （诗/文用法）尸骨；遗骸（e.g. Scatter my dust and ashes. 散去我的遗骸和骨灰。）

2. lead: *n.* a heavy bluish-grey soft ductile metal, the chemical element of atomic number 82. （化学元素）铅（符号：Pb）

3. sexton: *n.* a person who looks after a church and churchyard, typically acting as bell-ringer and gravedigger （照管教堂和教堂庭院墓地，主要从事敲钟、挖墓穴等工作的）教堂司事

4. idyllic: *adj.* (especially of a time or place) like an idyll; extremely happy, peaceful, or picturesque 田园式的；（生活）平静快乐的；（风景）宁静如画的（e.g. an attractive hotel in an idyllic setting 坐落于宁静如画环境里的迷人旅店）

5. churchyard: *n.* an enclosed area enclosed surrounding a church, especially as used for burials 教堂庭院（尤指墓地）

6. inn: *n.* a public house, typically one in the country, in some cases providing accommodation （尤指乡村的）酒馆；客栈

7. dim: *adj.* not clearly recalled or formulated in the mind （记忆或想法）不清晰的；模糊的 （e.g. She had dim memories of that time. 她对那时还有模糊的记忆。）

8. outworn: *adj.* out of date 过时的

9. sturdy: *adj.* showing confidence and determination 坚定的；坚强的；刚毅的（e.g. The townspeople have a sturdy independence. 市民们有坚定的独立精神。）

10. kindred: *n.* one's family and relations 亲戚；亲属

11. runic: *adj.* relating to or consisting of a similar mark of mysterious or magic significance to letters of an ancient Germanic alphabet, related to the Roman alphabet （与如尼字母相似的）神秘符号的；魔力符号的

12. epitaph: *n.* a phrase or form of words written in memory of a person who has died, especially as an inscription on a tombstone 纪念死者的文字；碑文

13. writ: *v.* (archaic) past participle of write （古旧用法）"write" 的过去分词

14. whit: *n.* a very small part or amount 一点点；丝毫 （e.g. The last whit of warmth was drawn off by the setting sun. 夕阳带走了最后一丝温暖。）

◆ *A Lead-in Note* （简明导读）

教堂司事主要负责打理教堂的墓园。在教堂司事眼里，月亮就是一座墓碑石的意象，这块墓碑石类似于其每天打理的教堂墓园中的墓碑石，不过月亮这块墓碑石上刻的是一些神秘的文字符号，这些符号是为人类书写的碑文。当然，教堂司事看不懂这些碑文的内容，只能在无人的夜晚听月亮述说碑文的内容。

◆ 教堂司事眼中的月亮

若干年内，我们的遗骸
将会随风而逝。
哪怕如今在乡亲们的哭声中
以铅封存，也是如此。

当这座田园般教堂墓园

变为城市中心区域，
车库或酒馆建在上边，
他们会将你的墓碑一推了事。

你的名字太模糊，磨蚀时间太久，
你的尸骨太靠近陆地表皮，
你最亲的人都死无寻处，
你的价值如何让人得知？

那就读一读月亮上的神秘字符——
人类的碑文，是深深刻下的字迹。
月亮说，这个世界是座巨大的坟，
里面葬着谁，月亮丝毫不在意。

月亮告诉世人要安宁地生活，
还要安宁地死去。
最起码，对我如是说的，是月亮——
天空的墓碑石。

097 Vachel Lindsay
韦切尔·林赛

◆ *The Poet's Profile* （诗人小档案）

韦切尔·林赛（1879—1931）：美国诗人及现代歌唱诗歌的奠基人。林赛的作品收集在《〈威廉·布思将军进入了天堂〉及其他诗集》（1913）、《〈刚果河〉及其他诗集》（1914）、《每一个灵魂都是一个轮回》（1929）等中。

◆ *What Semiramis Said*

The moon's a steaming chalice,
Of honey and venom-wine.
A little of it sipped by night
Makes the long hours divine.
But oh, my reckless lovers,
They drain the cup and wail,
Die at my feet with shaking limbs
And tender lips all pale.
Above them in the sky it bends
Empty and gray and dead.
To-morrow night 'tis full again,
Golden, and foaming red.

◆ *Annotations* （原诗注释）

1. Semiramis: *n.* (Greek Mythology) the daughter of an Assyrian goddess who married an Assyrian king. After his death she ruled for many years and became one of the founders of Babylon. She is thought to have been based on the historical queen Sammuramat (c.800 bc) （希腊神话）塞米勒米司：嫁给亚述国王的亚述女神之女。国王死后，她统治多年，成为巴比伦王国的创立者之一，她的原型被认为是历史上的女王塞姆拉迈特（约公元前800年）。

2. steaming: *adj.* giving off steam 冒蒸汽的 （e.g. a basin of steaming water 一盆冒着蒸汽的水）

3. chalice: *n.* (historical) a large cup or goblet, typically used for drinking wine （历史上的用法）大酒杯；高脚杯

4. venom: *n.* poisonous fluid secreted by animals such as snakes and scorpions and typically injected into prey or aggressors by biting or stinging （毒蛇、蝎子等分泌的）毒液

5. sip: *v.* drink (something) by taking small mouthfuls 小口地喝；啜饮；呷；抿

6. divine: *adj.* supremely good or beautiful; magnificent 神妙的；美妙的；绝世的

7. oh: *exc.* used to express a range of emotions including surprise, anger, disappointment, or joy, or when reacting to something that has just been said（表示惊讶、愤怒、失望、高兴等感情）噢；啊；哦；唉；哎呀

8. reckless: *adj.* (of a person or their actions) without thinking or caring about the consequences of an action （人或其行动）不顾后果的；鲁莽的；胡乱的；草率的；马马虎虎的

9. drain: *v.* (of a person) drink the entire contents of (a glass or other container) 喝干；喝光（杯子等）中的液体 （e.g. He seized the Scotch set before him and drained it. 他抓起面前的苏格兰威士忌一饮而尽。）

10. wail: *v.* give such a cry of pain, grief, or anger 恸哭；哀号；号啕

11. 'tis = it is

12. foaming: emitting or filled with bubbles as from carbonation or fermentation 布满泡沫的；冒出泡沫的 （e.g. bubbling champagne 冒着泡沫的香槟酒）

◆ *A Lead-in Note* （简明导读）

在美貌的塞米勒米司眼中，月亮成了一只杯子，里面盛的是毒酒。当然，毒酒里掺进了蜜汁，令其追求者欲罢不能，一饮而尽，成了她的爱情“俘虏”。

◆ 塞米勒米司眼中的月亮

月亮是只冒着气的大杯子，
杯里装的是毒酒加蜜汁。
黑夜仅抿了一小口，
就令悠长的时光曼妙无比。
哎呀，我那些莽撞的情人啊，
一饮而尽，却哀号不止，
四肢抽搐着，死在我的脚下：
柔弱的双唇苍白无力。
上方的天空里，弯弯的月亮
空洞而灰白，失去了生机。
明晚到来，月亮之杯再次满盈，
金灿灿又红彤彤，泡沫满溢。

098 Vachel Lindsay
韦切尔·林赛

◆ *The Poet's Profile* （诗人小档案）

韦切尔·林赛（1879—1931）：美国诗人及现代歌唱诗歌的奠基人。林赛的作品收集在《〈威廉·布思将军进入了天堂〉及其他诗集》（1913）、《〈刚果河〉及其他诗集》（1914）、《每一个灵魂都是一个轮回》（1929）等中。

◆ *What the Gray-winged Fairy Said*

The moon's a gong, hung in the wild,
Whose song the fays hold dear.
Of course you do not hear it, child.
It takes a FAIRY ear.

The full moon is a splendid gong
That beats as night grows still.
It sounds above the evening song
Of dove or whippoorwill.

◆ *Annotations* （原诗注释）

1. fairy: *n.* a small imaginary being of human form that has magical powers, especially a female one 小仙子；小仙女；小精灵

2. gong: *n.* a metal disc with a turned rim, giving a resonant note when struck 锣

3. wild: *n.* (the wild) a natural state or uncultivated or uninhabited region 天然状态；未开垦地区；蛮荒之地；荒地 （e.g. Kiwis are virtually extinct in the wild. 鹬鸵在野外几乎灭绝了。）

4. fay: *n.* (poetic/literary) a fairy （诗/文用法）仙子；仙女

5. fairy: *adj.* belonging to, resembling, or associated with fairies 属于（或关于）仙女的；仙女般的；有魔力的；精灵鬼怪的

6. whippoorwill: *n.* a North and Central American nightjar with a distinctive call 三声夜鹰；北美夜鹰

◆ *A Lead-in Note* （简明导读）

长有一双灰翅膀的仙女，有着超凡的想象和能力。在这位仙女的眼中，月亮是一面锣，“锣鸣如歌，仙女惜爱。”这样的声音，只有仙女的耳朵听得见，而普通人恐怕只能看到月亮和月光了。

完美的锣则是满月。月圆之夜，“夜深人静后，敲锣声传开。”高高在上的仙女听到“那声音在上方响起”，当然还有下方“鸽和鹰的夜晚之歌传来”。一切都是那么和谐。

◆ 灰翅膀仙女眼中的月亮

月亮是一面锣，悬挂于野外；
锣鸣如歌，仙女惜爱。
当然，孩子，你听不见；
你没长仙魔耳，能听见才怪。

满月是一面完美的锣，
夜深人静后，敲锣声传开。
那声音在上方响起，下方有
鸽和鹰的夜晚之歌传来。

099 Vachel Lindsay
韦切尔·林赛

◆ *The Poet's Profile* （诗人小档案）

韦切尔·林赛（1879—1931）：美国诗人及现代歌唱诗歌的奠基人。林赛的作品收集在《〈威廉·布思将军进入了天堂〉及其他诗集》（1913）、《〈刚果河〉及其他诗集》（1914）、《每一个灵魂都是一个轮回》（1929）等中。

◆ *What the Coal-heaver Said*

The moon's an open furnace door
Where all can see the blast,
We shovel in our blackest griefs,
Upon that grate are cast
Our aching burdens, loves and fears
And underneath them wait
Paper and tar and pitch and pine
Called strife and blood and hate.

Out of it all there comes a flame,
A splendid widening light.
Sorrow is turned to mystery
And Death into delight.

◆ *Annotations* （原诗注释）

1. heaver: *n.* a workman who heaves freight or bulk goods (especially at a dockyard) 举起者；挑夫

2. furnace: *n.* an enclosed structure in which material can be heated to very high temperatures 火炉；熔炉

3. blast: *n.* a strong current of air used in smelting （冶炼时用的）鼓风；吹风

4. shovel: *v.* move (coal, earth, snow, or similar) with a shovel 铲（煤、土、雪或类似之物）(e.g. She shovelled coal on the fire. 她把煤铲到火上。)

5. black: *adj.* (of a person's state of mind) full of gloom or misery; very depressed （心境）忧郁的；悲凉的；极为沮丧的 (e.g. Jean had disappeared and Mary was in a black mood. 吉恩走后，玛丽郁郁寡欢。)

6. grate: *n.* the recess of a fireplace or furnace 壁炉（或熔炉）的炉膛

7. tar: *n.* a dark, thick flammable liquid distilled from wood or coal, consisting of a mixture of hydrocarbons, resins, alcohols, and other compounds 柏油

8. pitch: *n.* a sticky resinous black or dark brown substance semi-liquid when hot, hard when cold, obtained by distilling tar or turpentine and used for waterproofing 沥青

9. strife: *n.* angry or bitter disagreement over fundamental issues; conflict 冲突；争吵；争斗；不和 (e.g. strife within the community 社区内部的冲突)

10. mystery: *n.* the condition or quality of being secret, strange, or difficult to explain 神秘性；神秘；隐秘性；不可思议性 (e.g. Much of her past is shrouded in mystery. 她过去的许多经历都笼罩在神秘之中。)

◆ *A Lead-in Note* （简明导读）

添煤工平凡无奇，做着简单而重复的繁重工作：往炉膛中添煤，但当他们抬头望见月亮，却心生不凡的想法。在添煤工的眼中，“月亮是一扇敞开

的锅炉门，人人都能看到炉内气流阵阵”。实质上，月亮是一种象征，令他们转忧为喜。他们用铲子像铲煤一样将“最悲凉的忧伤”，令他们“疼痛的负担、爱情和恐惧”，还有“争斗、流血和憎恨”，统统铲进月亮这扇锅炉门，让其在锅炉内部燃烧殆尽。

所以，在添煤工看来，人生的一切烦恼和不快，都可以铲进月亮里，月亮令人生变得美好。

◆ 添煤工眼中的月亮

月亮是一扇敞开的锅炉门，
人人都能看到炉内气流阵阵。
我们将最悲凉的忧伤铲入，
再往那个炉膛里抛进
令我们疼痛的负担、爱情和恐惧——
下面一层紧贴着它们，
是纸张、柏油、沥青和松木，
统称为争斗、流血和憎恨。

火焰蹿出，四处蔓延，
光线扩散，精彩绝伦。
悲伤转变成神秘，
死亡则转变成欢欣。

100 Vachel Lindsay
韦切尔·林赛

◆ *The Poet's Profile* （诗人小档案）

韦切尔·林赛（1879—1931）：美国诗人及现代歌唱诗歌的奠基人。林赛的作品收集在《〈威廉·布思将军进入了天堂〉及其他诗集》（1913）、《〈刚果河〉及其他诗集》（1914）、《每一个灵魂都是一个轮回》（1929）等中。

◆ *A Net to Snare the Moonlight (What the Man of Faith Said)*

The dew, the rain and moonlight
All prove our Father's mind.
The dew, the rain and moonlight
Descend to bless mankind.

Come, let us see that all men
Have land to catch the rain,
Have grass to snare the spheres of dew,
And fields spread for the grain.

Yea, we would give to each poor man
Ripe wheat and poppies red, —
A peaceful place at evening
With the stars just overhead:

A net to snare the moonlight,
A sod spread to the sun,
A place of toil by daytime,
Of dreams when toil is done.

◆ Annotations （原诗注释）

1. snare: *v.* catch (a bird or mammal) in a snare 用罗网捕（鸟或兽）

2. dew: *n.* tiny drops of water that form on cool surfaces at night, when atmospheric vapour condenses 露；露滴；露水 （e.g. A cold, heavy dew dripped from the leaves. 一滴滴冰冷、沉重的露珠从树叶上滚落。）

3. father: *n.* (poetic/literary) an ancestor （诗/文用法）祖先；父辈

4. descend: *v.* move or fall downwards 下降；落下

5. bless: *v.* (of a priest) pronounce words in a religious rite, to confer or invoke divine favour upon; ask God to look favourably on （牧师）为……祈神赐福；为……祈神保佑

6. sphere: *n.* a round solid figure, or its surface, with every point on its surface equidistant from its center 圆形实心体；球体；球面

7. yea: *adv.* used for emphasis, especially to introduce a stronger or more accurate word than one just used （用于强调）的确；诚然 （e.g. He was full, yea, crammed with anxieties. 的确，他忧心忡忡。）

8. ripe: *adj.* (of fruit or grain) developed to the point of readiness for harvesting and eating （果实或谷物）成熟的

9. poppy: *n.* a herbaceous plant with showy flowers, milky sap, and rounded seed capsules 罂粟

10. sod: *n.* the surface of the ground, with the grass growing on it 地表；草皮

11. toil: *n.* exhausting physical labour 苦干；累活

◆ *A Lead-in Note* （简明导读）

在有信心的人的眼中，月亮是月光的源泉，源源不断的月光自古至今造福人类。有信心的人要让我们看见所有人“都有土地接住雨，都有绿草托起颗颗露珠，都有场地晾晒谷粒”。同时他们认为，“有一张网，可网住月光”。因为月光造福人类，网住了月光，就等于拥有了幸福。

◆ 网住月光（有信心之人眼中的月亮）

露珠、雨水还有月光
都证明：我们祖辈有心智。
露珠、雨水还有月光
下凡赐福于人，添福祉。

来吧，让我们见证：所有人
都有土地接住雨，
都有绿草托起颗颗露珠，
都有场地晾晒谷粒。

没错，成熟的小麦和红红的罂粟，
我们会让每一位贫穷之人获取。
还要让他们夜晚有个安静之所，
那里头顶的天空，繁星熠熠——

有一张网，可网住月光；
有一块草皮，向太阳铺去。
有一个地方，白天劳作；
进入梦乡，若劳作完毕。

101 Vachel Lindsay 韦切尔·林赛

◆ *The Poet's Profile* （诗人小档案）

韦切尔·林赛（1879—1931）：美国诗人及现代歌唱诗歌的奠基人。林赛的作品收集在《〈威廉·布思将军进入了天堂〉及其他诗集》（1913）、《〈刚果河〉及其他诗集》（1914）、《每一个灵魂都是一个轮回》（1929）等中。

◆ *The Moon's the North Wind's Cooky (What the Little Girl Said)*

The Moon's the North Wind's cooky.
He bites it, day by day,
Until there's but a rim of scraps
That crumble all away.

The South Wind is a baker.
He kneads clouds in his den,
And bakes a crisp new moon that . . . greedy
North . . . Wind . . . eats . . . again!

◆ *Annotations* （原诗注释）

1. cooky = cookie, 甜饼干；曲奇饼
2. rim: *n.* the upper or outer edge of an object, typically something circular or

approximately circular （尤指圆形或近似圆形物的）边；缘；边缘

3. scrap: *n.* a small piece or amount of something, especially one that is left over after the greater part has been used 碎片；小块；少量

4. crumble: *v.* break or fall apart into small fragments, especially over a period of time as part of a process of deterioration 崩溃；瓦解 （e.g. their crumbling ancestral home 他们将要倒塌的祖屋）

5. baker: *n.* a person whose trade is making and selling bread and cakes 面包（糕饼）师；面包店主

6. knead: *v.* work (moistened flour or clay) into dough or paste with the hands 揉；捏（湿面或黏土）

7. den: *n.* a room that is comfortable and secluded （舒适而隐蔽的）房屋；屋子

8. crisp: *adj.* (of a substance) firm, dry, and brittle, especially in a way considered pleasing or attractive 干而脆的；松脆易碎的 （e.g. The snow is lovely and crisp. 雪松软可爱。）

◆ *A Lead-in Note* （简明导读）

在喜欢吃甜食的天真小女孩眼中，月亮就是一块圆圆的甜饼干，却一点一点被北风这个贪吃的家伙一天又一天啃咬着，一直“啃咬到只剩一条碎块，最终彻底破碎不见”。当然，这其实就是月亮本身圆缺的过程，但天真的小女孩还没有这样的科学意识。小女孩不忍心让北风把月亮啃咬殆尽，于是想象出南风这位好心的烘焙师来。烘焙师千辛万苦烘焙出一弯新月，结果“北风又 /来……吃……掉……真贪婪”。可以想象，小女孩该有多么失望啊！

◆ 月亮是北风的甜饼干（小女孩眼中的月亮）

月亮是北风的甜饼干，
北风啃咬着，一天又一天。
啃咬到只剩一条碎块，
最终彻底破碎不见。

南风是烘焙师，
在屋子里揉着云朵面团。
接着烘焙出松脆的新月……北风又
来……吃……掉……真贪婪！

Main Bibliography
主要参考文献

[1] LARKIN, Philip. Collected Poems [M]. New York, NY: Farrar, Straus & Giroux Inc, 2004.

[2] Longfellow, H.W. et al. 300 CLASSIC POEMS[M]. Tianjin, China: Tianjin Renmin Press, 2014.

[3] NEGRI, Paul. Great Short Poems (Dover Thrift Editions)[M]. Mineola, NY: Dover Publications, 2012.

[4] SMITH, Philip. 100 Best-Loved Poems(Dover Thrift Editions) [M]. Mineola, NY: Dover Publications, 1995.

[5] Academy of American Poets. Poets.org[DB/OL]. http://www.poets.org/.

[6] Bartleby.com, Inc. Bartleby.com[DB/OL]. http://bartleby.com/.

[7] Beamingnotes Team. Beaming Notes[DB/OL]. http://beamingnotes.com/.

[8] The Hypertexts[DB/OL]. http://www.thehypertexts.com/.

[9] Dictionary.com LLC's Online[DB/OL]. http://dictionary.reference.com/.

[10] Famous Literature, Poems and Stories [DB/OL]. http://www. eliteskills. com/classics.php.

[11] eNotes.com, Inc. eNotes[DB/OL]. http://www.enotes.com/.

[12] People living deeply have no fear of death [DB/OL]. EulogySpeech. net. EulogySpeech.net

[13] Famous Poets and Poems-Read and Enjoy Poetry [DB/OL]. http://

famouspoetsandpoems.com/.

[14]《新牛津英汉双解大词典》编译出版委员会.新牛津英汉双解大词典[M].上海:上海外语教育出版社,2007.

[15] 哈代.哈代诗选:英汉对照[M].飞白,译.北京:外语教学与研究出版社,2014.

[16] 黄杲炘.英诗汉译学[M].上海:上海外语教育出版社,2007.

[17] 商务印书馆辞书研究中心.新华成语词典[M].北京:商务印书馆,2002.

[18] 新华社译名室.世界人名翻译大辞典[M].北京:中国对外翻译出版公司,2007.

[19] 柯尔律治.柯尔律治诗选:英汉对照[M].杨德豫,译.北京:外语教学与研究出版社,2013.

[20] 周定国.世界地名翻译大辞典[M].北京:中国出版社集团、中国对外翻译出版社公司,2008.

Epilogue
后　记

译事之难，难于上青天。译诗之难，乃难中之难。

我们从浩如烟海的英语国家众多诗人作品中精选出一些月亮短诗，共计101首。这些诗不一定都十分出众，也不一定都名垂诗史，但是这些诗都具有一个共同的意象——月亮，或直接写月，或借月抒怀，读后让人有所思考，令人回味。为便于读者将其与中国诗人笔下的月亮意象作横向对比，我们对这些诗的汉语译文，即译诗，首先力求在意义和意象方面的贴切，再考虑形式的因素，特别是押韵方面。

我们在筛选、研究和翻译这101首月亮短诗的过程中，特别是在翻译的过程中，不时会遇到这样或那样的“坎坷”。诗人在创作过程中，为了格律的需要，避开了一些常用词，转而采用生僻的诗歌专用词，这就逼着译者硬着头皮去琢磨这样的词。另外，在译诗过程中，还要“观照”原诗的形式，特别是韵律方面，同时还要兼顾译语（即汉语）诗歌的形式，特别是译语读者的诗歌审美习惯。对于这样的“坎坷”，下笔前会来回踱步、反复思量、仔细斟酌。正如鲁迅先生在译完《死魂灵》后谈到翻译时所言：“我向来总以为翻译比创作容易，因为至少是无须构想。但到真的一译，就会遇着难关，譬如一个名词或动词，写不出，创作时候可以回避，翻译上却不成，也还得想，一直弄到头昏眼花，好像在脑子里面摸一个急于要开箱子的钥匙，却没有。”（鲁迅《“题未定”草·且介亭杂文二集》）

在筛选、研究和翻译这101首月亮短诗的过程中，我们还遇到了语言及文化差异方面的“绊脚石”，处理起来颇费脑筋。正如严复在《天演论》《译例言》中所言：“新理踵出，名目纷繁，索之中文，渺不可得，即有牵合，终嫌参差。译者遇此，独有自具衡量，即义定名。”另外，在翻译中对于查询无果的地方，也得认真加以思考，甚至经过了很长时间才“创造性”地下笔定论，可谓“一名之立，旬月踟蹰。我罪我知，是在明哲”（严复）。由此可见，译事之难也好，译诗之难也罢，不亚于李太白笔下的“蜀道之难，难于上青天”！

幸运的是，在对这101首月亮短诗进行筛选、研究和翻译的过程中，我们得到了许多朋友和同事热情的帮助和有力的支持。特别感激远在大洋彼岸、旅居美国的师姐钟亚梅女士，大学恩师路南女士以及同窗兄弟Peter You的热情帮助！在此，我们十分感谢安徽师范大学外国语学院及渤海大学外国语学院的领导和同事给予我们的热情的帮助和有力的支持！十分感谢安徽师范大学出版社所有工作人员在出版方面提供的有力支持！同时感谢为本研究提供帮助的所有朋友和同仁！

《礼记·中庸》里有言：“君子之道，譬如行远，必自迩，譬如登高，必自卑。”我们努力践行之。

王永胜　朱　红

2022年岁末